MW01415481

59 MINUTES

ALSO BY HOLLY SEDDON

The Short Straw
The Woman on the Bridge
The Hit List
Love Will Tear Us Apart
Don't Close Your Eyes
Try Not to Breathe

59 MINUTES

— *A Novel* —

HOLLY SEDDON

EMILY BESTLER BOOKS
ATRIA
New York   Amsterdam/Antwerp   London
Toronto   Sydney/Melbourne   New Delhi

EMILY BESTLER BOOKS

ATRIA

An Imprint of Simon & Schuster, LLC
1230 Avenue of the Americas
New York, NY 10020

For more than 100 years, Simon & Schuster has championed authors and the stories they create. By respecting the copyright of an author's intellectual property, you enable Simon & Schuster and the author to continue publishing exceptional books for years to come. We thank you for supporting the author's copyright by purchasing an authorized edition of this book.

No amount of this book may be reproduced or stored in any format, nor may it be uploaded to any website, database, language-learning model, or other repository, retrieval, or artificial intelligence system without express permission. All rights reserved. Inquiries may be directed to Simon & Schuster, 1230 Avenue of the Americas, New York, NY 10020 or permissions@simonandschuster.com.

This book is a work of fiction. Any references to historical events, real people, or real places are used fictitiously. Other names, characters, places, and events are products of the author's imagination, and any resemblance to actual events or places or persons, living or dead, is entirely coincidental.

Copyright © 2025 by Holly Seddon

All rights reserved, including the right to reproduce this book or portions thereof in any form whatsoever. For information, address Atria Books Subsidiary Rights Department, 1230 Avenue of the Americas, New York, NY 10020.

First Emily Bestler Books/Atria Books hardcover edition November 2025

EMILY BESTLER BOOKS/ATRIA BOOKS
and colophon are trademarks of Simon & Schuster, LLC

Simon & Schuster strongly believes in freedom of expression and stands against censorship in all its forms. For more information, visit BooksBelong.com.

Interior design by Jill Putorti

Manufactured in the United States of America

ISBN 978-1-6680-8769-5

For Mia, Alfie, Elliot, and Finch

"Only mothers can think of the future
because they give birth to it in their children."

—MAXIM GORKY

Part One

ALERT

IF

If a 1,200-kiloton bomb* strikes central London, a fireball will vaporize more than a kilometer of the city. Covent Garden, Westminster, Waterloo, all destroyed. Millions of people will be gone in a second. And they will be the lucky ones.

In Kennington, where some of my characters live, and as far out as Brixton, Hackney, and Hampstead, buildings will collapse, fires will spread, and there will be millions of fatalities. For those who do not die initially, burns and injuries will be universal. Many eyes will be blinded. Amputations will be commonplace.

Third-degree burns will be experienced by humans and animals all along the borders of Essex, Hertfordshire, Kent, and Surrey. Windows will smash, showering "survivors" in glass. Then, the fallout will come.

If one of Russia's giant nuclear torpedoes, known as Poseidon**, hits Plymouth, the effect will be a giant radioactive tsunami-type wave destroying the coast. This will be followed by unstoppable contamination spreading throughout Dartmoor and beyond, choking and burning the ponies and the people without discrimination. The countryside will be uninhabitable for many years.

The following story is fictional, the above details are not.

Data from Nuclearsecrecy.com/Stevens Institute of Technology.

---

*The largest nuclear bomb in the current US arsenal, but far from the largest bomb ever tested (the Soviets' Tsar Bomba).

**https://thebulletin.org/2023/06/one-nuclear-armed-poseidon-torpedo-could-decimate-a-coastal-city-russia-wants-30-of-them/

Chapter One

CARRIE

It is a beautiful day for the world to end. People in their winter coats are silhouetted against a postcard skyline. Raindrops loosen from lampposts and fall to wet pavements that shine like gold leaf. Luminous. Everything is luminous.

Fit for a finale, the South Bank has been threaded with fairy lights, peppered with market stalls, and scented with sweet, mulled wine. The Thames reflects the whole scene back to itself, an ouroboros of festivity.

A little farther down the river, under a stained concrete bridge, the seasonal standards of a brass band spill toward the London Eye. The cheerful music warms the waiting queue, which stamps its feet and puffs out cloudy breaths with something approaching rhythm.

This is the London that first drew Carrie, and on evenings like this, it lives up to every promise. The reward for enduring that other London of lockjaw morning tubes, piss-stink corners, and yellow crime signs.

And she's not just in London this evening, she's in Paris as she smells chestnuts and cigarettes. Or Vienna, as she trails her fingers along a wooden market stall. The tang of the river borrowed from Amsterdam's canals. A hundred different accents. An accordion of cities pressed together.

Carrie jogs up the concrete slope away from the Thames and walks past rows of early diners opposite the Southbank Centre. Happy hour cocktails and garlicky suppers. She has left work at the ad agency early, as most people do at the end of the week. It's technically still afternoon but it feels like Friday night has already swung into place, a gin blossom glow on the faces she passes.

The end of the week. *We made it.*

Just minutes to go until she's home with her family. Curly little Clementine, three years old, and Emma. Girlfriend, partner, twin heart. No label does her justice. Who gets lucky enough to fall in love with their best friend?

"Okay," Carrie will say, as she pours out two big glasses of Friday wine while Emma orders a takeaway on her phone. "Get ready for the download." And every detail from the day will gush out, exaggerated for comic effect. Emma will then pull the ripcord on her own day. All those inconveniences and irritations converted into amusements, trifles, to delight each other.

Later, bellies full, they will fall asleep halfway through watching a film in bed. Clementine will burrow under their duvet at some point during the night, boiling them all. They'll wake into the weekend and take it in turns to make cups of tea and fulfill Clementine's demands for juice, iPad, snack. Pj's all day. Absolutely nothing exceptional, and everything Carrie wants.

Carrie is so nearly there, but she's enjoying here too. As she skips, twists, drops a shoulder, nods her head, she leaves a trail of "excuse mes" behind her. She tangos around slow, entwined couples and smiles with delight as she engages in the brinkmanship of a mirrored sidestep, *after you, no, after you*, with a tremendously old man who doffs an imaginary hat as she glides past.

Down the steps. Across the road.

From the sparkle and cheer of the Southbank, the grim arches under Waterloo's tracks twang their minor chord. Cyclists weave with irritation as commuters march past the Archduke, which promises Cocktails, Steak, Jazz, in that order. Carrie buoys herself up, then charges headlong through this passage, breath held against the ammonia fizz, guiltily sidestepping a man rattling a can for charity. She would, she really would, but she never carries cash. Who carries cash anymore?

She thinks of Emma collecting Clementine from day care this afternoon, singing songs to her as she pushes her home. They take it in turns to do the nursery run, but Emma's new boss has little regard for her home life and for the last few weeks she has had to juggle work calls and WhatsApps with what Emma calls *Clemen-time*. Which is why, without really acknowledging it to herself, Carrie is rushing to relieve her of parenting duties. Why she will spend a few minutes on the tube rather than walk home in twenty-five. As she gets closer to the stone steps of Waterloo, she can feel Clementine's solid warmth in her arms and Emma wrapping her arms around both of them. They call it *Russian dolling* and it's the loveliest feeling. Until Clementine wriggles free, always busy. "She's already so tired of our nonsense," Emma will whisper in her ear as she often does. "What's she going to be like when she hits her teens?"

Carrie thunders up the steps, under the statue of Britannia and her torch, through the Victory Arch and into the belly of the station. This has always been Carrie's terminus, from when she and Emma were first allocated halls of residence in Kennington over a decade ago at the start of their degrees. A plan they'd made when they were ten and barely knew what university was. Just friends then. But never really "just" anything.

Carrie heads for the lower concourse, barely skimming the surface of the station before she'll be underground and away. The big clock suspended from the ceiling turns to 5:01 p.m. The place is filling up, strangers in coats plonking down next to each other at the tiny tables outside Starbucks and Pret A Manger. She wants to rally them as she passes. "We're almost there, home is in sight, don't give up now!"

Like airports, train terminals exude a kind of anything goes, international waters vibe. People shuffle into the Beer House as she's on her way to work in the morning. If someone fancies slurping down noodles at 3 p.m. on a tiny bench seat, they don't have to explain themselves to anyone. A person could lose themselves here.

Nearly at the steps now, she narrowly avoids a group of hyenas in school uniform. It makes Carrie think of her and Emma's school days. Always a pack of two. Laurel and Hardy, her dad called them.

She feels her phone buzz in her back pocket, hears it trill at the same time. She usually has it on silent but now somehow it's obnoxiously loud.

All around her, other phones vibrate and chirp loudly. A field of crickets. As she pulls hers out, she sees hundreds of hands reaching into pockets and bags, or pulling phones away from ears to frown at the screens. The laughter of the teenagers—their phones already palmed—grows unsure.

Carrie stares at the screen, not realizing she's stopped moving until someone clatters into her from behind and nearly knocks her down the steps.

"But?" she says to no one. She is holding her phone out in front of her like it's about to explode. Everyone is looking at their own phones, then at each other. The sound of the alert has died away, but Carrie can still hear it in her mind.

"It can't be real," says a heavily powdered woman in her fifties with a faux fur hat. But it's a question, not a statement. *It can't be real, can it?*

Carrie stares at the woman, then drops her eyes back to her own screen, reading the words again but understanding nothing.

SEVERE ALERT. NUCLEAR MISSILE THREAT TO SOUTH ENGLAND. 59 MINUTES UNTIL IMPACT. SEEK IMMEDIATE SHELTER. THIS IS NOT A TEST.

A confused murmur spreads through the now motionless crowd. Staff bunch at each platform entrance, looking at their own screens. Some have walkie-talkies stuck to their coat lapels, their heads tilted as they absorb instructions.

"No, it can't be real, it's just like that test," Carrie says emphatically to the woman in the hat, but she's not listening. She's now talking to a young man with a precise beard he must tend daily with tiny scissors. He puts his hand on the woman's arm and she places her hand on top of his, just briefly. Her fingers are thickened with rings.

For a fat second no one does anything. Then the station's public address system, which had fallen silent for the first time in Carrie's London lifetime, announces with calm detachment: "Would Inspector Sands report to security immediately."

At the same time, the huge advertising screen that runs the length of three platform entrances goes black. The giant digital Burger King Whopper that was squatting there like a fat toad has now gone. Across the width of the station, the rows of screens showing destinations start to flicker, the train times disappearing, the list of stops wiped.

Everyone holds their breath. Every screen in the station is now black. And then, all at once, they fill with an identical message:

SEEK IMMEDIATE SHELTER.

Chapter Two

FRANKIE

Frankie wakes in the passenger seat, bent-necked and Picassoed in the warped side-view mirror. She fell asleep somewhere near Bristol, although everywhere looks the same from the motorway. Warehoused fringes and constellations of Lego houses, their roofs just peeping out over the noiseproof fencing on either side of the roadway.

While she slept, the road thinned from a multilane monster into a fragile gray ribbon. No more bright service stations, just the empty shells of old Little Chef diners.

Cottages and trees now creep to the edge of the tarmac, dusted exhaust gray. Spread out and a million miles from a city, they look like locations from horror films or true crime shows, where young women break down in their cars, stumble into sex dungeons, and are never seen again. Then people like Frankie and Otis watch documentaries about them to unwind after work.

They are now in—or is it *on*?—Dartmoor, and Otis is threading his way between rust-colored banks, trees looming over them from either side.

"These names," Otis says at every signpost they pass. "Sticklepath!"

Frankie joins in. "Black-a-Tor Corpse."

"*Copse*." He laughs with a kind of manic delight. "Not *corpse*. You massive goth."

"Is that a Dartmoor pony?" she says dryly, pointing to a huge black horse, hair shining like granite, plodding along the fringe of a field.

"Yes." Otis laughs again. "Definitely."

They play the Dartmoor pony game as they pass sheep and cows too. And when three pheasants leap out and zigzag like nutters in front of them, Otis jokes that each one of them is a Dartmoor pony too. "And him, and him, and that fella too."

Booking this romantic weekend break for them was a typically Otis move, though she hadn't expected him to book somewhere so far away from Manchester. There are moors in the North, there is the epic beauty of the Lake District. But she likes a road trip, and she likes the two of them in his car, expanding their shared map. He has been reading guidebooks every night for the past three weeks, flipping through them in bed and reading aloud from the chapters he thinks she'll like best.

Signs for Princetown begin, and Otis says that's a euphemism for Dartmoor Prison. "Some really bad pennies in there, Frankie. Proper rotten eggs."

They sweep through a village called Chagford, so perfect it might have been pieced together from Pinterest boards. The Christmas lights and decorations are strung up already but not switched on, as if pencil-sketched over the mellow market square. And now they're out of the village again and weaving through a network of lanes that might be called paths in other circumstances.

A bright-red tractor appears, bearing down from the other direction. Most of the lanes have regular passing spaces bitten out of them but not this one. As the nonchalant farmer watches, Otis reverses jerkily and pulls into the driveway of a house, just a few minutes from the village but standing completely alone. She thinks again of the archetypal true crime setting, imagines what—or who—the householders might have in their cellar as Otis grinds the gears, his ears pink with embarrassment.

They finally reach their own rented holiday cottage. Square and squat, with cloudy walls of thick, creamy stone and a scratchy thatched roof. She nods that, yes, it is lovely, and keeps all her jokes about true crime to herself.

Visibly relieved, Otis grabs the weekend bags with gusto and jogs off to the front door. She follows slowly and finds Otis in the kitchen, rifling through the welcome basket like it's a Christmas stocking. A bottle of cider, some jams, a slab of homemade oat bar, a loaf of bread, an artisanal bag of crisps, and a froufrou bar of handmade soap that Frankie will take home and never use. The fridge is an empty shock of white but for one pint of milk and some local butter wrapped in paper.

In the bedroom upstairs, beams run up the walls and across the ceiling, caging them in like the ribs of a giant beast. They sit on the bed and bounce briefly in surprise, shoved from underneath by eager springs. It unbalances her so she tips toward Otis's torso and he wraps a solid arm around her, his hand then snaking down her side and grabbing her buttock.

"Oi," she says, but she loves it.

He smells of warm toast and black pepper. She closes her eyes and soaks up his heat, but when she opens them she sees Otis watching her in an ornate mirror. She can see how they must look to other people. Her, small, pale, and solemn, with thick, dark, bird's-nest hair. Him, huge, blond, tanned, and smiling, like a real-life Beach Boy. No one else gets it, but it works. It works perfectly.

"Are you okay?" he says, watching her in the mirror. "You're smiling."

"I am okay," she says, smiling even more now. "I'm really . . . really okay."

He sags with relief. "I think I love you," he says, resting his Labrador head on hers. He always says this, like a mantra. Ever since the first time, over fish and chips, squished together on a bench under the electric lights of Ancoats Green.

"I think I love you too," she replies, as she did then.

And now, suddenly, it is the perfect time. "And I have something . . . there's something I need to tell you."

Her phone makes a loud beeping sound on the bed next to her but the same sound also seems to come from downstairs. Is that his phone getting a text too? She ignores them both.

"What is it?" he says. "What do you have to tell me?"

"Well," she says, "the simple fact is that I'm pregnant. I am with child."

"What?" He laughs, and she realizes he's still watching her in the mirror. His laughter dies in his throat and his eyes bulge. "Like, actually?"

"Like, actually. God, is that all right?"

For a moment, he says nothing. Wets his lips, swallows. And finally smiles.

"Of course it's all right, you weirdo! It's bloody brilliant! How . . . how pregnant are you? You don't look pregnant."

"You don't get a massive belly on day one, dingus."

Her phone makes that same sound again. A long screech that she's never heard it make before. She doesn't mean to look at it, she means to answer Otis properly, to tell him that she did the test yesterday, that she is five days late and doesn't know quite how because they've always been so careful. Careful most of the time. Careful when sober. And that, while she has always been ambivalent about kids . . . now it's happened, with him, she is the very opposite of ambivalent. She's *super-bivalent*. She's fucking delighted. But she doesn't say any of this, because the screen is right there and she reads it before she realizes what she's doing. And her blood turns to ice.

SEVERE ALERT. NUCLEAR MISSILE THREAT TO SOUTH ENGLAND. 59 MINUTES UNTIL IMPACT. SEEK IMMEDIATE SHELTER. THIS IS NOT A TEST.

Chapter Three

MRS. DABB

Wipe eyes, straighten back, clear throat. Tomorrow she can unspool in private, but today she just has to knuckle through for a few more hours. She can do it. She's done it for so many years now. Even if it's getting harder, not easier, it is just one day.

The kitchen stove is lit but the warmth doesn't reach her bones. She can't even smell the baking stockpiled throughout the afternoon. Mounds of scones heaped on the side, a Victoria sponge, sticky jam tarts. It looks grotesque now, gluttony masquerading as a shrine. She never gets this day right, never knows how to mark the anniversary in a way that will mean something to Bunny while not peeling the skin slowly from herself.

It's Bunny who seems to know what to do with this date and has since she was tiny. At four, off her own back, she started the routine of beginning a joke before school and giving her mum the punchline when she gets home, "to stop you being sad all day." This morning, she'd barely got up in time to catch the bus, toast half-chewed, juice half-drunk, but still, "Knock knock," she shouted as she pulled on her shoes and grabbed her bag.

"Who's there?"

"Dejav."

"Dejav who?"

It hung in the air even after the door was slammed.

Any moment now, the school bus will deposit her daughter back home again. Then a swish of a school skirt, the rattle of a bag, and Bunny will be up the little path and bursting through the front door, bubbling with laughter as she blurts out the punchline. Immediately embroidering some joy over the pain.

An engine rumbles outside and she rushes to the window, squinting outside. The school bus takes so long to weave through all the villages that it is dark by the time it arrives. Through a gap in the shutters, the bus noses into view, shaking a little in its canine way as it appears to slow, but then moves off again without stopping. *That's not right.*

She pulls open the front door and jogs after the bus as it trundles away, until finally the driver spots her in his mirror and shudders to a stop twenty meters down the lane. The light from the vehicle renders everything around it dense black.

"All right there, Mrs. Dabb?" the driver says as he opens the door. He's nearing retirement but sits ramrod straight while she tries to catch her breath. God, she's so horribly unfit.

"My daughter should have got off," she puffs as she looks into the belly of the bus. "Bunny," she prompts, though he knows this very well.

There aren't many pupils left and they're dotted around the seats, all in the same uniform. She looks down at herself, at the flour dusted on her ratty old sweatshirt, slippers collapsing around her feet. Bunny would be mortified if she were here, but she's not. Where on earth is she?

The bus driver frowns. "She missed it today, love."

"What?"

"She was on here this morning, but a no-show tonight." He smiles, like he sees this all the time. Like he finds it whimsical. "Probably too busy nattering or something, lost track of time. Or maybe she was kept back at school and didn't want to tell Mum."

She shakes her head. Not Bunny. She's never been in trouble in her life and none of her friends, carefully vetted from the sidelines, would keep her "nattering." They are all Good Girls™. And besides, Bunny knows how important today is. It's important to her too. So even if she suddenly decided to tumble into teenage clichés, she wouldn't do it today. It's unfathomable.

"I'm sure she's fine, Mrs. Dabb," he says, his accent a local rumble. "But I really need to get this lot home."

"But—"

"Can't you just call her cell phone?" A hint of impatience, underscored by the wheeze of the bus.

"No, I . . . she doesn't have one."

The look he gives is clear. *Oh*, it says, *you're one of those.*

"I'm sure she'll show up, but I'll get on the radio to the other school bus drivers, tell 'em to keep an eye out. If they see her, they'll tell her Mum's worried. All right?"

She steps off the bus and onto the tarmac. "All right," she says, but feels anything but. He pulls away even before the door has fully closed. She troops back toward her own front door, left hanging wide open. They can still do that out here, leave doors open and cars unlocked. *They* can, but not her. She must be more careful.

Heart thundering, she looks at the little notepad next to the landline. Runs her finger down the short list of names of Bunny's friends' parents and starts to make calls. But no one has seen her since lunchtime and all their girls are safely home. "Jazzy says Bunny had a note from you excusing her for the afternoon," Jasmine's mum, Daphne, says. "Is that right?"

"What? What note?"

Muffled discussion. "Jazzy thinks it was a doctor's note but she's not sure."

"A doctor's note?"

"Maybe a doctor's note, she doesn't know for sure. Have you called Bunny's phone?"

"She doesn't have one. I . . . I was thinking of getting her one for Christmas." A lie.

"That's . . . hmm."

"What?"

"Well, I just thought Jazzy said she was on the phone to Bunny the other day."

"We have a landline, I'm talking on it now."

"No, it was when Jazzy was off sick and it was at lunchtime, so Bunny was at school. I must be . . . it must have been someone else. Hang on, I'll just check."

The conversation is muffled and protracted. What takes this long if the answer is a simple *no, of course she doesn't have a cell phone*?

"She says I must have heard wrong."

"What else did she say?" It comes out as a bark. "Why would my daughter be going to the doctor by herself anyway?"

There's a pause, then the sound of footsteps and a door closing. "I . . ." Daphne starts, her voice lowered. "Look, Bunny's obviously forged a note of some kind to get out of school."

"But she's not like that!"

"And Jasmine's insisting I'm wrong but I really thought she was talking to Bunny on the phone the other day, and she's definitely said something before about messaging her. I trust my daughter, I really do. Usually. But I think she might be covering."

"Covering for what?"

A pause. "Oh, I'm probably losing my marbles," Daphne says, and the moment is lost. "Perimenopause brain, probably. I put the electric kettle on the gas burner the other day."

"You think my daughter's hiding things from me?"

"No! I didn't . . . I wasn't saying anything like that, but . . . well, did you write her a note to get out of school?"

"No." It's almost a whisper.

"Look, I'll let you know if Jasmine gives me any other intel. But I'm sure Bunny will turn up. And you know, she's thirteen. Probably just trying to carve out a little independence."

"No," she says, her voice breaking. "Not Bunny. Bunny knows not to . . . She wouldn't do that to me, not today."

"I'm sorry, love," Daphne says, and though the words are kind, the tone is slightly impatient. "I have to go. Good luck."

She replaces the handset and looks at the time. Five o'clock. Bunny is now an hour late and has been unaccounted for since midday. It's dark, cold, and the anniversary of the worst day of her life. She pulls open the front door; the emptiness of the dark air slaps her in the face. "Oh, Bunny," she says, "why today?"

Silence is the reply.

But then it starts.

The sound reaches her ears, her hands, so that she crouches down, palms pressed against the sides of her head before her brain understands what it's heard. And still the sound whoops and whines, soaring and dipping like an electric bird.

The unmistakable wailing of a siren across the moor.

58 MINUTES UNTIL IMPACT

Chapter Four

CARRIE

Carrie is incapable of drawing breath, her senses reduced to nothing but a thunderous heartbeat. The crowd bulges around her and she looks for someone who knows what to do. Proper adults, trusty faces in crisp uniforms. But no one else seems to know how to act. The staff are still bunched by the platform gates, looking like children in their uniforms. Wild-eyed, they stare back at the crowds. Two members of staff at the nearest gate start to argue. Fragments of it reach Carrie.

. . . just let them on . . .

. . . need to follow procedure . . .

. . . nowhere to fucking go anyway . . .

People merge into soup. More bodies fill the space around her. Faces bleached of all detail by terror. Panic washes over the glass roof, up and down the escalators, sloshing over the platforms and onto the tracks. She can smell it.

A woman slips off her pointy-heeled shoes, throws them to the floor, and runs toward the underground entrance. This unleashes others. Normally calm, waves of commuters start to scramble to get belowground. *Seek immediate shelter.*

Carrie knows she should move but her body is not on board with her brain, and she feels herself grow smaller as she's bumped, shoved, lifted up, and moved. More people flood into the station from outside. Bodies press into the shops and food places.

"Please walk in an orderly fashion and remain calm," the station announcement says.

Where are the police? The army? She can hear sirens outside, but this is London and there are always sirens. *Look for the helpers,* that's the phrase, isn't it. But she can't see any and can barely move. But there must be something to do, somewhere to go, *a plan*. There is always a plan.

She gasps for air and twists to see behind her. Yet more people pour in from outside, through the entrance over there in the corner, and over there by the toilets, and at every other entrance she can see. People flow relentlessly inward. Not at speed, there isn't enough space for that, but slowly rolling in like boiling sugar.

The never-true-darkness of a London sky hangs heavily over them, just the other side of the glass roof.

Will that fill with blinding light?

An elbow glances off Carrie's chin as a tall man shuffles past, fighting his way toward the platforms and then goodness knows where. The trains are all canceled, and some passengers who had already boarded are jumping back off and cramming down the staircases that are cut into the platform surfaces, leading to the underground trains. The doors down there must be closed because people then start bubbling back up and spilling out onto the platform. Some shove their way toward the main concourse, scrambling over the barriers and joining the crush.

More people are jamming onto the trains, apparently hoping to flee for the countryside. She would do the same, most likely—a country-raised girl will usually return there in the end—but Clementine and Emma are not in the country, they are in Kennington. She can walk there in twenty-five minutes, run there in less. And they need to be together as a family, that's just a given.

And there's Pepper, who lives upstairs from them. Their landlord, but "landlord" barely covers it. Beloved friend. Father figure. De facto grandfather to Clementine. A man who, despite his acerbic and grumpy appearance, has one of the kindest hearts she's ever known. He will need help too. Anathema to him, but tough tits, Pepper. He's wound the neighbors up so much with his bitching and troublemaking that they'll all leave him well alone. So if Emma hasn't already, Carrie will get him to bring his supplies down to theirs, hunker down with them in their ground-floor flat. It's technically his flat anyway, he owns the whole building. And yes, it will be hard to pry him from his things. The photographs and paintings that cover every wall from artist friends, lovers, and enemies. The countless knickknacks. But she will carry him down if she has to, wriggling and kicking like Clementine when she's tired.

Yes, she thinks, *this is a plan.*

Even as she makes her decision, she's being shoved and shunted farther from the exits. She's closer to the now-open barriers of platform 17. A train that was due to leave for Woking sits crammed with people, their faces pressed against the windows in dreadful hope. "It's not gonna leave," a man in a train company jacket is shouting to anyone who'll listen, waving his arms at the windows. "You're gonna have to get off!"

She turns, sucks in a breath, and starts to elbow her way back toward the archway she came through just a few minutes ago. Some people instinctively shuffle to make space, others don't seem to see her at all. She catches more fragments.

. . . fuck is wrong with you, man, move your . . .

. . . nothing left of the city . . .

She starts off polite, timid, but after being pushed back twice and clobbered with a bag, she stops saying please and just starts shoving. Hard.

Chapter Five

FRANKIE

"This has to be rubbish, right?" Frankie holds her phone out in her palm like a rescued bird as Otis continues to stare at her belly in the mirror. The cottage is too warm, a smell of reheated dust tickling her throat. A chunky reclaimed radiator tuts as Frankie shoves her screen in Otis's face again. He frowns. The same look he has when she gets gloomy about climate change, politics, calories on menus, traffic accidents, and on and on until he tells her, gently, to shut up and have a bag of crisps. Life can't be that bad if we've still got crisps.

He starts to read out loud from her screen, stilted in a way that shows her exactly what he was like as a schoolboy. Eager to please, slightly guileless. She feels the burden of tears welling and coughs to stop all that. Because Otis is a grown man and not a little boy. Because this is a happy moment. Because this is not a real warning. It cannot be.

" 'Severe alert, nuclear missile threat.' *Nuclear missile threat?*" He looks up and then back at the phone. "Nah, that can't be real. Who sent it?"

"It wasn't a number, look, it's not a normal text, it just appeared on the screen."

"Like that test a few years ago?"

"I never received it." She'd joked about it at the time. Not one of the designated survivors, clearly.

"Maybe it's another test," he says, handing it back. "Or maybe they've sent an alert by accident. Anyway, I don't want to think about that, I want to think about . . ." He presses a big palm to her stomach and she instinctively sucks it in. ". . . our baby."

"Due on July nineteenth," she says, "and apparently the size of a poppy seed, but—"

"A poppy seed?" He pinches his fingers together. "How is that even possible?" He shows her his fingers. "How big is a poppy seed? Like this big?"

"Otis." She reaches for his hand and holds it.

"I don't know seeds," he says, frowning and allowing her to lace her fingers through his.

"Otis, I'm so happy you're happy, but can you just check your phone as well, just so we know for sure. I don't think we should assume . . ."

"Ay, all right." He gets up with a grunt, pats down his pockets, and then plods out of the room with a lack of urgency she finds reassuring. Of course it's bollocks, it has to be. It's total bollocks, and they'll celebrate with that fancy bag of crisps from the hamper, he'll bring them back up for sure. She's eating crisps for two now, that's the joke she'll make. It is waiting on her lips as he runs back up the stairs, his feet slapping the wooden steps so hard it shakes the floor. He has no crisps.

"I got it too," he says.

They thumb their phones, trying to find news. Nothing happens, the screens just hang. Frankie opens Twitter or whatever it's called now and tries to refresh it but it's just stuck on the timeline from when she last looked in the car, the same binary politics, sarcastic hot takes, and weird promoted tweets from crypto bros and elasticated bra companies. Otis doesn't even use social media, something she admires and finds annoying because it makes her feel bad about her own screen time.

Otis tries to call his mum. "Nothing's happening," he says, holding the phone away from his ear and trying again. "She'll be going mad."

Frankie tries to call her brother, Seb, back in Manchester, who always knows what to do. Nothing happens. She tries again but there's no ringing, no recorded message. Then she remembers he's in Dubai.

"If this is a hoax," she says, "it's still managed to jam the networks."

"There's a telly downstairs," Otis says, standing and offering her his hand, helping her up as if she's newly fragile. *Oh god*, she thinks, *I like that more than I should.*

The remote control for the TV sits on a handmade doily, which upsets Frankie for reasons she can't articulate. It feels so quiet and normal here in this gently fussy room, with its low beams and lacework, that she can feel hope holding her insides in place.

The news will tell us it's a hoax and then we can add this to our roster of things to joke about. Then get back to talking about our magical poppy-seed baby.

Poppy, she thinks, *that's a nice name.* She likes natural names like that, plants and animals. Countryside names for her city kid. She imagines Otis with a little girl called Poppy. Plaits and miniature Mary Jane shoes. Tiny fingers to wrap him around. He'll be the loveliest, most devoted dad. No beer benders and hangover-fueled rages. Their baby, *their Poppy,* will never be hidden in a cupboard "just in case" like Frankie and Seb during their father's worst years.

A beat in time, one last moment of hope, then she presses the power button and they watch the television screen come to life. Otis reaches for her hand and they stand in front of the telly, staring. There is no proper picture, just a black screen with a white crown on it, like the header of a government website. Subtitles roll along the bottom that match the calm voice speaking.

"—announcements will be made about the care of children in after-school and childcare settings, your food and water supply, delivery of stable iodine tablets, and care of animals and pets. Do not make mobile or landline phone calls—"

They look at each other, their hands becoming slick in each other's grip.

"—because the phone system could become overloaded. Any emergency notifications will still reach your phones even if the networks are down, so keep them charged for as long as you can."

The words start to swirl into one another. In the distance, Frankie can hear a siren. Army? Police?

"Further announcements will be made about the care of children in—"

"It's really real," Frankie says, putting her other hand on her stomach and allowing Otis to fold himself around her, muffling her words into his hoodie. His heart is the fastest she's ever heard it. A rabbit heart. Hunted and trapped. "Oh my god, Otis. What the hell are we going to do?"

school has called to check. Why did she do it? If she actually had a doctor's appointment there'd be no reason to keep that secret. And if it didn't say she had a doctor's appointment and Jasmine was either lying or guessing, what else could it have said to allow a thirteen-year-old out of school, unquestioned? Was she just buying time? Some kind of head start so she could run away? *Does she secretly hate me?*

Five hours at least before her absence was noted at home. How far could she have got in five hours? Multiple towns and cities. There's a train station near her school, she could have easily gone to Plymouth, Bristol, or Exeter. From Exeter, she could be in London in about three hours. Exeter St. Davids to Paddington. Or Exeter Central to Waterloo.

"Stop." She hears Miranda's stern voice. "There's no evidence she's left the area. You're spiraling and that won't help find your daughter." She flips the television on, usually set to the local BBC channel, sees the ticker tape news, and drops the remote.

"Oh my god."

She has to find Bunny, she has to find out where Bunny has gone, and drag her back to safety.

She thunders up the stairs.

Bunny's room is chaotic. Clothes strewn everywhere, schoolbooks dumped on the floor, *Bunny Dabb—French, Bunny Dabb—History* in colorful bubble writing. The air smells cruelly of her, a cloying mix of hair products and birthday-bought perfume, the slightly sour biscuit smell of the unmade bed, long overdue a stripping.

Heaps of dust create a new topography on every surface. Bunny is now responsible for cleaning her own room and so she just doesn't. *Oh, who cares. Why did I ever care?* She is such a good girl in all other ways, so what if she wants to live in age-appropriate squalor?

There is no "running away" note, no obvious signs of bags being packed, but it's such a mess, who knows?

Time is ticking, and she needs some kind of clue. She collapses down onto her knees and then all fours to rummage under the bed. Jigsaws they used to do together on a Sunday, piles of exercise books from previous school years, a photo album she can't bear to open. Nothing of any relevance to where she could be. When she stands up again, she

Chapter Six

MRS. DABB

"Breathe in one two three, out one two three."

She cannot see, panic whiting out her vision. She is on the floor, gripping the tiles with her bitten nails. Her ears amplify the sound so it swells through her skull, crushing all her thoughts. The air riffles her clothes, though she can't feel its chill.

But she is breathing. In, one, two, three. Out, one, two, three.

"This is a trauma response," her old therapist's voice says in her head. "You're not in actual danger, your body is just misidentifying risk because of..."

But this is a risk, she argues mentally, with a woman she's not seen in years. *This is a fucking siren, Miranda!*

She keeps breathing, as slow and steady as she can manage, until her vision clears and she is back in her body, able to scramble to a stand. *What is... Why is... Where is...* She tries to parse all her thoughts into separate strands, lay them out in the right order.

When she slams the front door closed, a faint siren can still be heard inside the cottage.

In the living room, she fumbles for the TV remote. She thinks, of course, of Devonport in nearby Plymouth. Of the nuclear submarines still being serviced there, despite everything. Of how fast the sea wind whips over the countryside toward Chagford, toward this little house, biting away at the soft stone, clawing its way inside. Twenty-eight miles from Devonport to here, as the crow flies. And she thinks of Bunny, out there in her thin coat, utterly unprotected.

Then she thinks of her daughter at some earlier point in time, carefully forging a note and doing a good enough job that no one from the notices Bunny's special teddy, Barnaby, lying on the pillow. There is no way she would run away without him. No way. This should calm her, but doesn't.

The desk in the corner is a graveyard of mugs and glasses, totally useless for writing on, but it has a drawer, which shrieks as she pulls it out. A sound she realizes she's heard coming from this room, vaguely noted and unidentified. Inside, amid the sweet wrappers, old stickers, and hairbands furred with brown strands, sits a bright-white phone charger.

Bunny really does have a secret phone.

54 MINUTES UNTIL IMPACT

Chapter Seven

CARRIE

It normally takes Carrie a few seconds to cross Waterloo's concourse but she's still only halfway to the nearest exit. Just in front of her, a man in a wheelchair is swallowed up by the crowd, she can just see the dome of his head and his shoulders busily working, trying to maneuver. She's seen this man many times before. He always wears the same color palette as a base—navies, grays, camels—but always with a little sprig of something bright. Mustard brogues or a vibrant red scarf. It should clash with his auburn hair, but instead it elevates it to gold. She's almost commented on it before, "I love your style," but worries it would sound patronizing.

His and her commutes often sync. Lots of these commutes do. In a crowded station in a crowded city, people still tread a shared path. A woman over there, gasping for air and pressing her chest, once gave Carrie fifty pence for the toilet back when there was still a charge.

A female member of staff who was talking into a walkie-talkie a few moments ago muscles past Carrie and toward the man in the wheelchair, who she thinks might be called Daniel but can't remember why. The uniformed woman pushes Maybe Daniel with her thick strong arms, her air of officialdom buying her more space than the rest of them. Carrie follows immediately in their slipstream, gripping on to the woman's coat like she's making her way to the toilets in a crowded pub, conga style.

With the wheelchair at the front, people automatically give all three of them a fraction more space. Carrie clings shamefully as the convoy reaches the wall near the exit, but then the uniformed woman unlocks a staff door, its No Entry sticker rubbed and faded. Carrie lets go as the woman pushes the man and his wheelchair inside. An institutional darkness swallows them up and the door locks behind them.

The exit archway is just a few feet away now, Britannia waiting bravely on the other side. Once out, Carrie will turn right and run through the taxi rank, dodging whatever is happening there. She can almost taste the air outside, sweet and smoky from exhaust fumes.

There is a staircase down to the back of the station that'll bring her out near the beginning of Kennington Road and she can simply follow it all the way home, turning at the last moment into Prince's Street and then finally Prince's Square, the cluster of Georgian houses and converted apartments in which they live, huddled around a little communal garden. She can almost see their front door, can smell Pepper's cooking from upstairs, can feel Clementine's baked-potato warmth in her arms, and can picture Emma, Zoom-fashionable from the waist up, crying. Because Emma cries at everything, she's even worse than Carrie. Sad films, happy endings, Christmas commercials, dogs in sweaters, videos of baby goats. She cried when Carrie first said that, yes, she did love her *like that*. Like more than friends. Like together forever.

Emma cries in panic and fear too.

Carrie doesn't jog as much as she used to pre-baby, but today she can feel energy prickling, an impetus growing in her chest to suck in oxygen and pump it out through her legs. To run, as hard and fast as she can, the way she and Emma used to thunder down the path between each other's houses, or freewheel on their bikes. If she runs, she will get home with enough time to do whatever you're supposed to do. Maybe Pepper has already started sorting things out. He lived in Eastern Europe in the seventies when the threat of nuclear war danced all along the border with the West. Not that he talks about it much—preferring to brag about assignations with household names and other dubious claims—but he'll know what to do.

Hundreds of heads, elbows, knees, and bags block the way out. There are only fifty-three minutes until a missile devastates this part of the country, but people still talk in low voices and murmurs. No one is screaming, although some are crying. A pregnant woman is pressed against the front of Foyles bookshop, holding her stomach, protecting it from the surge of people. The woman's face is shiny with tears but her mouth is clamped shut. She doesn't ask for help and no one is offering it. Inside the doorway, people press themselves against the old ticket booths repurposed as pretty book displays.

Would Carrie have asked for help if she were still pregnant? She puts a hand on her empty stomach and thinks of Clementine. She cannot help this woman, and hates herself for it, but she leans in and wishes her luck as she passes.

Surprisingly, people part easily as she reaches the exit arch. And then she sees why. The thick glass doors are closed. Locked. Four police officers stand on the other side of the glass, at the top of the steps, holding large and complicated-looking guns.

Climbing up the external steps on their knees, getting as close to the police as they dare, is a crouching, begging sea of people. As she reaches the glass from the inside, she sees a sketch of herself reflected. Pale white skin, slipped makeup, bleached hair, off-brand coat. Nobody special, nobody more important than anyone else in here or out there.

"Those people outside are all trying to get in," a voice says in her ear. "But there's no space."

Carrie bangs on the glass. "Let me out! Please!" Only one of the officers out there turns to look over his shoulder into the station, his gun still facing forward at the people on their knees.

"Please! One of those people can have my place!"

"Miss, use your head." That voice again. Carrie turns to see a teenage girl in school uniform, navy with royal-blue piping. Fierce eyes, pretty brown face, and curly hair pulled into a tight knot behind her head. The girl shifts her schoolbag back onto her shoulder but it's immediately knocked off again.

"If they open the door to let you out," the girl says, as if she's explaining complex physics to a small child, "all of them out there will rush in." Carrie stares at the glass doors and then back at the girl, whose frown softens, her voice wavering slightly as she adds, "And then we're all dead."

Carrie tries to look across to the other exits but all she can see is more people.

"Are all the doors closed?"

"Yes."

"Surely not? What about the bridge to Waterloo East?"

"Yes, we're completely shut in, so *please,* please stop banging, miss."

Carrie looks again at the girl's face, her eyes. How easy it was to mistake fear for fury. This child is terrified.

"I'm sorry," she says, but the girl has turned away.

Chapter Eight

FRANKIE

The kitchen tap sprays back into Frankie's face as she fills every bowl she can find, intending to fill every container in this unfamiliar house while the water is still clean. She grips the sink and closes her eyes, struck by a sudden nausea that could be the pregnancy or could be existential doom. To think that she used to actively lean into such concepts. She shudders at the memory of her mum scrubbing off the gloomy lyrics she'd carefully penned onto her bedroom wall. "I don't know what's wrong with you, but if Dad sees this, he'll flip his lid and I won't be able to stop him."

"You could try."

Frankie leaves the next bowl filling and goes into the living room. The TV is their only source of information, and it flips through several messages, each as dystopian as the others.

". . . before water becomes contaminated, fill every sink and bath available, ensuring a tight seal is made by any plugs. Check for leaks and, if necessary, use plastic sheeting or anything available to . . ."

She turns off the kitchen tap and pants up to the bathroom. This is not her bath; how can you tell if it'll leak? She pushes the rubber plug into place so hard her fingertips throb. Then she pulls the plastic shower curtain off its rail in one angry motion, her ribs aching at the movement. Laying it across the bottom of the bath, she turns on the cold tap. Water trickles out slowly now; everyone around here must be doing the same thing.

She runs breathlessly back downstairs to find Otis holding a pile of blankets he's found somewhere. "It's going to get cold," he says. He dumps them on the velvet sofa, covering the brush marks made by whoever cleaned all traces of the last guests. The TV rattles on in the background, the other message again now.

"Further announcements will be made about the care of children in after-school and childcare settings, your food and water supply, delivery of stable iodine tablets, and care of animals and pets."

Food and water supply . . .

"Otis," she says. "This isn't going to work."

He looks at the blanket fort he's been building. "The TV said to—"

"No, no, not this, this is . . . no, it's food. We can't go out to get any once it happens and we don't have enough to last."

Otis, always the counterpoint to her pessimism, stares back but then lowers his head, defeated. "I think you're right," he says.

Chapter Nine

MRS. DABB

Why today? Has her family not suffered enough on this date?

She closes her eyes and knuckles her temples, as if she might find her daughter hiding in the dark there.

Think.

There is only one other person who would have bought Bunny a phone . . . aka the softest touch in town. Bunny's grandmother. Back in the hallway, she picks up the handset and presses the programmed number for *Mary Dabb*. Nothing happens. She tries *Mary—cell*. Nothing.

This is not totally unexpected, especially today. Mary pulls it out from the wall on difficult days, throws her cell phone across the room, pulls the curtains, and doesn't answer the door. On the most difficult days of all, Mary switches her hearing aid off and powers down, just outright rejects the world. And this is definitely a difficult day. Does Mary know what's happening? Can she even hear the siren?

If she bought Bunny this phone in secret, what else might she know about her granddaughter? Does she know about the fake note? God, did she *write it*? No, that's insane. She's an indulgent grandmother, not a partner in crime. But maybe she knows something that explains where Bunny might have gone. Maybe she knows something without realizing its importance.

Sometimes secrets skip a generation.

Outside, an old injury tingles like a warning for rain but the skies are still a solid moonlit gray. Fog slowly closing in on the world out here. It's bizarrely dry for November, but bizarre weather is nothing new here.

The air is crisp and smoky from the pump-out of the stoves, almost festive. Along the hedge, Christmas trees are lined up in size order like the von Trapp children. Each one an aide-mémoire. An archive of Christmases past that mirrors the different heights of a growing girl, whose notches are immortalized on the inside of the cellar door. At ten, she was as tall as her grandmother. At eleven, she caught up to her mother, who will soon have to stand on a stool to score the line across the wood.

Despite her height, though, she is still a little girl. "We're cozy girls, Mum," Bunny likes to say. Both homebodies, preferring to be bundled from top to toe. Most evenings after school, homework diligently done despite the mess she does it in, Bunny will appear in the living room swathed in flannel pajamas and an ancient dressing gown. Her feet are usually in rabbit slippers whose soft ears droop toward the floor. They'll each curl themselves into a corner of the sofa and watch old films and comedies they've seen eight, ten, twenty times already. It's a small and peaceful life. So why isn't Bunny here living it?

On the gravel drive, an ancient Land Rover sits next to a newer, much smaller electric car. The former can cover all terrain but it's unreliable, and the last thing she needs is to break down in the middle of nowhere, the threat growing closer and no sign of Bunny.

She climbs into the small car and looks back at their home as she pulls away. The cottage seems tiny and vulnerable. Over a mile from its neighbor in one direction—a holiday cottage often empty. And Mary the other way, herself tiny and vulnerable.

She stamps on the accelerator, pulling herself forward toward the windshield and squinting out into the fog as she goes faster still. The car whistles along in near silence, no growling engine to warn people she's coming. The roads will be treacherous enough for people not used to them, but she only cares about one person. And if anyone on these roads gets in her way, she'll drive straight over them.

The television said to stay home but the television does not have a daughter out here. Loose, unprotected, and maybe totally unaware of what's happening.

51 MINUTES
UNTIL IMPACT

Chapter Ten

CARRIE

The armed people in uniforms are inside now. Carrie doesn't know if they're police, ordinary soldiers, some kind of secret military unit, or something else entirely. What she does know is that these long guns and masked faces have not brought her the reassurance she'd hoped. Clusters of identikit armored bodies that have beetled out of handleless doors, hidden around the station like military anthills. A uniformed group stands rigidly at every visible exit.

Now that no one else can get in, those already inside have rearranged themselves in the pockets of space. While a huge number must be down in the underground, people left at surface level have filed into the shops and restaurants, wedged themselves in the bathrooms, or simply pressed their bodies against the wall. A man nearby is crying, his head on another man's shoulder. Not soft sobs but great ragged cries. Both are suited, black-shoed. They look shiny and professional. They both look like they'd have a lovely "signature scent," a favorite sour cocktail, and an annual bonus. From what Carrie can make out, the crying man's wife is currently giving birth in another part of London, one he can no longer reach. "He'll be born poisoned," the man weeps. "Or he won't be born at all."

Babies. New lives. She is winded by thoughts of Clementine's soft skin. Of her this morning, refusing to wear the outfit put out for her by Emma, before she left for work at the recruitment agency. A hated job so at odds with everything about Emma that Carrie trips over that detail as if it's not true.

Picking Clementine's clothes is a way for Emma to weave herself into their daughter's day before leaving for work. But Clementine was having none of it this morning. Oblivious to the bittersweet ritual, she stood defiant. The concave of her lower back pronounced, shoulder blades so sharp they could split open and sprout angel wings. Three years old but still baby-shaped, her belly jutting out like an apple.

Does Clementine even remember this morning? Did she hold on to the frown, the outrage of the "wrong jeans, Mummy"? Does she remember being briskly wrestled into different jeans and a neon-yellow sweater of her choosing instead? Does she remember the laughter afterward? The goodbye kiss at nursery? Carrie's lips had barely grazed her puffball cheek. Why didn't Carrie just stay home with her? Call them both in sick? Better yet, get Emma to call in sick too. The whole family hunkering down together. Why didn't they just do that every day?

Some people are filming on their phones, taking photos of the huge "seek shelter" warnings. Others are smiling into their screens as they record, talking rapidly of happy memories. "The way you looked at me that day," a man in his fifties says into his phone, "was worth a million lifetimes."

There is currently no way to post on social accounts or send videos anywhere, the network is still down, but maybe it's a soothing habit. Maybe they just have no better ideas right now. A woman a bit younger than Carrie sits cross-legged on the floor, recording a video into her phone. She is also sobbing as she says, "If I don't survive and you find this video, please get it to my family at 17 Dungordan Gardens in Wednesbury. Please tell them I love them."

Behind her, a fight is brewing. It's not spilled over yet, but she can tell the vibe shift from the sounds alone. The grumble of male voices overlapping, the shuffle of heavy feet circling each other.

Whatever is going on has attracted the attention of the uniforms and they stand rigid, watching the fracas carefully, no longer interested in her but still unwilling to let her through. If only she could . . . An idea forms. Her agency filmed a commercial here last year. It could only be shot in the early hours, when the station was almost empty, and she'd volunteered. Carrie can never resist a sneak peek into a secret place. And on that night last year, she and her colleagues were all guided through a warren of tunnels, a disused bit of track that led to . . .

Yes. She knows what to do.

People press themselves to the wall ahead of her, oblivious to the secret door set into it. But. But.

If they open the door to let you out, all of them out there will rush in.

The same applies here. An open door will attract a flood and it will become as dangerous down there as it is up here. A crush in the dark, on the stairs, on the tracks. She tries to look incidental as she weaves her way toward it, brain wheeling for a way to slip through unnoticed.

When she's a few feet away, a bony hand grabs her arm. She looks at the fingers in alarm, then up into an old man's face. "Help me, please," he says, clutching his chest with his other hand. "It's my heart."

She watched her dad have a heart attack and that looked totally different. But she helped her mum through plenty of panic attacks after he died, and those looked just like this.

The man's rheumy eyes hold her gaze and she knows she could reassure him. But. But.

Carrie pries his soft, cold fingers off, one by one. "Just keep breathing slowly and you'll be okay," she whispers as he stares back, pupils ringed in white.

"Help!" she shouts. Her voice a whipcrack against the communal hum. "This man needs medical attention!"

"What?" he gasps, pressing both hands onto his chest.

"Help!" Carrie screams now. "Is there a doctor here? Anyone?"

The crowd pulsates; people jostle and move slightly closer to rubberneck. No one is looking in the direction of the secret door anymore, they are all looking at Carrie and the old man.

"I'm a doctor," a middle-aged woman says hesitantly. She wears a bright-yellow jacket that makes her look nautical. As the medic walks hesitantly toward the old man, the sea-crowd parts around her. They are still watching the doctor when Carrie slips away, unnoticed.

Chapter Eleven

FRANKIE

"How far was that village we passed?"

"I'll go now." Otis is already holding his car keys.

"I'm coming with you."

"It might not be safe, Frankie."

"If you don't get back in time . . . and we're separated when . . ."

It is an unbearable thought to finish and instead he hugs her, just quickly, and then they scramble out of the living room and down the unfamiliar hallway. The little wooden door to the downstairs toilet is open. Frankie really needs to pee but that's out of the question. Everything is out of the question.

They run out the front door, Otis's face as grim as hers must be. She's not used to him sharing her pessimism and it chills her. He needs to be the yang to her yin, but it's all yin right now.

"You must remain inside," the radio says as they buckle up. Otis flashes her a look, then turns the key.

As he reverses at speed and zooms back down the lane, her stomach surges. The denim-blue paintwork of Otis's car scrapes along tree roots, knotty banks and low-hanging tree branches. He cared so much about his paintwork just hours, minutes ago. Neither of them is speaking, Frankie's left hand snakes up to grip the grab handle over the door. She feels hot with panic, her heart audible in her ears, her bladder prickling.

Mist starts to settle on the road in front of them, almost solid in the headlights. Gray shapes slide through the silver air, dissolving into aggressive hedgerows.

Otis is bull-breathing, fast and deep, as he white-knuckles the wheel and leans forward, pressing faster. The radio fills the silence but Frankie thinks for a moment that she can hear a distant siren.

Maybe the army is driving around in a truck, maybe it's their war cry. Maybe it's someone who will help them, and it won't all come down to this, a mad shopping-cart dash in an unfamiliar place. Will there be anything left in any shops? Will it be full *Mad Max* in that pretty little village?

"Shit!"

A rabbit springs out from a hedge and Otis swerves automatically, just missing it and nearly sliding head-on into another car, which whips into a gateway just in time, beeping its horn.

Frankie closes her eyes, and when she opens them, they're still on the lane, still racing along. Otis normally drives this car like it's a Fabergé egg. Now he's driving like he's in a video game.

Her skin itches from the adrenaline and she feels like she could wet herself. Should they have caught that rabbit for food? *Jesus Christ.* She's not sure if she's ridiculous for thinking that or crazy to dismiss it. She's vegetarian. How will that work with limited supplies? She thinks of horror films. The way people turn, pick each other off, consume each other. Did Wes Craven and George A. Romero do a better job of preparing her for the future than her schoolteachers?

The same calm male voice keeps its vigil on the radio. An updated message on loop. How many of these have they got prepared? Did someone know this was happening? The voice urges them not to travel, but what choice do they have? He tells them to seek shelter, to conserve water, batteries, food, and fuel. That it is unlikely that emergency services will be able to help the majority of people. He says this in the same flat tones as a Revenue and Customs ad reminding people to file their tax return or risk a penalty charge.

The voice changes to a woman; she's speaking faster, as if catching her breath. Frankie looks up at Otis, but he's staring at the road. He looks gaunt somehow, like his stuffing has been seeping out into the footwell as he drives.

"This is an emergency news broadcast from Pirate FM," the radio woman says, more somberly than the station name would suggest.

"Speaking from a secure location, the prime minister has sent the following message to all radio stations." There is a click and a pause. When the prime minister's voice starts, it sounds like it's been recorded in a train lavatory.

"Good evening, Britain. I am speaking to you directly to urge you to remain calm but act with haste and diligence. We have faced tough times before, and I am cheered to think of London during the Blitz and our National Health Service heroes during the Covid crisis. Then, as now, we endure.

"I am under no illusion about the incredibly tough times to come, the likes of which we have never before seen. But with hard work and common sense, Britain will emerge, in some form, ready to rise and rebuild. They will not defeat us. God bless you all, and God save the King."

"God save the King," Otis says slowly, but it sounds like a question.

Above them the sky hangs swollen and black, but dead ahead is nothing but solid gray mist, a migraine aura. She grinds her teeth, working them so hard that a snap of pain shoots up one side of her skull.

The recorded messages return, telling them to make sure they seal any water bottles and keep some for washing as well as drinking. The voice coolly reminds listeners that the very worst thing to do now is go outside.

As Otis turns a sharp corner, he briefly loses control and judders across the barely visible road. There is no one else out, no engine sounds, no lights. Not a tractor, car, or truckload of military people coming to save the day. The headlights swing loose as Otis rights himself and Frankie catches the outline of three horses, hanging their heads over a heavy metal gate.

Their breath blends with the mist and the car has passed them before Frankie can even wonder what they're doing out after dark. What can they sense that's got them het up? Are they a family? She realizes her hand is on her belly again.

Is that a Dartmoor pony? she thinks. Was that really today?

Chapter Twelve

MRS. DABB

Any anger about Bunny keeping secrets has entirely disappeared. Relegated to the before times. Now it's about survival. About finding her daughter in time, getting her home, and battening down the cottage to wait this out. Locks. Bolts. Shutters.

A stab of guilt. She cares about Mary too, of course, but right now Mary is a destination. A hope. *Please let her know where Bunny is. Please let her be able to call this secret phone and negotiate with Bunny to return home or at least give up her location so she can be collected.* Maybe Bunny is already at Mary's cottage, and that's why Mary isn't answering. Maybe she called Mary to collect her from school or the doctor hours ago and they're cooking together, preparing food to mark their family's loss, more jam tarts and cupcakes that will end up in the freezer. *Please let them both be tucked up safely, oblivious for now, simply tending their grief.*

The fog is thickening in front of her, layer upon layer of white gossamer until it's impenetrable. Her pedal foot twitches but she can't go any faster, she literally can't see the road. This car is low and lightweight. Insignificant. The banks loom high on either side. Endless and all the same.

She lowers the window for air as nausea bubbles up, but the siren cries out, louder now, its waves breaking against her ears. A rush of it. A bird swooping in the dark, then flying off toward the hidden horizon. It repeats, arcing in volume as she follows the undulations and ancient turns of the road.

It's an incongruous sound out here, a gross punchline, and carries thoughts of blue lights, crime tape, and panic. She forces herself to think instead of Mary's homemade cakes and a warm fire, of Bunny sitting on the beanbag she always opts for, of them looking through old photos of—

Shit!

She swings out of the way as a car, slick and fast as a snake, slithers around the corner and nearly hits her. Her little vehicle whistles to a stop and she closes her eyes for a moment, takes a breath, and then carries on.

People are acting irrationally, and she tries not to think about where that can lead. She cannot remember bolting her back door or turning both keys in the front. She cannot even remember pulling on her coat or stepping outside. Her brain is an organ of instinct and it has not kept a record. Did she leave the security lights on or off? Did she lock her back door?

A familiar creeping dread builds from the pit of her stomach and radiates down her legs and along her arms. Her temples are sweating. She wipes them on her coat sleeve, taps the accelerator, and pierces the fog that is still circling, slowing everybody down and hiding god knows what—or who—in its folds.

The lane twirls away to the right and she follows it until Mary's cottage is dead ahead. There's a glow from the bottom right window and Mary's old 4x4 is in the drive.

She pulls behind it in the drive, curling a wave of gravel into the air, hurls open the door, and jumps down.

She slams the car door and a moment of silence settles. She hears herself breathing, fast and panicked, but then the siren returns, reedy but insistent, like it will outlive everyone.

48 MINUTES UNTIL IMPACT

Chapter Thirteen

CARRIE

The door closes behind her and Carrie presses her back to it for one second, two. Oh thank goodness. This *is* the right place. And she is alone.

The air in this dimly lit corridor is as cold as it was when her agency filmed that deodorant ad. The veteran stuntwoman in a *Die Hard* vest, Daisy Dukes, and heels performing action film feats while the other woman, the twenty-one-year-old whose face they used for the close-ups, sat on a step rubbing her arms, sipping endless energy drinks, and sending up clouds of blueberry vape.

After the panicked hum of hundreds of people, the silence in here is unnerving. Why was this place unlocked? There's no sign of anyone, but perhaps some staff are already down here, maybe sheltering in secret. Is this a trap? Dangerous in some way? A dead end that she's misremembered? But Carrie hasn't got time to overthink it, she just has to move.

The windowless corridor is papered with posters and safety signs. A clipboard hangs from a nail. Everything is dusty, tides of black dirt beached along the floor, the space lit halfheartedly by security lights. As she rushes along, she automatically looks at her phone, expecting to see a message from Emma, about to thumb her way to Favorites to call. *I'm on my way, give Clementine a kiss from me, I love you both, see you soon. Kiss kiss.* As if she were simply leaving work and heading home. But the screen has been taken over by the parasitic message and nothing else is working.

She doesn't remember it being so dark when she was here last time. Maybe they turn up the lights for corporate customers. Even as she thinks these pointless things, Carrie is running along the narrow space, past flapping pieces of paper that brush against her puffy coat. Her sneakers slap the floor so if there are any staff are down here, they'll certainly know she's coming.

She reaches the staircase at the end of the corridor, sucks in a breath, then steps down.

All those desperate people back there, and she's slipped away from them, burrowing her way secretly under the city.

The staircase twirls below her, corkscrewing under the earth, tiled in the old style of the tube. The sounds of her feet on the second, third, fourth step don't so much echo as swirl, dancing up and down the dark space so it sounds like she is a small army. This is a repurposed old elevator shaft. She and her colleagues were told this as they stifled yawns, Carrie thinking at the time that she should write these facts down like she was on a school trip.

The stairs seem to stretch away as she runs down, tricking the eye like an Escher illustration. The wall tiles disappear, it's just rough gray concrete now. This was never meant to be seen.

She's glad to be traveling light, no dangling bag. Everything she needs is right here in her pockets. Well, nothing she truly needs but everything she has.

After stomping down as fast as she can, Carrie reaches the end of the stairs, knees wobbling uncertainly, suspicious of the flat ground. The echo of her steps continues for a moment.

A gust of chilled air hits her ankles, exposed and prickling above her sneakers. She is in an alcove, the dark walls thick with foamy, fungal dirt. When she ventures outside of this corner, she is almost sick with relief. She is on a stub of platform, the very same one from the commercial.

A mistake, a quirk of the train company changing design during the building of an extension, having to avoid some unknown pipe or other. Occasionally it's used for dragging broken cars out of the way but mostly it's just forgotten. More importantly, it leads onto the main track of either the Northern Line or the Bakerloo—she doesn't remember which. Maybe she should have written things down after all.

The whole crush of London is up there, over her head, but she really does have a chance of getting to her family. She can do this.

Chapter Fourteen

FRANKIE

We're never going to do this, Frankie thinks. *We don't know the area, we don't have anyone to ask for help, we don't even know if the shop is open.*

They are passing clusters of houses now, gray sketches and smudged glows barely visible through the mist. They've just learned that the car doesn't have fog lights.

Otis swings the car into a blind bend, slamming into more mist as Frankie's bladder sloshes. She could wet herself, really. For the first time as an adult, she actually might. If this were any other time, anyone else at the wheel, she'd be screaming at them not to drive like such a dick.

Instead, she reaches her hand toward Otis's leg. She often drapes her fingers on him when she's in the passenger seat, squeezing his thigh muscles absent-mindedly, proprietorially, but she pulls her hand back. It would just distract rather than reassure him.

He swings the car again, his tendons and nerves straining. A glow of lights bounces past from the other direction but the vehicle they belong to is invisible. Luckily the road is wide here because neither driver attempted to slow down. She catches sight of herself in the windshield, looking twice her thirty-six years, bulky in her sweatshirt and for once not giving a solitary shit. And all it took to shake off body-shame was the end of the fucking world.

The ghost of a siren seems to skim over the surface of the fields, coil around the silver twists of the roads, and dissolve into the mist.

"Do you hear that?" she asks, but Otis doesn't reply, won't let a single drop of concentration fall away from the road.

Is she just imagining a siren because she expects to hear one? It sounds pretty clear to her, but do they even have sirens like that anymore? It's not World War II.

"Oh my god," she says, the thought gulping out of her. "Is this World War Three?"

"What?"

This is . . . a nuclear strike is, well, that could be it, couldn't it? Not just here, not just for them, but for everyone eventually. Because the UK will fire back, right? And then the countries on each side will set off their weapons and then everyone is dead. That's how mutually assured destruction works. "Like *Dr. Strangelove*," she says, but he's not engaging. She doubts he's watched it and feels, unfairly, irritated to be alone in her references.

Is there any point to this wild-goose chase? But she looks at Otis and she thinks of a new family, of a poppy seed that deserves to flower, and knows they have to try.

Otis stamps on the accelerator so hard they lurch forward suddenly. When she looks over at the dashboard, they're barely skimming fifty miles an hour but it's so twisty and fogged that it feels like a ninety-mile-an-hour slalom.

The radio is still burbling away and she focuses on that, trying to ignore the car sickness.

"Stay inside and seek shelter where you are," the detached male voice says with a crackle. Frankie imagines some actor doing this for a flat fee years ago, forgetting the weird job as time passed. Is he sitting by a radio somewhere hearing himself? Maybe he's long dead and his children are finding some last tiny comfort from this unknown recording.

"It is important to conserve supplies, it is unlikely you will be able to buy more in the coming weeks. Gather batteries, food, and fuel. Keep water supplies covered. It is unlikely that the emergency services will be able to help the majority of people once the strike occurs. You will need to stay inside; the fallout will be extremely dangerous."

Once the strike occurs. Is "once" a when or an if? And if it's not occurred yet, could it be diverted? Shot down? Could any kind of help come? Does it work like that? It feels unlikely and childish to even imagine it.

"Stay inside and seek shelter," continues the dispassionate freelance voice artist who may or may not be dead.

How can we seek shelter while also gathering batteries, food, and fuel? We can't be the only people without a well-stocked larder and a fallout shelter?!

Has the siren stopped? She looks at her phone, hoping a new emergency alert will appear, undoing the last one. "Sorry, we pressed the wrong button. As you were." A great big catastrophic lol. But no. Of course not.

Either the siren was never there or it's now hidden under the radio, but she can hear a new sound. A low buzzing, almost like a growl. She looks at Otis but he's still frowning at the road ahead, swinging around another corner and into a narrow cottage-lined lane.

He stamps the brakes before she's processed what she's seeing. Zigzagged, abandoned. A graveyard of cars, engines still running.

Chapter Fifteen

MRS. DABB

"It's me," she says, banging on the door and then reaching into her pocket for her set of keys. "I'm coming in, Mary."

She shoves the sticky door with her shoulder. Inside, the cottage is a hot box, causing an instant sweat on the upper lip. The faux logs glow, the old radiators click like tongues. The living room curtains hang half-pulled, the television blaring at full volume. Mary has steadily lost her hearing over the last ten years but she's only recently got aids fitted and frequently forgets to charge them—or chooses not to.

Mary is perched on the edge of her sofa, shoulders slumped in defeat. She looks as tired as this room with its heavy, old-fashioned curtains that she made herself, decades ago. The dusty school photos in their brown cardboard frames, warped with time, too painful for anyone to look at.

Mary's face is bleached by the glare of the screen, whitewashing her lines and wrinkles, rendering her moon-white and decades younger. The smiling, jolly woman she once was, only the nub of whom is still inside this older lady. Like a fruit stone.

Mary's eyes are pink from crying. She gestures to the screen, frowning and shaking her head. She knows.

"Is Bunny here?"

Mary looks up with a snap of her neck.

"No," Mary says, frowning. "She knows I always come to you on—"

"She faked a note from me to get out of school this afternoon and then didn't come home on the bus. Her friend Jasmine thinks the note said she had a doctor's appointment but that could be total bollocks or just guesswork and I don't know what to do, Mary!"

"What do you mean?"

The glow of the screen has already stripped Mary of any complexion, but she seems to go whiter still. "Nothing," she says quickly. "Just at thirteen, girls are looking inward. You remember that, surely? And her mum is the last person to know anything. Have you tried her friends? What about her best friend?" Mary gives her a loaded look then. "I know you're close as anything but you're still her mum. It's best friends that know everything about thirteen-year-olds."

Jasmine.

Mary claps a hand over her mouth and struggles to a stand, then reaches to grab her hands, just briefly. "She's out there with all this going on?"

"I don't know. I don't know where she is! I hoped she might be here. She didn't say anything to you?"

"No," Mary says. A flicker of something, a question or a thought. She purses her lips, just slightly, but then shakes her head. "No," she says, firmer this time. "Have you tried the doctor's?"

"It won't be open now, you know it won't."

"There might be someone there, it's worth—"

"Did you know she has a phone?"

"A phone?" The confusion on Mary's face seems genuine.

"Did you buy her a cell phone?"

"What?"

"I don't care, Mary, I won't be cross, I just need to know because then we can call it and—"

"Of course I didn't buy her a phone, I know your feelings about . . . all of that."

"Did you give her any money?"

Mary sits back down with a grunt. "I sometimes give her bits and bobs, you know I do," she says quietly. "Not enough for a phone, nothing like that."

"She could have saved it up, she could—"

"A couple of quid here and there, enough for sweets, not gadgets."

"Enough for a train ticket?"

"A train ticket?"

"To Plymouth or London. I'm worried she's—"

"Oh dear god," Mary cries then. "No, darling, I haven't given her enough for a train ticket to bloody London. That's more than a phone would cost these days. Why would she think to—"

"Because . . ." *Because what?* Because it's a place that lures people away.

"Darling," Mary says softly. "Today is hard enough but now there's all this." She waves her hand at the screen. "You're not thinking straight. Bunny doesn't know anyone in London now. Or Plymouth. Or Bristol for that matter. You need to look closer to home."

45 MINUTES UNTIL IMPACT

Chapter Sixteen

CARRIE

The tube trains have apparently been stopped; that's what they announced when she was still on the concourse, and she can't hear any coming.

This fake station is empty and dimly lit. It's still gussied up from whatever was last filmed here, a wartime romance maybe, the kind for which Carrie has a soft spot. All those tea dresses, waistcoats, and lovely hats.

Fake posters line the walls, warning Londoners to wear something white and carry a flashlight, to be careful alighting in the blackout, never to chance a journey without a gas mask. And a real sign, crusted with dirt. It bears only the classic roundel and three capitalized words: LINE IS LIVE.

She walks to the edge of the platform. She can hear a slight sizzling sound, which must be the electricity. She turns and lowers herself until she is sitting on the edge of the line. Humpty Dumptying with death. Can she really do this?

She thinks of Clementine and Emma and steps down between the tracks.

Carrie has ridden the tube thousands of times in the last thirteen years but she has never paid any attention to what's underneath the trains, what makes up the metallic veins and arteries. And now she must walk among it all.

When she sweeps the flashlight of her phone around, it's a confusion of tracks, metal boxes, and mechanical-looking oddities. She doesn't know which bits are electrified, maybe all of them. The sizzling mingles with the pulse in her ears.

There is no color. Everything around the tracks is the same dark sooty gray. She listens intently. The noises separate and clarify until she can tell which tracks are making the sizzling noise.

She starts to walk carefully along the narrow edge of the track, the platform level with her torso. A shock of cold bites her as soon as she steps into the tunnel; every muscle in her body clenches.

She holds her phone in her left hand and uses her right to guide her along the platform wall, greasy dirt coating her fingertips. The space she's in now is completely circular overhead, it's unbelievable that a whole train can fit in here. If one were to come along now, there'd be nowhere for her body to go. No platform, no exits. Ahead, a red light glows on a spike.

Her steps are babied by the dark and the constant reminder that she could be electrocuted if she slips. Running down those stairs from the station, she'd felt like she had ample time to get home. Now she feels time leaking away into the thick dirt floor of this tunnel.

Shit!

What the hell is that?

A tiny mouse, brown and tailless. Part of an innumerable tube colony, wriggling wildly through the network, multiplying like a virus. She knows they're harmless. She knows that *rationally*.

Her narrow shaft of light picks out more movement. She keeps on stepping rhythmically, thinking of Clementine and trying not to imagine these little bodies busying themselves up the hem of her jeans and writhing around against her skin.

"Oh, go away," she says to them, her voice bouncing around the tunnel and back to her. "Piss off!" A gasp comes in reply. A pocket of wind.

This is the most constructed place she has ever been. There is not a scrap of anything natural. The only organic things are her and the vermin, just their soft tissue and hers tickling this metal throat.

She reaches the connection to the main line, although it looks exactly the same as this spur. With time ebbing away fast, it's essential she goes in the right direction, left or right. She thinks it must be to the right, but if she makes the wrong choice, she will worm her way right back under the station and toward the river, boomeranging along the South Bank toward her office. If she doesn't get out soon and run home, or if she's too far away when she does emerge, she won't make it in time.

If Clementine survives and Carrie doesn't, if she's fried by the train line or blown to pieces by the missile, or poisoned by whatever the hell is loaded into it . . . she's made no will. She and Emma aren't married because *forever* was already established. But Emma doesn't yet have parental responsibility for Clementine. The half-filled-out form is still wedged next to the fridge. Would Emma and Mum fight each other for custody?

Stop fucking spiraling and make a decision.

She steps out to the right, shouting at the mice as she goes. Her throat fills with something that makes her cough. Her skin, somehow, is both cold and sweating, clothes coated in filth from brushing against the wall. Every few meters there's another small red light. A glowing signal meant for drivers. She forces herself into a shuffling jog, her footsteps echoing.

When her flashlight catches a slice of her white sneakers, they're filthy with the dried grease that must be inches deep on this floor, pasted there by nearly a century of trains rushing through.

She kicks something and it wriggles away in the dark. But as she starts to hurry on, she hears something new. Something clear. The shuffle of feet. An uncertain cough. Another.

And then, "Excuse me, miss?"

Chapter Seventeen

FRANKIE

"We can't get through," Otis says, staring at the cluster of abandoned cars. As his engine idles, he drags both hands down his face, *Scream*-masking himself. He reverses a few meters, keeping some space all around the old Mercedes, which suddenly feels enormous.

The lane snakes around a tight bend; it is impossible to know how many cars are ahead. Frankie swallows back her rising nausea.

Otis squeezes her hand quickly, shuts off the engine, and gets out. She wrestles out of her seat belt and opens the door. Her coat is back at the cottage and the cold air smarts her skin, the wind feels like a personal attack.

"Can you run in those?" He points to her clumpy boots.

"I'll have to try." His much bigger hand swallows hers like a mitt and then, hefty in her boots, she starts to run.

They weave and dodge through cars, some nosed up on the pavement, some two abreast, or diagonal. People clearly tried to do this neatly at first, even in panic. But it didn't work.

They pass a Fiat 500 with a tiny Yorkie dog going nuts on the back seat, his desperate teeth chomping at the windows, limbs whirling. The small car is entirely wedged in; will his owner be able to get him out? Get him home? How many dogs will be left outside, cats too . . . it's not like they'll have received the emergency alert. Oh god, all the ponies.

As they skim the car, the Yorkie cries plaintively and Frankie has to look away or she'll be breaking in to rescue him. He looks just like her parents' dog, out in Spain.

"Cough the dog" was originally called Bartholomew, which her mum thought was distinguished. He got told to "fuck off" from under her dad's big feet so many times he started responding to the name. Fuck off. Cough. Cough the dog. She wonders if they're—

"Ow!"

"God, are you okay?" Otis stops suddenly, his hand dropping from hers and moving toward her hip, but she pushes him away, panicked.

"I," she gasps.

She'd not seen the side mirror there, jutting like a prank, clipping her hard on the side as she squeezed through. How had she not seen it? It was right there. But Otis was pulling her and she was miles away, thinking about her parents and . . .

"The baby," Otis says, but it's a question. She rubs her side; it's not her belly, so she shakes her head.

"We need to go," he says gently.

"Don't pull me so fucking hard," she says, even though she knows it's not his fault. He looks wounded, but he starts to move again and she follows.

Otis strides ahead and Frankie shuffles after him. He clearly wants to run but every step for her is hard in these boots and she doesn't even have the spare breath to ask him to slow down, let alone to run with him. She's never been sporty, unlike Otis, and, for most of her life, stayed thin the same way her mum and her aunties did. The smoking of cigarettes and the denial of pleasure.

They follow a conch shell of lanes, turn a corner, and finally see the village. The skeletal decorations still hang dormant. Will everyone still be sheltering at Christmas? Will anyone be keeping track of the date by then? How many people in this village will die, either from the strike or the fallout? They should have lit these decorations today, had one last hurrah.

Just down the road, a queue leads to a grocery shop. It is unnervingly orderly. As they join the back of the queue, she says, "We shouldn't have left the fucking North." She says this instead of saying she's terrified and her hip hurts. That she hates how dependent she's being on him. That she was always so worried she'd end up like her mum, negotiating a marriage that was more like a terror campaign. She was so happy, just eighteen minutes ago, to know that her child would never experience that kind of fear. And now, in utero, they face something immeasurably worse.

"I thought you wanted to go away," Otis says. "You seemed really happy."

"I was really happy," she says, louder than intended. Two waxed-jacketed women queuing in front of them turn to look, then turn back. "I *was* really happy. Otis, I was so fucking happy. I'm sorry."

A woman rushes out of the shop ahead of them, hugging a full shopping bag to her body as she runs down the road away from the village square. A rumble of disapproval spreads. "There'll be nothing left," one of the women in front says as they all take a collective step forward.

"This is my fault," Otis says, pulling at his hair. "I shouldn't have brought you all this way, I shouldn't have risked you or—"

"We'll be okay," one of the waxed jackets says to Otis, her voice kind. She gestures to the church behind them. "He will look after us." She smiles and pats Otis on the arm. "Just trust in Him."

For a moment no one says anything else. The crowd turns back, and then Frankie looks at Otis and he at her.

Her shoulders start to shake with delirious laughter. When people in films laugh during a crisis, she rolls her eyes. *That would never happen. Unrealistic.* But it does now. She shakes and laughs, a fraction away from hysteria. She feels like she did when she first ate a chocolate brownie loaded with weed, a million years ago. Laughter that took her over, threw her around like a rag doll.

Otis watches her, alarmed at first. Then his own shoulders shake and his face folds and he is laughing, and she is laughing, and then he is crying and she is holding him and he's gulping great wretched sobs and she's telling him it's really not his fault, none of it, and she's trying to convince herself that she doesn't blame him, not at all. Even though the Lake District was right there.

Chapter Eighteen

MRS. DABB

"I need to speak to Jasmine."

"Call her from here," Mary says, her eyes pleading. She doesn't want to be left alone, clearly.

"I don't have any phone numbers with me and I had to go through her mum last time. No, I need to speak to her in person and look her in the eye."

"I'll come." Mary struggles to a stand, joints clicking like she's been crunched into a stiff position for hours. "We can check the doctor's on the way."

"No, just . . . you just stay here, safe and warm. We're not supposed to be out and about."

"I can't just stay here like a useless lump, not with Bunny out there and everything else." Mary's voice is going higher, wobblier. She used to be so sure of herself but in this moment, she seems younger than Bunny.

"You've got your key for my place, haven't you?"

Mary nods.

"Wrap up the food and bring it to mine. Secure your place properly before you go, lock your doors when you're driving, and don't pull over for anyone. Okay?"

"Darling, I—"

"I mean it, Mary, it's not bloody safe. Okay?"

"Okay."

"Just let yourself into ours and hopefully Bunny will get home even before I do and we can all just . . . we can get through this together. Okay?"

"Okay."

"Please, Mary, be careful, you don't know what desperate people will do."

A pause. "Yes, I do," she says, her voice no longer unsure. She walks into the kitchen to start wrapping up food.

Mary's 4x4 is a relic but it's built like a tank. So long as she doesn't stop for anyone en route, no matter how convincing they are, she should be okay. She can't get hung up on that now anyway, Bunny has to be the priority.

The little electric car is still warm from earlier. Her temples hum and her neck starts to sweat as soon as she sits down. She loosens her coat and turns down the heater but there's no time to stop and peel any layers off as she pulls out into the lane, trying to think about the quickest route to Jasmine's house on the other side of Chagford. She's dropped Bunny there before, made small talk with her mother on the doorstep while peering surreptitiously over the woman's shoulder to look for evidence of . . . not something bad as such, more evidence of care. Of kindness and safety. That the girls wouldn't be allowed to roam unprotected.

Chagford will be full of cars right now, full of people flooding into the church. The thought of all those people makes her throat constrict, but Mary is right, she should check at the doctor's just in case. As she picks up the pace, the car doors lock automatically, sealing her in with a mechanical gulp.

The siren is still wailing and the fog has strangled all visibility. Dartmoor is held together by myths, and her favorite was always the pixies. While most of the others are scary or tragic, the pixies come out to help people, especially in weather like this. They lead the lost back to the roads and help travelers find their way. Where are the pixies tonight, with the weather conspiring against locals and visitors alike? Do they help anyone, no matter who they are or what they've done? She checks the door locks instinctively, but of course they're still locked.

A prickle of something or someone in the car with her. Her eyes flash up to the mirror but the back seats are empty. A ghost sensation, ridiculous but hard to shake. For a moment, she pictures the little girl that Bunny once was, fast asleep in her booster in the middle of the back seat, positioned so she was always visible. The unbearable thought of letting her out of sight, loose in the unknown . . .

But that's exactly what I have done.

She snaps on the radio but it doesn't tell her anything new so she turns it off. Sometimes it's worse to know.

42 MINUTES UNTIL IMPACT

Chapter Nineteen

CARRIE

"Miss, did you hear me?"

Breathing hard, Carrie stays stock-still, brain wheeling through the possibilities. Transit staff? British Transport Police? A Victorian ghost? *Am I dead?*

"I didn't mean to scare you, miss," the voice says. "I wanted to say something before but you seemed busy shouting at the mice."

Carrie turns then, raising the beam of the phone flashlight so that the silhouetted person covers their face. Carrie lowers the light just a little until the blur of a dirty white sleeve moves down and the schoolgirl's blinking eyes are visible. The blazer she was wearing earlier is gone, her sweater now tied around her waist in a way that takes Carrie immediately back to school, rolled waistband, tie stuffed in her pocket.

"It's you," Carrie says, "from up there."

The girl walks along the tracks toward Carrie now, treading carefully, palms out in front of her, her schoolbag on both shoulders.

"I followed you."

"Why?"

"I didn't want to stay in that meat market and I thought you looked like you knew something."

Carrie says nothing.

"And then I saw you starting beef with the mice and realized you didn't know anything either but it was too late and I didn't want to go back without a light of my own."

"How old are you?"

The girl hesitates. "Thirteen," she says, frowning a little like *what's that got to do with anything?* and she's right, but it's the only thing Carrie ever thinks to ask kids.

"Where are you going?"

"Well, I was following you, but—"

"Where do you want to go? Are you trying to get home?"

At this, the brave rigidity softens and the girl nods. "I live in Lambeth, and they'll be there without me."

"Whereabouts?"

"What?"

"Which bit of Lambeth, which road?"

"Elm Walk, d'you know it? It's off—"

"Kennington Road. I live just the other side but, hang on, what's your name?"

"Grace, miss."

"Hi, Grace. But look, I can't slow down. I've got to get back to my partner and daughter, no matter what—"

"And I need to get back to my whole family, so let's get going, yeah?" It's false bravado and Carrie knows it, but she nods.

"Okay. But please stop calling me miss, I'm not a teacher."

"Okay."

"My name's Carrie."

"Okay, Carrie."

They walk either side of a live rail, the sizzling sound constant. It has been twenty minutes since the warning came but Carrie doesn't know how far they've walked, or how far there is left to go. Her nostrils are gummed up with stale air and dust, her eyes stinging.

"You ever experienced anything like this before?" Grace asks.

"Not like this, no."

"My mum was caught up in the 7/7 bombings," Grace says. "Before she had me."

"God, was she?"

"Yeah. She was on the next train at Edgware Road. She doesn't talk about it, though, I only know because Granddad told me."

"I was about your age when that happened," Carrie says, her feet settling back into the rhythm of before. "But I didn't live here then."

A faraway tragedy brought to the screen in Technicolor when she got back from school, though the news had already gone around the playground. Her beloved dad had lowered his eyes from the screen, muttering things that sounded angry and unlike him. For her mother, it was a simple confirmation that London was a bad place full of bad people making bad decisions. "What do they expect," her mum said, watching footage of stoic Londoners as they walked home in work clothes and sneakers, spreading across empty roads where buses and cabs would normally be. "They chose to live there."

London, to her parents, was a Pied Piper of a city, leading people off a cliff. But Carrie had watched that footage, head tilted, tuning out her parents. The news didn't put her off. Instead, it confirmed London as special. A place where news was made.

Carrie thinks now of those brave pedestrians on their open roads, walking with determination toward their boroughs. Of Grace's mum, not talking about it but continuing to live in the capital, to raise her family there. She thinks of the courage with which Londoners remounted buses the next day, shuffled down escalators into the bowels of the underground. She thinks of everyone sardined at Waterloo. The closed exits. Guns.

"Right, we need to find a way out before we get to the next station," Carrie says.

"What if there isn't a way out before the next station?"

She hadn't thought about that. Maybe they'll have to fight their way through. Just her and this plucky kid. Maybe there'll be fewer guards at the next stop than there were at Waterloo. Maybe. Or maybe they could keep going, crawl along the line and hope no one sees them, keep going all the way home. But then what? Same again, a fight to get out, a bullet for their trouble. And what if they're not even on the Northern Line? Or they are but she chose wrong and they're headed north instead of south? Emerging at Westminster . . . She gulps the air but it doesn't help.

"Are you okay?" Grace's hand, wavering and light, touches her shoulder.

"Yeah," she manages. But she's thinking about Westminster. If they are heading that way, they're already dead. Because you don't have to know anything about anything to know the seat of government will be a prime target. And now this girl has hitched her wagon and Carrie is responsible for her too. Why does she always end up taking responsibility for other people and complicating her own plans? Why does she always think the best and never plan for the worst?

Okay, think. Maybe they could get a boat at the Embankment, sail it down to Vauxhall Bridge.

"Do you know anything about boats?" she says weakly.

"What?"

As if there'll be any boats left. They'll have fled down the river toward the coast, to France or Ireland. Or simply capsized under the crowds.

"No, sorry, forget it. I'm just being mad. There'll be an exit soon. Of course there will. Maintenance people must have to get down to the line between stations."

"You sure?"

No.

"Yes."

She just needs to get back to Clementine and Emma. *And Pepper.* She owes it to him too to get back. As she picks carefully through the tunnel, she pictures what Pepper will be doing now. Gathering, as usual, the artifacts he has curated from a life that has spun around so many different coils. Things gathered during his theater years and the precious few relics from his childhood in Poland. Is her and Emma's flat already stuffed with his mementos when it should be filled with canned food and water? What should they be doing back home? What should she be doing *now*?

Carrie thinks of every disaster movie she's yawned through, fallen asleep halfway through. No useful techniques stuck and she has no witty lines. But she has a sidekick now. Having a sidekick and being on an epic quest means Carrie's undeniably the hero of this film. And heroes and their sidekicks always survive. Don't they?

Grace stops suddenly, grabbing Carrie's arm and then dropping it just as quickly. "Look, do you see that?"

"What?"

Almost everything ahead of them is pitch-black, except for a tiny block of light. *Is that . . . ?*

"Oh thank god," says Carrie. "It's an exit sign."

"You're definite?"

"Yes." Carrie almost laughs. "I really, actually am."

Chapter Twenty

FRANKIE

There are twelve human heads in front of them, another three have just gone inside, and two more have just appeared from different directions and joined the queue behind her. Two red-faced, middle-aged men, one in a bodywarmer, the other a waxed jacket. They nod to each other, and then to Frankie as she watches. Silent and frowning, but with no sign of panic.

Chagford is clearly a village that coped well with the pandemic a few years ago. Thrived, even. Bicycle deliveries, collection slots, shopping rotas for the vulnerable, Zoom book clubs, and alfresco church services. Frankie can tell they know what they're doing here, with their calm, collective community organization.

Outside the shop, there's a boy of eighteen, nineteen tops, wearing a grocery store uniform, letting people in and out. He is tall and scatter-limbed like a baby deer. Open-faced and reed-thin, he'd have no hope of stopping anyone, but people have submitted fully to this queueing system. No shouting. Or pleading. Despite that church clock over there showing forty-two minutes until . . . until what? She can't begin to fathom. Until an explosion? Until something hits the ground hundreds of miles away in London and the fallout from it drifts slowly this way? Until the whole of the South of England melts and—

"Jesus, you okay?" Otis looks at her in alarm. "You've gone dead pale."

"I'm just . . . this is a lot."

"It's too much, that's what it is."

"Zero out of ten," she says, as he hugs her tightly again.

Otis jiggles his legs, his knees bashing into her as the queue tightens. A tic that happens when he's being forced to wait, the impetus to move crackling through him. The opposite of her, who knows never to get involved, Otis is a doer, a fidgeter, a fixer. It's how they first met after all, him coming to fix the broken blind in her dried-flower studio early last year. A happy handyman who lingered when he was finished, asking dumb questions about flowers to which he obviously didn't need the answers. Just a nice guy, four years younger than her, who said she was his last job and did she fancy a drink.

That drink in a pub turned into a few more drinks back at hers, turned into going to bed. She assumed that was the end of that, and that was okay, that was safer all round. No chance of anyone getting hurt. But the next morning, he was still there, and that felt, somehow, safer still. Only now he is the father of her child and the person with whom she will spend the last normal moments of life. And nobody is safe.

A woman joins the queue behind them; other people who are waiting greet her with weary tones and nodded heads. There's an acceptance to all this that unnerves Frankie.

"If we don't get into the shop soon, we're cutting it too fine to get back and do everything we need to do," Frankie says.

For a moment, she thinks Otis hasn't heard her. Then he turns, cups her face, and says, "Just for once, can you pretend to be an optimist?" Then he kisses her mouth before she can protest this statement. Optimism, when the missiles are already locked and loaded? Sure, why not.

The queue grows restless. The orderly silence of a few minutes ago blisters into little snippets of sharp conversation, of complaint. There's an edge to it now. It wasn't calm collectivism they'd stepped into, Frankie realizes now, it was dormant British rage.

"... enough water?"

"Jim's doing all of that back home, we've got the bath, two, no, three buckets, every mug..."

"Well, it's good you've got your Jim then, isn't it, Sheila? Dave's stuck in Plymouth."

"Oh. Oh, I'm so sorry, Della. Does he still work at—"

"Devonport. Yes."

Silence comes like a handbrake.

Frankie waits for more, looking at the woman she now knows is Della.

Her hair is auburn, a sliver of soft silver at the roots. She wears a waxed jacket with a torn pocket and sturdy walking boots. Her eyes are red-rimmed but steely, cheeks scribbled with rosacea. She catches Frankie's gaze before she can look away.

"Not from round here?" she asks, her voice booming militarily. Frankie shakes her head. "Ah, I see. Well, Devonport is where they refit the subs."

Otis and Frankie look at each other, like, *does that mean—*

"Nuclear subs," Della says. Everyone in the queue is silent now, listening as if this is new information when it must really be information they've tried to forget.

"I didn't know," Frankie says quietly. "Will that make it a—"

"Target? Of course it will," Della says. "It's only twenty-five miles from here, as the crow flies. Didn't you hear the siren?"

"I hoped I was imagining it," Frankie manages to say.

Chapter Twenty-One

MRS. DABB

She looks at the time and thinks of people streaming through cities, fighting for space. She thinks too of strangers offering kindness, of perfect strangers gripping hands and bracing for their worlds to end. She thinks of dogs howling, of pets bundled into cars that then slam into traffic, of families sheared in two by distance. Parents at work with no hope of getting home in time, children stuck at school. People jumping in crowded boats, motorway pileups, and housebreaking. She can barely breathe, her lungs stuffed with thoughts of all the desperate people doing things they would never normally do.

As she whips faster through the gray air, she thinks guiltily of Mary. Will Mary really be okay getting herself to the cottage? Can she even carry all that food? She could have come along after all, secured in the passenger seat, knees blanketed, strapped in place. Today, of all days, she should not be on her own.

She did tell Mary not to open the door to anyone once she got to the cottage, *didn't she*? To lock it tight and wait for only her and Bunny?

I'm not a child, Mary's voice chides her, and she isn't. She's not old and batty either, which would be the easy thing to suggest. But she is riddled with holes. She wears the moth-worn fabric of the grieving, and sometimes those clothes are so heavy that all Mary can do, all anyone grieving can do, is curl up in them, close her eyes, and opt out. And when that happens, mistakes are made, risks are taken or creep in unseen.

There is no room for more risk today, the atmosphere is already crackling with it.

It's been an hour and twenty minutes since Bunny should have been home. Over four hours since she was last seen at school. Out there, with a secret phone, but one she hasn't used to call home, to reassure her mother. Why? Surely she knows that even though she's broken multiple rules in lying, sneaking, and using something she's banned from using, being safe trumps all that. Unless someone has stopped her making that call.

She shakes her head; it is simply not the time for thinking the worst. "Picture a time that you thought something bad was going to happen but everything turned out for the best," she hears her therapist, Miranda, say in her head. *Oh, Miranda, you do not know what can of worms you're hacking into.*

Light floods the road ahead of her, turning the fog atomic white. She sucks in a breath, squints, and slows, just slightly, Overhead, the roar of a helicopter shakes the car's outer skeleton as her own organs seem to liquefy inside it. *Stay on track, don't let them scare you off course.*

Whoever they're looking for from up there, they're unlikely to find them in this weather, among all these knotted hedgerows draped with fog. The last time these big beasts flew around here in any number was during the floods, not that long after they'd moved into the cottage. Terrified, she and Bunny had taken refuge upstairs in her bedroom, bringing up the old TV and DVD player that came with the place, watching cartoons from decades earlier, and eating food she'd shoved into a picnic basket, imagining the rest of the kitchen would be lost to the filthy water. She'd laced the lower floors with sandbags, buckets at the ready; "We will just have to learn to sail," she'd said to Bunny, who didn't fall for the fake jollity but pretended not to be scared for her mother's sake. The two of them, locked into mirror acts of fear and denial.

They'd been spared, too high above sea level to be affected, just as Mary had reassured them they would be. She couldn't explain to Mary that it was the helicopters, and not the water, that scared her the most.

The helicopter swings away, apparently happy that her little car needs no further investigation, dimming the air again. She breathes out slowly, but even with the helicopter gone, there's plenty to fear.

Oh, Bunny, why today?

She hardly gets given any pocket money, so if Mary didn't buy her a phone, who did? Surely not a boyfriend?

Thoughts of cars and trucks squealing around, no seat belts. Zitty chins and greasy fingers. Men five, ten, fifteen years older, too immature for women their own age, too gross, too demanding. Creeps. Older creeps. Slipping their arms around narrow young waists, convincing girls they're women, that they're lucky to have been noticed. When these beautiful young girls shine brighter than they ever could.

But she's only thirteen, and a young thirteen at that. Still so loving. Resting her chin on her mother's head, already so much taller, her laughter reverberating through both their skulls. She still sucks her thumb, hooking one finger over her nose, eyes glazing over as she watches the screen. Still the milk-drunk baby she once was. *Still my baby.*

Should I go to the police?

The thought makes her press harder on the accelerator.

Don't be ridiculous. They have enough on today. Christ.

She pulls onto a little-known track that will take her via a back road to Chagford, just showing as a hazy glow through the fog. The streets will be full already. Faces she might see often at the produce exchange or the community beehive will now be strangered in their anguish.

39 MINUTES UNTIL IMPACT

Chapter Twenty-Two

CARRIE

As Carrie and Grace approach the exit sign, the noise of the next station along starts to reach them through the tunnel. A burble of announcements, indecipherable but in the same detached tone as all the others. Carrie has an overwhelming urge to grab Grace's hand but resists. No need to make this insane situation any more weird.

A new sound hits them from underneath the recorded voice. A kind of moaning, vibrating hum. Carrie concentrates, trying to parse it into sense and detail.

People. Lots of people.

Weeping and moaning, sniffing, wailing, and talking. The tinkle of children's voices. Their young sentences rising to question marks at the end. How on earth are parents finding any answers to give them?

"Do you hear that?" she asks.

"Course," Grace says.

A small voice breaks through the distant hum. "Mummy!"

Clementine!

Carrie stumbles, knowing even as she does that it can't be her child, but it's too late . . .

She is falling, hard and chaotic.

Her phone spins away from her, lighting up snatches of black dirt.

Her feet scrabble.

Her arms flail.

She is falling onto the live line.

Pain.

Carrie has landed face down, her mouth filled with the taste of dirt, metal, and the blood around banged teeth. Her hands and face are smeared in whatever. But she's not been electrocuted. *I am still alive.* How?

Carrie realizes, as the sounds stretching and flexing around her start to make sense, that one noise is now missing. The sizzling sound of the live rails has stopped. They must have turned them off. Did other people fall on them, is that why? Maybe people were throwing themselves... She shakes that thought away. *No, no, nope.*

"Carrie, oh my god, are you okay?"

She feels Grace's hands on her arm, tugging her up. She's in pain. She caught her right knee on one of the rails, her other knee landed in the middle dip—the so-called suicide pit. Her head throbs from smacking against something on the way down, her teeth feel loose. But she is alive. The pain proves that. She feels around for her phone, finds it face down not far away. The screen is smashed, little pieces of glass falling out as she lifts it.

"Oh man."

Grace helps her to her feet. They look at each other but say nothing. And then, ignoring the pain from her legs and face, Carrie and Grace start to run as fast as they can for the illuminated door. No longer careful. No longer afraid of frying.

As they get closer to the door and the station some distance beyond, the rumbles separate out into individual voices.

"This is hell, man!"

"Nah, mate, hell is coming."

These are the sounds of things about to turn. Grace looks warily at Carrie, but if she's asking a question, Carrie doesn't know the answer. The calm drone of the announcer becomes crisper through the grate in the wall, offering yet more appeals for calm and promises of water.

"Where the fuck *is* the water?!" a woman shouts.

Carrie grabs Grace's arm and they reach the door together, their bodies slamming into it. With filthy shirtsleeves and smeared hands, Grace reaches for the handle and turns it hard.

The door swings slowly inward and away from the tracks, a grinding sound blocking out all the people noise. They look at each other with relief. Grace looks younger now, as her eyes widen.

The light pouring out from this doorway is overwhelming, a white flood that springs tears. When Grace sees Carrie's illuminated face she flinches.

"That bad?" Carrie says, reaching up and touching her tender face. Grace shrugs but then nods. They blink as they step inside and Grace closes the door behind them. Carrie can see her own hands properly for the first time, the dirt so thick it looks like she's wearing dark gloves. Her own blue jeans are black now, her shoes unrecognizable. Grace's school sweater has fallen off, her bag is gone, her white shirt is lousy with sooty slime, but she's smiling now. For the first time since Carrie met her, she's smiling.

They're inside a small antechamber, like an airlock. Another door ahead of them reads Fire Door—Keep Closed. The walls are dull gray but smattered in jargoned signs, maintenance guidelines snapped into clipboards, suspended from nails. She fumbles to pick one of them up, streaking it immediately with black dirt.

"Where are we then?" she says to herself, but Grace starts rifling through bits of paper too.

"Look," Grace says, pointing to a word at the top of one of them.

" 'Bakerloo,' " Carrie reads. "We just need to know which side of Waterloo."

"It doesn't really matter, Carrie, we have to get out here anyway or we'll be stuck."

For the briefest moment Carrie is affronted. *You're thirteen,* she wants to say, *I should be in charge here.* But Grace is right.

Carrie wipes her hands on the concrete wall, Grace does the same, and then Carrie reaches for the next door handle.

Chapter Twenty-Three

FRANKIE

Frankie had thought there was some level of safety in Dartmoor, that there was nothing to bomb here.

"Do we stand any chance?" she says, not to Della or Otis or anyone in particular. But a man a few paces away answers, his power belly swinging around as he turns to face her.

"We don't know where the targets are, how many missiles are coming or where they're coming from. The warning was longer than I'd expect for the obvious candidates," he says. His red jacket is zipped tight and he's coiled a purple scarf around his neck that he loosens as he speaks, his voice soft but intense. "We've no idea whether it or they are coming by air or sea, or how strong the payload could be. If they send a missile by air to Devonport, the whole Plymouth region will be vaporized, totally destroyed."

"Robert!" Sheila hisses at the portly man, flicking her eyes at her queue neighbor, Della.

"I am aware," Della says. She stares ahead and straightens her back, but Frankie can see her hands trembling.

"But we'd be okay this far out?" Frankie asks, even though she can feel Otis's hand on her shoulder, trying to stop her. For her sake or his, she doesn't know.

The man—Robert—looks at her so closely she backs away. "Do you actually want the truth?" he says, wiping his slick forehead on his coat sleeve and pulling his scarf clean off, bundling it under his arm.

"Hope for the best and plan for the worst," she says, trying and failing to find a smile. She can see more and more people arriving and bulging at the back of the queue, as if forming an audience to hear this man speak.

He swallows. "Well, see, I'm retired now but I worked at Devonport for a very long time and we did a lot of drills and scenarios, 'specially in the early eighties. From what I was told back then, well, if a missile hit Plymouth, then out here, yes, some of us won't die straightaway. Maybe you can call that 'being okay,' but I'm not sure I would."

Otis shifts beside her as she asks, "What would you call it?"

"Robert," Sheila says again, pleading now. "Don't."

He looks at Sheila but then addresses Frankie. "Well," he says. His voice is growing harder, more confident. This is his area of expertise and he's been brought out of retirement for this special occasion. "Those who don't die will be seriously injured. And I mean seriously. We'll all be burned, every one of us here. And it won't be safe. What little food and water is left will have to last for god knows how long because we'll be too toxic for anyone to come and help us. And the food we have will become toxic from the radiation anyway."

He pauses and pulls one of his fingers to crack the knuckle.

"Buildings will collapse, fires will rip through all the villages. There'll be no . . ." He looks across the pretty village square. "It'll never look like this again, and the fallout, the radiation poisoning, the water supply . . . the bombs they have now have never been fired at populations. So we just don't know. We don't know anything. And now the Russkies have nuclear torpedoes that cause radioactive tsunamis . . . according to them, anyway, and if *they* hit Plymouth—"

"What if they don't hit Plymouth at all," Otis says. "What if it's just London?"

"Then we have a chance, maybe, of some kind of afterlife. But there's no such thing as 'just London,' we all breathe the same air eventually. And if our capital city's vaporized, that's our government, banking centers, all sorts. And millions and millions of people just wiped out. Can you fathom that?"

"No," Otis says. "I can't."

"That's if it doesn't trigger a retaliation and a full-scale nuclear war," Robert says. His face is pink and waxy, and he wipes his sleeve over it again. He's no longer making eye contact with anyone. "Then it's not just about us, not about England. It's about all life on the planet."

"But why are they bloody doing this to us?" an old man with a strong Devon accent cries out. "What have we ever done to them? We're not the bloody government, we didn't do nothing."

"You boomers voted for the bloody government," a teenage girl of sixteen or seventeen says, hugging herself in her duffle coat, tears and eye makeup all down her face. "You know who our MP is, what he's—"

"I didn't vote for anyone," the man says in alarm. "Not one of those bastards, they're all the same."

"Jesus, well, if you didn't even bother to vote—" the girl starts, but her companion, her mother by the looks of it, tells her to stop.

"It's the Russians, it has to be," another old man four heads down says, his voice a bark.

"Oh come on," says Sheila, stamping her feet as if to stay warm. "They've got their hands full, 'aven't they, would they really—"

"It's out of spite. Because we helped the Ukrainians. You remember what they're like, you know what they did to the Germans after—"

"Yeah, an' I know what the Germans did to us and we don't—"

"You weren't even born then," the old man barks, and turns to face her. "What would you know?" Sheila takes a step back, colliding with the covered window of the shop and letting out a sudden whimper.

"That's enough," Della says to the aggressive old man, pushing her body between him and Sheila.

"I just mean," Sheila says, her face flushing, "that all of that was a long time ago and we can't base our opinions on the past."

"What else is there to base our opinions on?" the old man says, genuinely surprised.

For a moment no one says anything, and then an old woman near the front of the line calls over to the old man: "They'll be in on it with the Chinese, I'd say."

"Mum," the teenage girl says, "we need to get in the shop now and get home quick. You heard what Robert said, we need to be inside and we need to get any food we can. And we need to be with Dad and Matty, to make sure they're running the taps and that. You know what Dad's like."

The mother is a hall-of-mirrors version of her daughter, softer and more rounded. Both wear woolly hats, blue for the mum, green for the girl. Even in this situation, people are wearing hats and wrapping up warm. Were they wearing these getups anyway when the message came, or was it just autopilot for them to layer up? It's mild for November but it's still cold, and Frankie realizes she's trembling, that her jaw has clenched again. *The whole of London will be vaporized.* What must be happening in the city now? But even here ... skin burns and fires and radiation and ... Otis holds her up as her knees start to buckle. "It's okay," he whispers. But it's nothing like okay.

More people have arrived since Frankie and Otis got here, the queue now billowing and ballooning from a line to a crowd.

"We just need to wait our turn, we'll be in soon enough."

"It's going to be too late at this rate, Mum!"

The old man who blames the Russians looks up, hedgerow eyebrows knitted together. "Yes it will, my maid, it will be too late." As if they've rehearsed it, the old man and the teenage girl push past the young lad on the door. For a moment, no one does anything else. A held breath.

And then, mayhem.

Frankie and Otis are jostled from all angles as people stream past them into the shop. The genteel waxed-jacketed villagers have become looters in an instant, fighting their neighbors for food. Robert crunches an elbow into Della's shoulder, his pink face shining.

"We need to go in as well, there'll be nothing left," Frankie says, but Otis grabs her arm and pulls her back.

"No, just me. It's too volatile."

"But—"

"No," he says again, with a firmness she's never heard from him. "It's not just about you. I'll be able to focus on getting more stuff if I'm not worrying about you and the baby. You find somewhere safe on the way back to the car and just wait for me. Okay?"

He has elbowed his way inside before she can reply.

Chapter Twenty-Four

MRS. DABB

She follows the little lane toward the glow of the brightly lit church. Approaching from the back, one of the huge stained glass windows, ancient and vulnerable, is just visible through the fog. A blur of red, blue, and green, but she can picture it exactly, her memory filling it in from the hours she spent in the churchyard while her daughter was at the little church-run preschool. Unable to bring herself to go home. *Just in case.* It wasn't until primary school, when she was seen repeatedly lurking and asked to leave the school gates, that she finally broke the habit. *It's hard for her to settle if she sees you, Mrs. Dabb, and some of the other parents are uncomfortable. . . .*

As she gets closer, she can hear singing from the belly of St. Michael's. Nothing organized, not a proper service, just bursts of song. Practice runs from people nervously waiting. She slides the little car through the narrow lane, just avoiding some collapsed cardboard boxes and an old picnic basket someone is throwing away.

She picks her way around the edge of the main square, desperate to avoid anyone still out. She'd expected a police presence. They would be too busy to help her look for Bunny, and the thought of them makes her sick with nerves, but to see no uniforms at all is somehow even more unnerving.

The doctor's office is a few streets away and she pulls up outside the same building where she came for those humiliating and unhelpful sessions with Miranda, years earlier. "I sense you're still keeping something back," the therapist gently suggested, during the last appointment. She could taste the replies on her tongue, each word curdling.

If I tell you what I'm keeping back, you'll take my daughter away.

If I tell you what I'm keeping back, you might hand my daughter over to monsters.

If I tell you what I'm keeping back, you will think I'm the monster.

If I tell you what I'm keeping back, you will know I am.

"There's nothing more to say," she'd replied, standing and gathering her things. She has avoided coming here ever since.

Did Bunny pick up on her mother's reticence, and figure she'd have to go it alone if she ever got ill? *Is Bunny ill?!*

She climbs out of the car and rushes over to the front door. It's locked. The windows are shuttered from the inside, but she bangs on one anyway, then presses her ear to the pane to listen for signs of life. Nothing.

"I'm looking for my daughter!" she shouts, before moving back to the door and kicking it a couple of times. No one comes. If Bunny was here earlier, she's not here now.

Back in the car, she reverses with a squeal and heads back out of the village toward Jasmine's road.

Empty cars dot the roads but it's not as bad as she thought it would be. Maybe everyone is already inside. Secured wherever they wanted to be for 5:59 p.m.

Everyone but her and Bunny.

36 MINUTES UNTIL IMPACT

Chapter Twenty-Five

CARRIE

Carrie and Grace are now at the bottom of an unending corkscrew. The curved walls are lined with metal ribs, gray-black from dirt and age. A great steel esophagus.

They climb, and climb. Hands smearing the metal handrail, dull footsteps echoing.

"Not long now," she says to Grace. "We'll get you home."

Grace doesn't reply, but a sound that could be a sob echoes up and down the shaft.

Lactic acid spikes, shins clip steps, and toes scuff. Her thighs burn. It is insane, Carrie thinks, that she can still notice any discomfort. Can feel bruises from her earlier fall seeping across her skin like inkblots, can taste the blood from her gums. How can she think of anything besides the imminent attack on her city, of Clementine and Emma unnaturally separated from her?

Clementine will be oblivious, and although Emma will know what's happening in the big picture sense, she'll have no idea Carrie is on her way home. Will she hope for the best or assume all chance is lost? Might Emma even *pray*? They both went to a church primary school, half-learned parables about donkeys and Good Samaritans, but praying has certainly not crossed her own mind.

"Are you okay?" Grace asks as they march up and up.

"Just thinking about God."

"God?" Grace says. "Oh, are you religious or something?"

"No, just desperate." They march in silence for a moment.

"Actually, I was thinking about Emma more than God," Carrie says.

"Emma?"

"My partner."

"You're not married then? God, sorry, I don't know why I said that. My mum and dad weren't married either, it's not like I—"

"Don't be sorry, it's a good question. I guess . . . I guess we just didn't need to get married, we were already . . . no, that's not it really."

"You really don't have to answer, I'm sorry. My mum always says I'm too curious for my own good."

"Stop, it's nice to talk about this. About her. Honestly, I think it's actually that . . . well, it's a few things. Some of our good friends, our older friends, never got to marry the people they loved. And even though we can now, we wouldn't want to do it in a half-assed way. And there's always something more urgent to spend the money on. It's expensive raising a kid in London. But, to be honest, I guess we didn't want to change anything in case it changed us."

"I get it, I think. Like, my mum and dad used to say the same kind of thing, like they didn't need a piece of paper to . . . um . . . and then . . ."

"And then what?"

"Nothing, just . . . tell me about Emma. What's she like and stuff?"

Emma, she thinks. *Let me tell you about Emma.* Her hair is the color of ketchup but she always smells of peaches. Everyone has their own smell, and that's hers. The quieter she tries to be the louder she gets. She has the sweetest tooth Carrie has ever known, can eat Brighton rock candy like a carrot stick. She loves pick'n'mix sweets more than anything and sometimes she'll go into the cinema and not see a film, just buy a huge bucket of pick'n'mix and bring it home so they can all eat it in front of the telly. Even though they had all these plans about how Clementine wasn't going to eat sugar until she was at least six.

Emma can cook amazing meals from guesswork and imagination but can't follow the instructions on a packet of noodles. Charlotte Upton broke her heart in year ten and Carrie put dog poo in Charlotte's bag and got caught and had after-school detentions for weeks, but it was worth it to stop Emma crying. Stupid that she hadn't realized then . . . she was almost sick with jealousy when they got together.

Emma says there's no excuse for being uncomfortable and takes slippers on train and plane journeys. Emma never knew her dad and says she doesn't care about that unless she's drunk and then she and Carrie whip themselves into a Nancy Drew fever doing Facebook investigations into people with his name, but they're never him. Only when they're really, really drunk do they acknowledge that Clementine may someday have these same questions. Emma's stepdad is nice but he's quite thick, and the only music he listens to is novelty comedy records. His cell ringtone is "Star Trekkin' " by The Firm. Emma loves her mum more than almost anyone. Maybe even neck and neck with Carrie and Clementine. Emma drops it into conversation like it's just a vague idea and thinks she's being subtle, but she's desperate to live in Brighton and smell the sea every day. *Why didn't we move to Brighton?*

"She's amazing," Carrie says. "She's a brilliant mum, she's the best partner, she's . . . I *should* marry her, frankly."

"Mmm," says Grace.

The light overhead changes. An almost imperceptible shimmer that sets her eyes watering again. She can see slivers of white ceiling lights. The top.

"There's a door!" Grace shouts from above, hidden in the upper coils. "There's a door!"

"Just wait," Carrie pants. "Just a minute, you don't know what's on the other side."

"I'll be okay."

"I need to keep you safe, what would your mum say?"

"She'd say hurry up, the end of the world is coming."

"How much time do we have left?"

"I don't know." Grace's voice bounces around the stairwell, a sudden chorus of teenagers. "My phone died at Waterloo."

"Fuck. Sorry. Fiddlesticks."

"Oh my god, Carrie, it doesn't matter. Just say 'fuck.' "

Carrie reaches into her coat pocket and pulls out her filthy, smashed-up phone as she puffs her way up. She can't even see the time. She can't see anything. If the network comes back, she cannot call Emma, or Pepper, or her mum. All her photos of Clementine are gone too, as she's never bothered with the cloud. Three years and thousands of moments. Three years. How can someone that little be living through this?

Facing final moments.

No, not final.

"No."

"What?"

"It doesn't matter." Carrie finally gets her legs to run.

Chapter Twenty-Six

FRANKIE

"Otis," Frankie shouts, elbowing her way inside the shop. He has already been swallowed by the liquid flow of people that is filling up every space. Some have multiple bags, shoving anything they can into them, even bread and milk, which will spoil in days. Others jostle for what's left of the long-life supplies, hands clawing around tins of fruit and jars of Marmite. There's a new vibration in here, a fevered look in people's eyes.

She feels a thud against her legs from behind; an elderly woman with a wheeled tartan shopping bag nearly knocks her flat. Frankie stumbles to the side. "Out of my bloody way," the woman growls. Otis was right, this is dangerous. Frankie fights her way back out, covering her stomach with one arm and leading with the other elbow.

Even as she stands on the pavement, she's knocked out of the way by new arrivals, a hand managing to strike her lower belly. She wraps her arms around herself protectively.

Find somewhere safe on the way to the car, that's what he said. She looks around the square, a movement to her left catching her eye. A middle-aged man, swinging a golf club at the window of a fancy little cheese shop. Behind her, she hears glass smashing and turns to see a woman in a waxed jacket reaching through the shattered pane of a tiny greengrocer's shop.

Frankie jogs away from the square, past the shuttered pub and a pretty little wine shop. Will that soon be looted? Maybe getting leathered and passing out is the wisest move. Next to it is an intact bakery, no use taking bread that will mold over in days. Next to the bakery is an archway leading to an alley. She looks up it but it's empty, no one there, just a big blue dumpster at the top. She spins to look behind her but Otis isn't out yet. Realizing she still needs to pee, she shuffles up toward the bin, slipping behind it.

She dries herself with a bit of pocket tissue and pulls everything up, then stumbles back out of her alley and toward the main square. She emerges carefully, looking to the left at the grocery shop a few doors down. People are still approaching it, but is anyone able to move in there?

In the doorway, a man with an empty bag is howling, Frankie doesn't know who he's shouting at or what he's looking for. The old man who hates Russians nudges the howling man out of the doorway, and is now telling the people arriving that they can't come in, it's too crowded. They move him out of the way like he's made of paper and he drops his bags. Fig Rolls and boxes of chocolate tumble out as he stoops to gather them, getting trampled as he tries.

As she heads up the slight hill away from the shop, she can hear people behind her, others yelling from upstairs in the pub. There is no one ahead of her as she walks in the direction of the church. It's not so much a ghost town as a film set, the crew behind the scenes, the actors out of shot.

She follows the mild slope away from the village square. The cars have thinned out now and the air feels cool and clean, Frankie gulps it while she can. Behind her, she hears footsteps. Otis? She turns, but it's two shell-shocked young women, running in the other direction with splitting grocery bags in their arms.

Another pretty pub now, leadlight windows with curtains and blinds drawn inside. How many people will spend the next . . . god knows . . . however long they have to spend, sheltering in that pub? There must be people for whom that was a fantasy. Her dad in his younger days, for one. A perennial lock-in. But how long until the beer runs out? The patience? She thinks of her dad at the end of a bender, imagines others like him stuck in close quarters. No thank you.

The churchyard is on the left. And after this comes the narrowing road, the sharp corner, and then Otis's car and then back to shelter at the cottage. And the burns, the fires, the radiation, the . . . *What the fuck is that sound?*

Chapter Twenty-Seven

MRS. DABB

She squints into the fog to find Jasmine's house. It should appear any moment, a rosebud cottage at the front and a modern extension at the back, all sleek black metal doors and polished concrete. A checklist of must-have features that Bunny once asked why their own house is lacking: a garbage disposal and a solar hot tub and an instant boiling water tap and on and on. "I do my best," she'd snapped, thinking of the two incomes Jasmine's household has. And that her parents are ten years older, proper adults who planned it all out and have a remote-controlled orangery roof to show for it.

She imagines that delicate roof fracturing into tiny pieces that fall like rain onto the family.

She pulls into the driveway and fumbles to get out. The shutters are down, but there's a car in the drive. She bangs on the front door, rings the video doorbell, slaps the nearest window. She looks mad, undoubtedly, but this is a time for madness.

The front door is yanked open, a little boy of eight or nine staring back at her with moon eyes.

"Is Jasmine here?" she asks him, but before he can answer, Jasmine's mum, Daphne, skids into view at the end of the hallway. "Don't open that door," she's shouting, though it's too late. Reaching the doorway, she hisses, "Upstairs," to the boy, then grips the doorjamb, peering out to check who else might be there, before finally focusing on her visitor.

"I need to speak to Jasmine."

"What? Why?"

"I know for sure Bunny has a phone, I found the charger and—"

Daphne sags. "Is she not home yet?"

"No." It comes out as a sob.

"I'm sorry," Daphne says, opening the door wider. "I really thought she'd be back by now. Come in a minute."

The door is closed and locked behind her, and now she's engulfed by the smell of a warm, posh home. Orange peel curls and cinnamon, real logs popping and smoking on the fire though god knows how much they must cost.

"My husband works in Princetown," Daphne whispers then, "and he's not back yet either so the kids are really rattled. Be gentle with Jasmine." She turns and calls up the stairs for her daughter. It feels insane to be standing still, fingers tangling, drumming, waiting. Daphne looks at her, her eyes backlit with questions, but she doesn't open her mouth again.

Jasmine appears skittishly at the top of the stairs. Out of school uniform she looks older than thirteen. Older than Bunny, even though Jasmine is shorter. She steps down slowly like she's walking to the gallows, her glossy long ponytail swinging.

"Jasmine," Daphne says, "we really don't have time for this today, so can you please tell Mrs. Dabb anything you know about where Bunny might be."

"I honestly don't know, Mum, she told me she had a doctor's appointment."

"So it was a doctor's appointment," Mrs. Dabb says. "You said you didn't know."

"I didn't . . . I think she told me that or maybe I just . . . maybe I thought that's what she said."

"And you didn't push to find out?" she interrupts, even though Daphne casts a warning look. "You didn't ask if she was okay?"

Jasmine looks down at her slipper-socked feet and shakes her head.

"I told my best friend everything when I was your age." It comes out with more anger than intended, and Daphne moves her body slightly in front of her daughter.

"Bunny's mum knows she has a phone, Jazzy," she says, raising her eyebrows at her daughter, prompting, but Jasmine just stares back in panic.

"I do, Jasmine. And it's okay, she's not in any trouble, I just really need to know what the number is and who gave it to her."

"I don't know," the girl says, her eyes pleading at her mum.

"I'm sorry, but I think you're lying, I need—"

"Okay, all right," Jasmine's mum says to her then. "I know you're worried, but we're all dealing with . . . look, if Jasmine says she doesn't know, then she probably doesn't know."

"But she does know, I can tell, and you can too. Look, Jasmine, it's not the time for covering for your friends, this is life and . . . just please tell me where she got the phone, I won't tell her you told me."

At the top of the stairs, the moon-eyed boy crouches down, spying. Everyone is holding their breath.

"I think it's something to do with her dad," Jasmine says finally.

33 MINUTES UNTIL IMPACT

Chapter Twenty-Eight

CARRIE

Carrie's eyes water from staring at the strip light at the top of the dark staircase but she will not stop looking, nervous on some level that it's just a mirage and if she looks away, it will disappear.

Carrie's clothes are sweat-drenched and she can feel her hair sticking to her face, every step now exhausting and painful. When she finally approaches the top, she can see neither an exit nor Grace. "Where are you?" Her voice is whiny, childish, when she—the adult—should be the one in control.

"I'm here!"

She turns a final corkscrew and there it is. EMERGENCY EXIT.

And there Grace is, beaming underneath the exit sign, angelic in the electric light. Her fingers are on the door handle already, her face shining with sweat and smeared with grease. Without thinking, Carrie grabs and hugs her. Grace stiffens but then exhales into the hug.

The door is curved, almost hidden in the wall like a prank. They still don't know where they'll come out, how close they are to their homes, to their people. Nodding to each other, and in one shared movement, they pull the handle down and push the door open.

"Oh my god," Grace says, as Carrie moves in front of her without thinking and then steps out into some kind of apocalyptic video game.

Sirens scream from all angles. People rush past Carrie and Grace as they step out cautiously into the crisp evening. Carrie blinks and looks frantically around for something familiar, a landmark. But this place is unrecognizable. *Carnage.* Biblical scenes of mayhem and horror. People shoving and stumbling, charging at the closed doors of shops, banging on shuttered windows.

A cyclist is knocked off her bike nearby, her thin body skidding across the road, insectile. The man who pushed her is already on it and frantically pedaling away. Everyone is trying to get wherever they need.

"Where are we?" Grace says.

Carrie spins desperately, trying to get her bearings, to see some kind of static landmark behind the frantic movement.

And then . . . a tall dark hotel building to their left, so large she didn't see it there, pasted onto the sky. A railway bridge behind it. Waterloo Station behind that. They're barely one hundred meters from where they first got the warning.

St. Thomas' Hospital is just along there, though not visible. Where she and Emma first held Clementine, first smelled her soft apricot skin.

Oh god, there must be babies being born right now.
In this.
And what of people in surgery?

"We need to go, Carrie." She feels a small hand gripping hers, pulling her gently. They inch carefully along the street, still holding hands.

Wild-eyed, they dodge the staggering, the running, and the injured. A car swerves the wrong way to avoid a taxi ricocheting between lanes and abandoned cars. They turn a corner, but Carrie knew already. The relief is gravitational; she spins in her shoes like a compass magnet and now she's facing the Lambeth North underground station. She touches the bloodred tiles and grounds herself. She chose the right direction, down there in the sizzling dark.

And now they're on their way home.

Chapter Twenty-Nine

FRANKIE

The sound comes from inside the churchyard. Four women, none younger than sixty, wear pink T-shirts under open coats. On their chests, carefully stitched sequins spell out Chagford Rock Choir. They hold hands tightly and catch each other's eyes, voices breaking then harmonizing as they somehow find the fortitude to sing an a cappella version of "Don't Stop Me Now." They have no microphones, no speakers, and their voices are almost lost to the evening wind.

Frankie barely noticed the church earlier, when they rushed past it to get to the shop, but now sees it glowing like a beacon. Light streams up from the grounds and paints the old stone walls golden.

She's always loved graveyards. The stillness, the reminder that it's all happened before and it'll all happen again and, if you're lucky, someone will read your name aloud centuries later and, just for a moment, wonder who you were.

Soon there will be too many bodies to bury anywhere formal. She thinks of London, all those people in the street, on the tube, whizzing around in taxis. In just over half an hour, they'll be turned to powder, their ashes too toxic to be scattered by anyone who loves them. Do they all know that? Are they all lying motionless on the floor right now like they're in a Radiohead video, the catastrophic realization of their fate too heavy to bear?

A large stained glass window glows above the entrance archway. The church sits in a dip with the graveyard sloping gently toward it. The church door is open and people inside squirm for space. She's reminded of news footage after earthquakes and landslides, the dusty bodies of survivors moving molasses-slow through community spaces.

The song finishes and the choir women huddle. Then, still holding hands, one of them counts to three. They start a new song, their performance so tight it's like they've prepared for this moment their whole lives. They sing "We Have All the Time in the World."

It is simply too much. As she carries on up the slope, wishing Otis would hurry up, a loud metallic voice booms from behind.

She turns as megaphone-amplified words crackle out from the window of a muddy pickup truck growling toward her, the noise so distorted it's just an angry roar.

"... shelter ... home ... authorized ... shoot ... danger ... shelter ..."

The patchy megaphone drowns out the choir's singing but their mouths are still moving, eyes on each other, fixedly ignoring the truck. Frankie is reminded of the band on the sinking *Titanic*.

Under the dust, the truck is the color of flames, and it crunches its way up the road, clipping cars indiscriminately. On the roof of the truck, a flashing light rotates; it looks taped on and not remotely official, but who is she to know?

The truck pulls up beside her, engine idling to a rumble. It's big, far taller than her, so that even if all the tinted windows were down, she'd not be able to see inside fully. It's the kind of truck a crew of builders might use—her dad used to get picked up in this kind of thing when he was a brickie in the nineties. She thinks, just briefly, of puffs of smoke out of windows, wages in brown envelopes, early starts but early finishes too so Dad would slink home half-cut after drinking the afternoon away and weaseling his way into some random woman's bed. Or he'd come back steaming so Frankie and her brother, Seb, would scramble, run to an auntie's house or hide together in one of their bedrooms.

Frankie doesn't like it. Not the memories or the reality, which pants its diesel breath in front of her.

She flinches when the megaphone withdraws and the window slides fully down. Two men sit in the front and both wear balaclavas. Sprigs of beard poke through the mouth holes, their eyes are in shadow. What she can see of their clothes looks like old army shirts, the type popular in the nineties. The ones dirtbag boys at high school wore. She would scoff at these blokes, were this not a nuclear emergency and—more urgently—if the man in the passenger seat weren't holding a gun.

She swallows and takes a step back.

It looks like a rifle, not that she knows anything about guns, but it's long, thin, and horrible.

"You need to get inside your home," the man in the passenger seat says, the megaphone now out of view but the gun in his hand poking casually out of the window like it's nothing. His voice is low, almost amused. The other man in a balaclava sits mutely in the driver's seat, his blank head facing forward.

"I'm going back now," she says.

"What's your address?" the passenger says, running his eyes over Frankie, her messy hair, her chest shrouded in baggy clothes. *They think I'm alone.*

"My boyfriend will be here any minute."

The man's face shifts under the skin of the balaclava as his cheeks curdle around a smile. "You sure about that?" He has the same accent as the villagers but it sounds rougher, looser. A mouthful of gravel. She is ever more aware of her own flat Mancunian tones even as she tries to soften them, finding herself using the peacekeeping tones of her mother.

"Please don't worry about me," she says, attempting a smile. "Our place isn't far and there are other people who need your help."

"We're not offering help," another amused voice says from deeper in the truck. A third man whose voice is muffled but whose meaning is clear. For a moment, no one says anything. Where is Otis? She looks behind her, but he's still not there.

"What he means," the man in the passenger seat says to Frankie, his voice more friendly, "is that it's not optional because we're getting everyone to safety. Get in, love."

"But our car is just around that corner," she says, pointing up past the church.

"Oh, there's no way through there," the passenger says with a slight laugh. "You'll never make it to your place if it's that way."

"We can get there on foot," Frankie lies, "it's not far."

"You heard what my brother said," the driver says, his voice quieter than the others. "You'll never make it. The only way to survive is by getting in with us."

Frankie takes a step back. "I need to wait for my boyfriend, he'll be here any minute."

"We'll come back for him," says the passenger, his dark, wool-ringed eyes finding Frankie's. "We've got everything you'll need at ours." He smiles again. A salesman's smile. "Plenty of food and water. Comfortable beds." His irises are dark, the lashes the same rusty brown as his beard.

The old ladies are still singing. She looks at them, pleading with her eyes, but they're not looking her way.

The man in the driver's seat gestures their way and says something inaudible. The passenger laughs, an elbow drifting casually out of the window, megaphone loose in one hand, gun in the other. "My brother says we've got better music at our place too. The Devon Militia, my love, are always prepared. Now, pop that back door open and slide in."

She cannot get inside this truck. That is Frankie's overriding thought. She's never heard of the Devon Militia, but she knows red flags when she sees them.

"Frankie!" she hears Otis call, and turns to see him jogging toward her from the square, a hundred meters or so away. He has a six-pack of water bottles in one hand, a bulging shopping bag in the other. Thank god. How did he manage to find the water? She starts to walk back to him, the relief nearly buckling her. But then she hears the truck door opening, heavy boots landing on the tarmac behind her.

She feels arms wrap around her from behind and even as she's screaming Otis's name, even as she sees him throw his precious cargo on the ground and sprint, she is being turned and bent over, folded into the truck headfirst.

Her body hits the back seat of the truck, her face slamming into the lap of a terrified teenage girl, who screams in alarm. The man who grabbed Frankie laughs as he jumps in behind her and pulls the door closed.

The truck squeals away.

Chapter Thirty

MRS. DABB

"Bunny doesn't have a dad." The words sound like they're coming from underwater, from someone else's submerged mouth and not her own. She grips the glossy finial at the bottom of this family's staircase but her hand grows slick and slips off.

Jasmine shuffles her weight from foot to foot, looking down at the plush carpet. "I know . . . like . . . that she doesn't, like, live with her dad but—"

"She doesn't *have* a dad." The words are sharper, more true.

"Why doesn't Jasmine's friend have a dad?" the little boy calls down from the top of the stairs, before being shushed by his mother.

"Her biological father has absolutely nothing to do with her and she doesn't even—she's never met him and there's no way she ever could have."

"Is he dead?" says the boy.

"Rudy!" Daphne shouts then. "Go and sort your things out like I told you!"

"He's as good as dead."

"It wasn't actually him," Jasmine says, still looking at her feet the whole time. "Not her . . . biological father. But I think it was one of his relatives who gave her the phone. It was outside school, a few weeks ago, and—"

"Oh no," Daphne mutters. "You silly, silly girls."

"Which relatives? She doesn't—which bloody relatives?" She is submerged again, drowning. This is not possible. It cannot be possible.

"Whoever it was had an old truck, that's all I know. They called her over to them but I didn't see who was inside because it was a little bit away from me and I was talking to Sacha and I wasn't really looking. But Bunny wouldn't talk about it at all afterward, honestly, she wouldn't." Jasmine looks at her mother now, who massages one temple. "Honestly, Mum, I tried to get her to open up but—"

"Never mind that, Jasmine," her mum says, sharp and serious now. "What's the number for this phone? We know you have it."

"I don't know, my phone's upstairs." She's close to tears but her mum has clearly run out of patience.

"Well, bloody go and get it then, Jazzy, we don't have time for this shit today!" A gasp comes from upstairs. "And you go to your bloody room, Rudy!"

Jasmine runs up the stairs now, sliding in her socks. A sob slipping out as she goes.

"I'm so sorry," Daphne says, reaching out a hand but letting it fall. "I really didn't know."

"But this can't be true, she can't . . ."

"Is he . . ." Daphne pauses. "Is he a bad egg?"

"A bad egg?" It comes out in a maniacal barking laugh.

"That bad?"

"Much worse than you can possibly imagine. I've spent the last thirteen years making sure he has nothing to do with her, that he doesn't even—"

Jasmine appears on the stairs, the phone held out in front of her like a holy tablet.

"Call her!"

Jasmine looks between the two women. "But it won't . . . it won't work."

"Just try," Daphne says, "just in case."

Still standing on the bottom step of the luxuriously carpeted stairs, Jasmine presses a few buttons and then holds the phone to her ear. Everyone waits, but she shakes her head almost instantly. "I told you," she addresses her mother. "It doesn't work."

"Write the number down for her mum and then we really need to get sorted." Daphne is speaking to Jasmine but the implication is clear. *Time is up, you need to leave.*

Jasmine trots down the hall to a little bureau table where a notepad sits next to a vintage-looking phone, an old-fashioned pen, and a fancy scent diffuser. She copies the number carefully from her phone and tears off the sheet. At the top of the paper is the family's name and address in gold lettering. Jasmine avoids everyone's eyes as she hands it over.

"Good luck," Daphne says, pulling open the front door.

30 MINUTES UNTIL IMPACT

might otherwise be demanding to board a plane first, protesting that he has gold frequent flyer status. "You are being derelict in your duties," he shouts at the closed church door, turning to display his outrage, his shock, to the others around him.

The church is not calling anyone to prayer, its bells are silent. Are they usually silent?

From the road, a chunky man in ill-fitting jeans and a fisherman's sweater runs past and collides with Carrie's shoulder, spinning her round as he vaults the low fence of the church and belly flops face down on the chessboard-tiled ground. Obviously hurt, he still scrambles to his knees, praying and crying. The frequent flyer watches in disgust, then smooths his own coat.

"Are you okay?" Grace asks as Carrie tentatively rubs her shoulder. She nods. She's already smashed her knee, her teeth, her hands. Her whole body is tenderized with bruises that should hurt. But she can't feel anything under her skin now, which prickles with adrenaline. Even her legs, which felt on the brink of collapse while climbing those metal stairs, are now thrumming with movement, with readiness.

On the opposite side of the road is the Hercules pub, on whose wooden benches she and Emma spent their first official afternoon as a couple, having spent thousands of similar afternoons as friends, sinking misty glasses of rosé and cheesy fries. She didn't know then that she was already pregnant with Clementine.

Now men and women bang on the pub doors. Benches are shoved askew, some lie on their sides.

A school building now. Faces collaged in its windows. "They're wearing the same uniform as you," Carrie realizes.

Grace nods. "Yeah."

"Any friends?" she says, thinking of herself at thirteen, of Emma.

"I've got friends," Grace says, a hurt in her voice that Carrie hasn't heard before.

"Of course you do. I mean, do you see any of your friends in there?"

Grace shakes her head but doesn't say more, only ever giving what she must. Is that mistrust or confidence? Either way, she's the opposite of Carrie, who will overshare so uncontrollably she'll lie awake replaying

Chapter Thirty-One

CARRIE

Carrie and Grace stagger along the street in silence. C
are wedged into shops, their faces pressed ashy against
frightened faces stare from upper floors. Outside, gro
against doors and shutters, begging, banging, threaten
of people who might never otherwise meet. Tailored
jackets, straggle-haired men and snooty-looking wor
between all their legs, little kids in winter clothes. All
ing. Do the children understand or are they just nat
The way Clementine will clap when Carrie claps, po
when Emma does that to her, join in with her mo
they're singing along to all-banger playlists while cool

Away from the groups, lone figures zip frantically a
or cycle or skitter, one way, then another. Parents r
pushing wiry strollers loaded with children, sheddi
boxes into the road.

Grace and Carrie cling together, stumbling as i
race. The sports day at the end of the world.

"Back in the hood," Carrie says. Grace looks at he
"I know that's what the kids say, so don't give me
"Oh my god."

A silvery dog, loose from its owner, barrels into
just briefly, watching it rush off behind them. Its lea
it yelps and runs frantically toward stationary traffic

A small crowd beats the door of a brutalist chur
you have to give us sanctuary!" shouts the man at th
his coat neatly buttoned, his scarf poised *just so*.

her monologues and torturing herself for weeks about what she's told to whom. All except one secret. The worst possible secret.

"How come you were at Waterloo then? You live in the opposite direction."

"I went into town after school," Grace says. Her voice falters. "Wanted to get a present for my little brother. It's his birthday the day after tomorrow." Whatever Grace got, it must now be lost in her long-abandoned bag, sinking into tube filth.

"I've never not been with him on his birthday," Grace says.

"You will be."

Grace says nothing.

There is a roadblock at the junction of Lambeth Road and Kennington Road. It stops cars attempting to head toward the A3. A terrified-looking police officer lifts a megaphone to her lips as several of her colleagues flank her. "Kennington Road, Lambeth Road, and the A3 are now emergency service roads, you cannot pass."

Cars beep, raggedly queued, jammed any which way. Kennington Road ahead of them is eerily empty save for a huge fire engine, racing away toward the main road. Horns blare throughout the queue of vehicles and—almost as if they've planned it—several men simultaneously leap from the various cars nearest to the roadblock and charge at the police. The officer with the megaphone lifts it again, even as a wiry man fights to pull it from her.

"These are now emergency service roads." Her shaking voice ricochets from nearby buildings, followed by a screech of feedback. She tries to say more but another man knocks the megaphone from her hands as her colleagues put up riot shields, the synchronized sound like a chorus of plastic crickets.

There is a solid, immovable layer of cars at all angles coming from Lambeth Bridge and Waterloo. Where have they emerged from? Were they all lying in wait in the center of the city, dormant in underground parking garages?

A bus horn blows from somewhere as more people tumble out of their cars, running to join the angry swell at the roadblock. As Carrie and Grace run past, down Kennington Road, the police behind them are so overwhelmed that a car smashes straight through the blockade. More cars start to flood the road now, the other protestors peeling away to take up positions behind steering wheels, getting through while they can.

At first, traffic creeps forward and it seems almost normal. Just for a moment, this is the same Kennington Road it always is. Stop/start, but flowing. And then the cars at the front—now beyond Carrie's viewpoint—must have reached another roadblock because a sea of urgent brake lights and shrieking tires spreads backward toward them like a wave. The crunch is louder than anything she's heard before, and even as she runs, Carrie covers her head with her right arm and, without thinking of personal space or consent or any of that, puts her left arm around Grace's head to protect her. Cars have slammed into one another, abandoned cars shunted along with them. People scramble out of the way as vehicles mount the pavement. A small silver car narrowly misses Grace before crashing into the white wall of a four-story Georgian building.

For a moment, nothing more happens, but as they run past the little silver car, the driver's door opens and a woman tumbles out, frees herself from a tangled seat belt, yanks open the back door, and pulls out a screaming baby.

"Oh no," Carrie says. "We should help them." Before they can do anything, the woman bundles the baby under her arm like a rolled-up carpet and sprints away, leaving her car door open. Its radio is still on.

"Do not attempt to travel," says a crisp voice through the car speakers. "Roads are expected to be impassable. Stay in your homes or places of business. If you are not currently inside, seek shelter at the nearest building to you."

As they pass a crashed taxi lying sideways in the road, a different voice brings breaking news. "We can reassure Britons that the King and his immediate family have been taken to safety," it says.

"Fuck the King!" someone shouts.

They push on faster, past the Three Stags, crowded with faces, across the crammed and stationary crossroads. The traffic lights merrily flicking through in turn, as if cars were still able to drive, as if people were still standing at the crossings, patiently waiting for the walk signal. As if the whole of Kennington Road wasn't a scrapyard, and people weren't scrambling, bloodied, from scuffed and crushed cars.

The Imperial War Museum lawn is dotted with people holding on to trees, crouching like animals, some with their foreheads pressed against bark, others with their arms wrapped around the trunks. Are they misguidedly hoping for shelter or just giving up? They are all looking inward, into the bark, not out at the carnage.

A few meters away, she realizes there is a couple lying on the grass, a woman on the ground, skirt up and tights down. A man on top of her. They claw at each other, kissing fiercely. Another couple, two men, press up against a tree.

Carrie moves slightly in front of Grace. "Just focus on where we're going, it's not long now till you're home." Grace keeps looking over anyway. *Right, distraction needed.*

"Hey," Carrie says, "what will you miss most about normal life?"

Grace stops, just briefly. She looks as if she wants to correct Carrie, to chastise her. "For me," Carrie plows on, "it's Nando's, McDonald's breakfasts, cheesy fries from an oily van at the end of a night out, a big bag of candy on a long journey, and—"

"That's all food," Grace says.

"Yeah, you're right, I need a drink too. Put in—"

"Put in?" Grace laughs now, what a lovely sound. "Put in where?"

"The time capsule or whatever, the list of stuff we'll miss. Add in a black-and-white shake from Shake Shack. With whipped cream."

"That's just more food, basically," Grace says. "So what you're actually asking me is what junk food I'll miss." They jog along the pavement littered with glass, smashed bottles and the frothy fragments of safety glass windshields, pushed out in escape.

"I guess I am," Carrie says. "Yeah."

People are still flooding into the museum, its every door flung open. People must be pressing themselves into the exhibition tanks, clinging under the fuselage of long-cold RAF planes, and taking refuge in the gift shop. To have a war museum, it suddenly strikes Carrie, when war is still so very present—what a ludicrous world.

"Papa Johns barbecue meat feast, XXL original crust, with chicken poppers," Grace says. "And put in two liters of Dr Pepper."

Chapter Thirty-Two

FRANKIE

The truck she's been shoved into is large, but Frankie's being tumbled around among other legs, grasping hands. She feels like she's drowning. The teenage girl in the back seat scrunches up against the far door, trembling, the driver revs into the mist, and the front passenger slaps his legs with excitement.

She hears the chunky confirmation of central locking. Feels the gritty carpet under her sock. When did one of her boots come off?

"Otis!"

The man's hand is over her mouth then; she gags at the taste of his dirty fingers as the truck lurches forward again, so fast she sprawls sideways. She's half lying on the man now, his soft bulk beneath her. Her head is back so she can only see the upholstered ceiling. Frankie thrashes, but the man is too strong, and besides, the man in the front passenger seat has turned around now and is pointing his gun at her. Directly at her head. She freezes. The girl lets out a whimper.

"Martial law, love," the man who grabbed her says in her ear, his voice similar to the others. Her newly sensitive pregnancy nose smells fruitcake and sour orange juice on his breath. When did he eat fruitcake, before or after the alert? "Now, sit up and behave."

He slides from under her with a grunt, pressing himself against the door and pushing her between his right thigh and the left thigh of the girl, who recoils as if Frankie is a fat spider who has just dropped down from the ceiling. It's a roomy truck with a high ceiling, but it's still a crush, with three of them in the back and two of them swollen with fear.

She puts her hand on her stomach. *Four.* There are four of them back here.

"Please," she says, "just let me out."

"No can do," the passenger says. "We've told you already, this is a rescue mission."

They turn sharply into the lane where Otis left the car; some of the other vehicles have thinned out but there are still some dotted haphazardly, and the truck just plows through them, sloughing side-view mirrors and nearly snapping off an open door. The Fiat 500 with the little dog has gone.

The driver fiddles with something on the side of the steering wheel and then everything ahead of them gets clearer. Fog lights, of course, a prerequisite if you live around here. Through the windshield, she can make out Otis's car up ahead where they left it. The color of dried delphiniums, a little blue oasis on the road. It will still smell of them, their journey mess still dotted in the cup holders like artifacts, their CD soundtrack still in the old stereo.

This car is still intact, with enough room to maneuver. They would have been okay if they'd just got to it in time. If he'd just left the shop a bit sooner, if they'd not separated, if she'd not taken a piss. They'd still be together.

She cranes her neck, desperate to see a flash of Otis's gray hoodie racing after them, but everything swirls with mist, the mellow streetlights behind them showing glimpses of abandoned cars, nothing more. She can feel the truck moving faster, flashing past tight little cottages and empty cars.

They whip past the Mercedes now and she watches it become a blue smear in the rearview mirror, going nowhere. The last link to her old life. To Manchester. What if these people keep her captive forever? Will the fallout keep her captive for them? *Will Otis ever meet our baby? Will I live to have our baby? Will our baby live?*

"Where are we going?" Her voice is high and pleading and she hates it. Hates the whine, the desperation.

"Sanctuary," the man in the passenger seat says, with a laugh.

Overhead, two planes cross the sky in quick succession. The air force? Are they monitoring movement? Can they see anything through the mist? They're gone again in seconds. Is there anyone who can save her from these bloody nutters?

The girl has her head pressed against the window, staring out, her fingers turning an out-of-battery cell phone over and over in her lap. "Please let me go," she says quietly, "I just want my mum."

The men ignore her.

"What's your name?" Frankie says, but the girl just stares out of the window, tears streaming now.

"I just want my mum," she says again.

"Where do you live?" Frankie tries. "Could you get there if they let you out?" The girl nods, but doesn't turn around. "Can't we just let her out?" Frankie says, appealing to the man next to her, who laughs.

"What?" he snorts, eyes dancing with amusement. "Because we've got you now, you think we don't need her?"

"She's got a mam waiting for her," Frankie says. "And she doesn't want to be here."

"She belongs with us," the driver says gruffly.

"But her mam must be terrified, you can't just—"

The passenger turns back with a warning in his eyes. The gun bobs in and out of view between the two front seats. "That's enough," he says, snapping the radio on.

"Gather batteries, food, and fuel. Keep water supplies covered. It is unlikely that the emergency services will be able to help the majority of people once the strike occurs. You will need to stay inside; the fallout will be extremely dangerous."

"Does your mam know where you are?" Frankie whispers to the girl.

Without lifting her head from the window, she whispers back, "No, she has no idea."

Chapter Thirty-Three

MRS. DABB

"Fuck! Fuck! Fuck!"

She is outside Jasmine's house, somehow back inside her car with no memory of getting in it, slapping the steering wheel so hard that the horn sounds and her slightly loose ring cuts into her finger. Nearby, curtains and shutters flicker. This is impossible. What Jasmine said can't be true. But even as she's thinking it, she knows that's wishful thinking. Clearly they got to Bunny, ensnared and corrupted her. Forced her to lie to her best friend and her mother. The school too. And now they must have her, where else could she be? Why else would she write a note to get away?

She starts the car and flies into the fog without thinking about any other vehicles. Tears stream and her throat is sore from shouting, but she has to hold it together. She cannot waste time screaming and crying, collapsing inward. A heavy hourglass settles on her chest, Bunny breaking into tiny pieces of sand and slipping through. She is running out of time.

She always convinced herself that she could keep everything—everyone—separate. That Bunny knew nothing about him, had no way to find him, and couldn't be convinced and cajoled even if he did get to her via some kind of intermediary. And while Bunny didn't know he was her father, she certainly knows his family's name. Everyone knows them, they're notorious. That should have been enough to scare her off completely, before any cajoling could even begin.

But no. All it took was a phone, passed out of a truck window, in broad daylight.

The siren continues in the distance. She glances at the dashboard clock and presses the accelerator harder.

The rest of the country seems to have been rebuilt from the ground up during her lifetime but the lanes she drives on now have never changed. Even in this grayness, the same sturdy red banks and looming foliage frame the road, the iron gates and passing places are centuries old. She has to squint into the fog to stay on track. If she weren't concentrating so hard, she might not have seen the man running a few meters up the road, at the fringed edge of the fog. Has he just run from the village?

He is wearing gray, perhaps deliberately trying to hide in the fog, but his rapidity marks him out even against the monochrome backdrop. He's big, she can see that, and she reaches to lock the door even though the central locking is automatic and already on. As she passes him, she sees him wave in the mirror, trying to flag her down. No chance.

Shit. She didn't mean to come this way again, back through the village. Her and the car on autopilot, heading for home. But she's not going home, she's going somewhere she never ever wanted to go. Straight into the hornet's nest.

27 MINUTES UNTIL IMPACT

Chapter Thirty-Four

CARRIE

Kennington Road is thick with people; those already running and stumbling have now been joined by those drivers and passengers still able to get out of their cars. Others, trapped in their vehicles, push through windows and thump their fists against unbreakable sunroofs.

Carrie wants to tell Grace not to look but it's not Grace who is looking and slowing them down, it's her.

Any minute, more police will arrive with guns like at Waterloo, the army maybe, goodness knows. Carrie grabs Grace tighter, dodging people and bikes and baby strollers. Oh god, baby strollers.

People stumble from all angles, running, shouting. A heavily pregnant woman screams outside a beautiful Georgian house on the other side of the road. She has a toddler in a thin stroller, the kind you'd take on holiday because it folds tiny enough for the plane. Carrie and Emma have one from when they took Clementine to Crete in September, a bottle of sunscreen still trapped in the folded basket, shoved in the everything cupboard.

The pregnant woman lifts the whole thing almost over her head, presenting the child to the faces watching from the middle-floor windows.

"Michael, please, you have to let us in!"

The toddler screams.

Grace stumbles to a stop, staring at the stroller in the woman's shaking arms.

"Tell me about your brother," Carrie says, guessing.

"He's so little," Grace says. "He won't know what's going on, he'll never—"

"How old is he?"

Grace opens her mouth but then shakes her head. "It's easier if I don't talk about him, actually."

The side roads they pass are emptying as exhausted Londoners stumble up steps and slide behind front doors. Most people must either be in their own homes or have barged their way into sheltering in other people's. Where are all the homeless people that she would usually see whenever she walks home? The man by the Pret near the Park Plaza, who always tells her he loves her when she buys him a latte. She hopes he is inside the Pret for once, drinking a huge milky coffee.

With each road they pass, fewer people are out in the open but their presence is felt through sound. Radios and TVs chunter behind windows. They play the same recorded messages, but the millisecond delays create a discordant orchestra of the same horrifying information.

A brief lull settles, as they leave the worst of the crashed cars behind. The radios and TVs have paused and instead, through covered windows, they hear the sounds of crying, talking, kettles boiling, furniture being dragged about. Carrie is holding her breath, without fully knowing why. But when the broadcasts start again, it's just more of the same. As if someone somewhere had to rewind an old tape.

"This is an announcement from the Health Security Agency. A radiation emergency is expected in your region in the coming days, depending on the amount of radiation carried by the incoming missiles and the area they strike."

"They don't even know what's coming!" someone shouts. The crowd stills and Carrie and Grace slow with it. Back to the early bewilderment of Waterloo, people looking at each other for answers, no one knowing anything. "Are we running about for nothing?" a man says. The woman nearest to him shrugs and starts to move away.

"The potential scale of emergencies will vary from site to site," the radio continues. "Food and water supplies will be adversely affected, and it may not be possible to seek emergency care from hospitals or other health services. It will be vital to stay inside your homes as fallout will be extremely dangerous. There is a plan for the supply of iodine tablets to the general public."

"I don't even know what iodine is," Carrie says as they move away again, leaving some people still motionless behind them.

"Potassium iodine?" Grace says, like she's prompting Carrie to remember a film. *You know, the one with Brad Pitt where he's not really there?*

"I . . . don't know what that is. Sorry."

"It's a stable form of iodine, it helps block, well, sort of block radiation poisoning. It's like the good kind of iodine that battles against the bad type—"

"The radioactive type?" Carrie says.

"Exactly."

"God, you're so clever, I didn't know any of that when I was your age."

"You don't know any of it now," Grace says, and then covers her mouth. Carrie laughs, she can't help it. Oh god, it's coming out manic. *I've turned,* she thinks. *I've lost it now.*

"But, Carrie," Grace says, and her tone stops Carrie's laughter like a brake. "You do know that . . ."

"What?"

"Like, iodine and sheltering and . . . all that stuff they're saying?"

"Yeah?"

"Well, you know it's . . . that's not going to . . . it's just to keep us all . . ."

"What?"

"Do you really want to know?" Grace says.

"Yes."

"I'm not sure you do."

"Why?"

"It's just . . . what happens next," Grace says. "I read . . . I read a lot about this when the Ukraine stuff first happened and I asked my physics teacher."

"And?"

"And I don't think it's going to go how people think."

"What do you mean?"

"Carrie, the whole city will be—" She stops like she's run out of air. "Actually, I don't think I should . . . look, just focus on getting home and spending these last minutes with your kid."

"What do you mean, last minutes?"

As they jog, Carrie notices a man just ahead of them standing in the entrance to an alleyway. He is static. As static as any of the abandoned cars.

"Grace," she says again, "what do you mean, last minutes?"

Grace doesn't answer. Grace is gone. At least, Carrie can't see her. She can't see anything, the whole street has just gone pitch-black. No streetlights anymore, no light leaking from the barricaded windows or under doors. The power is out.

"Grace!"

She hears a muffled sound, a voice, but even as her eyes adjust and black turns to gray turns to a bruise of shapes and smears, Grace is still not here.

She grapples in the empty darkness, arms finding nothing to connect with.

"Grace!"

Chapter Thirty-Five

FRANKIE

Frankie watches the woolen heads of the men bob to and fro in the front of the truck, the rhythm determined by these bumpy, swinging lanes that they seem to know intimately. The man next to her presses against her leg. She inches away and feels the tremor of the girl against her other leg.

The mist outside swirls and the air inside the truck feels thin and finite. The individual smells not mingling at all but at war. She can almost taste the cake breath of the man next to her and the sour tang from the girl. The smell of fear, leaking out into this confined space. She smelled it enough on herself and Seb when they were little, back when their dad still drank. Will he start again after this? Maybe he reached for a can as soon as he heard the news. Will Mum be safe? Will Cough? She feels a pang, something dormant stirring.

"We're going to be nice and cozy back at ours," the man next to her says as he jostles for space, reconnecting with her leg. "A couple of nice girls, a good lot of grub, and all the time in the world." The passenger in the front laughs at this. Everyone here is facing the same existential crisis, a missile literally on its way followed by poisonous fallout . . . but they're acting like they're throwing a party.

Next to her, Frankie feels the girl gulping back tears. Her whole body is trembling, still wrapped in her school coat. Frankie offers her hand and the girl grabs it and threads her fingers through Frankie's. The girl's phone drops to the floor.

Frankie's parents are in Palma, not just Spain but an island off Spain, surely one of the safest places in Europe to be. Her brother is even farther, her silly, caring brother and his whip-smart wife and lovely children, all in Dubai. And to think, she'd been uneasy when he said they were headed there for winter sun. So far away, so hot, so near to places that made her vaguely uneasy. In that sense she's lucky, everyone she loves is accounted for, even her aunties. They'll be better off in Manchester than here. But they won't know where she is. Maybe they'll never know and that will be their form of fallout. She touches her tattoo through her sleeve. *A heap of broken images*. Her favorite line from "The Waste Land." Will she be identified by it one day? What about this girl? Will her family ever know what happened to her? A wave of nausea breaks across Frankie's gut.

"I feel sick," she says. "Is it much farther?"

"Not much farther," grunts the driver.

"I need to get out or I'll throw up," she says, and realizes it might be true.

"You complain a lot," says the front passenger.

"It's been said."

"We're not stopping now," the front passenger says, more to the driver than her. "But we'll crack a window."

The man nearest her presses a button and the window slides down slowly. He stops it halfway, the gap not even big enough to fit her head through, but a rush of cold air now tousles her hair and chills her skin. It is strangely invigorating. Proof of life.

"Where are we actually going?" Frankie asks. "Are you sure your house is big enough for extra people?"

"It's not a house," says the man next to her. "It's a farm."

"It's a compound," the driver says sharply.

"It's a base, is what it is," says the passenger cheerfully. "An HQ."

"For what?" Frankie says. The men pause, and the driver and passenger look at each other.

"We told you," the passenger says, puffing his chest just a little under his green faux fatigues. "The Devon Militia."

"You're not from round here so we can't expect you to know," the driver says, his voice softer. "Last line of defense since 1558. The militia defended Devon through every major war until—"

"Until now," the passenger cuts in. "Don't matter what they say, it never really stopped. *We* never stopped."

"Do you mean," Frankie says carefully, "like *Dad's Army*?"

There is silence.

"Not like fucking *Dad's Army*," the passenger says and slaps the dash. The driver accelerates in response and the girl grips Frankie's hand even tighter.

As the truck swings around the bend, the moonlit side mirror shows a glimpse of something following them. A shape, a blur almost invisible through the mist. It disappears as the truck turns. She holds her breath, looks carefully at the others' faces, but they don't seem to have noticed.

Another bend, another quick slice of reflection.

It's a car. Silent in the mist.

Could it be Otis?

She stares but it's gone again, the angle lost. Still, no one seems to have noticed. She takes a long, deep breath to try to slow her racing heart, closes her eyes, and bites her lip to stop from making a sound.

The men are now arguing over the exact nature of the Devon Militia, which sounds like a tissue-thin, deadly mix of bad ideas, historical hubris, and rural weaponry.

Meanwhile Frankie's mind wheels around, trying to work out what Otis will do next—if it is him?

The men are arguing about other "soldiers" who have passed through the "ranks." Cousins, second cousins, and uncles, from the sound of things. They argue over whether they'll have lived up to the pledges made when they were sworn in. They seem to think that other "soldiers" like them will also be scraping their way through Devon, gathering up the vulnerable and dragging them into their trucks, heading to this farm-cum-HQ. How many other women and girls will be forced there? How did they snatch this girl?

Frankie peers carefully into the rearview mirror but the angle is unhelpful and all she can see is her own terrified face.

Whoever it is could be seen if they follow too closely. She saw the car, after all. And if these men see the car, they could shoot whoever is driving. And even if it is Otis and he's not seen, will he simply follow them all the way to this compound of nutters? He has no idea who these people are or what they're like, he can't have seen how many there are let alone know how many could be waiting. Outnumbered and outgunned by all these blood relations.

Even if it's just these three and the others have abandoned their posts—that's still three to one. Unless... She looks at the girl. Could she help somehow? Plus Frankie and Otis... that's three against three. Three unarmed, uncoordinated, untrained strangers against three men with a gun, who have been waiting for this moment all of their rotten lives.

Fuck.

Chapter Thirty-Six

MRS. DABB

The solar streetlights are wan and create more shadows than light as she heads out of Chagford again, passing shuttered cottages, parked cars, vans, and trucks.

Could it have been just some random creep in a random truck, enticing girls with free gadgets? But if so, why just Bunny? And why wouldn't she tell Jasmine? Why wouldn't she tell her own family, for that matter? She's been drilled on the importance of speaking up if strangers approach her; did she really want a phone that badly?

No, she thinks with a jagged swallow and a sinking heart, there was nothing random about this. Bunny was clearly nursing unasked questions, and someone slid down their window right on cue to answer them.

The last time Bunny asked anything about *that side*, the only real time, was years ago, and it was theoretical, broad. Some jerk kid at primary school had said something and Bunny came home, fidgeting and wriggling with questions.

"It's up to you what you tell her," Mary had said, when she asked for advice but actually wanted reassurance. "But you have to tell her something or she'll fill in the blanks herself, and that doesn't always go well."

"I don't know what more to say. I said she's lucky to have people who love her, that she's being raised by a village—"

"Raised by a village? She's being raised by a mother who won't give her a straight answer, no wonder she's confused."

It had hung in the air too long, silence burning the oxygen in the room until Mary had apologized. The whole thing was then punted down the line. And here's where it had landed.

The light from the headlamps shimmers in the fog, picking out the berry-bare brambles that have consumed these hedgerows.

A car shoots past, just missing her. Its lights are so faint it may as well not have any. She sucks in a breath, feels her pulse hammering in her temples, but stays on course. It wouldn't be the first time someone had crashed in these lanes. Not her problem, though. Not today.

Don't be mean, Mum.

The voice appears fully formed in her head, as if her daughter had climbed inside her thoughts.

You don't understand, she tells an imaginary Bunny. *You can't understand until you've been unable to fix someone.*

She looks at the clock, so much time lost already. The fog seems slightly lighter now, which helps her go faster. She doesn't want to get to her destination, she never wanted to return there, but she must. Somehow, it's become her only hope.

The last time she saw inside his house was when she woke up there, fourteen years ago, with a mouth that tasted of bad decisions and a stomach churning with guilt.

He was lying across the bed, hairy arse out, one arm pinning her into position. The coverless duvet was in a heap on the floor, the sheets smelling of sweat, cum, and booze. And all she could think, as her eyeballs throbbed in their sockets, was *You're not my person. You will never be my person.*

A month later, holding the positive test result in one hand while her actual person made breakfast the other side of the bathroom door, she vowed that whoever this little baby turned into would never know how he or she came to be. It seemed simple. Bunny would never be his, but now he's got to her anyway.

As she swings around the bend, a truck up ahead slides into view.

Whoever it was had an old truck, that's all I know. They called her over to them but I didn't see who was inside.

She presses harder on the accelerator.

24 MINUTES UNTIL IMPACT

Chapter Thirty-Seven

CARRIE

"Grace!"

The power is still out and Carrie gropes around her, trying to find Grace or some trace of where she could be. Why isn't she speaking?

This is a kind of darkness Carrie has never seen in the city. The streetlights have been snuffed, the nearby houses and shops are without power. Only the dim orange glow from a distant pile of crashed cars smears the darkness with its thumb.

This is war. A sudden, alien thought. London has done this before, blacking out for the Blitz. Is that what they're doing now? Surely modern missiles are more high tech than this? Do they need visibility? Isn't it all done with computers? *Why the hell haven't I paid attention?*

Something metallic collides with her leg and she nearly falls over. It's a bike—she can hear the rattle of the wheels and just make out the shape of the rider as they whip away into the night.

Nearby, people are shouting and crying, but they're just gray shapes; the whole picture of Kennington Road is like dark papier-mâché, shapes on shapes, torn out and undefined.

Her eyes adjust more. Shopfronts and houses are penciled in, she sees people darting around. She can see the cyclist who clipped her, zigzagging around people in the dark like a dying wasp. But she can't see Grace.

People have started using their phone flashlights, the whole road seemingly dotted with fireflies. She can see colors now, of sleeves and coats. Grace cannot have gone far.

She tries to remember what she could see just before the power went. An alleyway, a man. She hears scuffling nearby. *Oh fuck.*

She can see the opening to the alleyway, still totally dark. But she can definitely hear movement. "Grace, come out," she says, but it's clear she won't. Or more likely she can't. Because she's not alone in there.

Carrie takes a cautious step inside and her foot sends a glass bottle spinning noisily, smashing against the wall. A muffled cry comes from a few meters away. Carrie stoops and gropes for a piece of the smashed bottle, her hand shaking so much she can barely grasp it. "I'm armed," she says, and it sounds ludicrous. "Just let her go, and no one will ever know."

A muffled sob.

"Come on," she says, "we've only got minutes left of life as we know it, do you want to spend it hurting a young girl?"

"Yes," comes a voice. Reedy and robotic.

Carrie stands up straighter, the anger moving through her like adrenaline, as she steps farther into the alleyway. She grips the bottle tightly as the streetlights around sputter into life and she sees him. He's standing in front of a wheelie bin, his arms holding Grace tightly. A small, wimpy man, about fifty. A shopping bag has been pulled over Grace's head and pinched together under her chin. As she breathes—rapid, animal—the plastic sucks tight around her mouth. "Jesus Christ!" Carrie shouts. Devoid of a better idea, she throws the bottle just behind him. He cowers. A rat man in his rat alley. His grip on Grace slackens and she runs full-pelt toward Carrie, tearing the bag off as they collide.

"You evil prick," Grace shouts over her shoulder as they run from him, tangled together.

It hits Carrie like a punch. Even now, even in this, the chance to hurt women and girls is still all-consuming to some men. And if there's him, there'll be a hundred, a thousand men more. All the men who have shouted things at her and Emma, or not believed her when she's said she's not interested. Are they still stalking the city today? Will they be waiting around the next corner?

Carrie pulls Grace close and tries to comfort her, but she shakes herself loose and turns back to shout, "You deserve what's coming!"

Chapter Thirty-Eight

FRANKIE

"Do you have any games at your place?" the girl says suddenly, her voice aimed at the two men in the front. Her voice is overloud, drunk with nerves; she is gripping Frankie's fingers so tightly she nearly cries out in pain.

"What, like Monopoly?" says the passenger. "Because if you mean PlayStation an' that, it won't work. Not after. The generator's for emergencies only."

"I meant like Monopoly then, Clue and stuff," the girl says. "Board games."

"We've got Risk," the passenger says. "But we can make our own fun anyway." The driver stares at him sharply but says nothing.

The girl looks at Frankie. It's just for one moment, but it's a look she would recognize anywhere. A ladies' toilet look. An *I saw someone was bothering you so let's walk out together* look. It tells Frankie that this girl has also seen the car. That to stand a chance of them getting out of this, the men mustn't spot whoever is following. The men must be distracted by any means possible.

"What are your names, guys?" Frankie asks. It comes out stiff and wooden. For a moment, the men say nothing, and she swallows dryly, imagining that they've also seen the moonlit outline of the car. That any second, the truck will shudder to a stop and they'll pile out like kids playing soldiers. Then shoot whoever is following them in the head.

The passenger shrugs at the driver. "The young one knows full well who we are, what does it matter if this one knows our names too? I'm Jimmy."

"I'm Ashley," the driver mutters. "Ash, to friends."

"And I'm Sandy," barks the one in the back, right in Frankie's ear. She feels his hand grab hers awkwardly and he pumps it up and down, looking amused. *This is funny to them?*

"And we'll be your flight attendants for this journey into the apocalypse," says Jimmy.

Yes. This is funny to them.

"I'm Frankie," she says. "And I'd love to know more about where we're going. Did you say it used to be a farm?"

"Used to be, yeah," Sandy says. "Do you have farms where you're from?"

"Are you joking?" The pause suggests not. "Yes, we have farms in the north of England."

He's fidgeting next to her, his spreading legs land-grabbing more and more space so she can feel the muscles in his leg against hers, the flesh of their hips pressed together. She gasps for air and tries to hide it. She nearly slips off the seat as they turn a corner and then notices a seat belt dangling from the ceiling, designed for the middle passenger. She pulls it down, expecting to be met with derision or complaint, but when she tries to clip it in, Sandy lifts one buttock out of the way and lets her. She nods at the girl to do the same.

"I love farms actually," she says, and it sounds like total bollocks. Because it is. "Will you tell me about yours?"

"Well, for starters, it's not a farm anymore. We told you that." It's Ashley butting in from the front, but the snarl feels put on.

"Sorry," she says, but it's probably obvious she's not. Resting Bitch Voice, Seb calls it. "What, um, what's it like, how big is your . . . ex-farm?"

"Our compound," Sandy says.

"Yeah, sorry, your compound." *You deranged pricks.*

"We've not got as much land as we used to," Jimmy says. "We used to have a hundred acres but most of it was owned by the Duchy and when Mum fucked off and then Dad died . . ." He and Sandy interrupt each other to tell a complicated story about the King when he was still the Prince and how the Duke of Cornwall owns this and that and does this and doesn't do that. Or shouldn't do that. She can't follow it, she doesn't give a wild shit, but it's keeping them distracted, and they're not looking in the mirrors. Right now, that is the only thing that matters. One life/death challenge at a time.

Otis drives a rattly old work van by day, with bumps and dents that Frankie's never thought about before. Has he already bashed into a pole?

Hit another car? Slid too close to the hedge and banked it? Or is it him following carefully, just out of sight?

The Mercedes is the great love of his life. A vintage powder blue, older than him, with little nubs instead of proper back seats, an engine that needs perfect conditions to start—too cold, too hot, too wet, no hope—and an ancient CD player and radio. Nowhere to put a baby's car seat, but there is ... there was ... plenty of time for that.

He loves that car and he drives it almost holding his breath, like any scratch or nick will appear gouged out of his own skin in sympathy stigmata. He hand-washes and waxes it himself every Sunday and—

Thud.

"What the fuck?" shouts the man in the passenger seat as the truck is suddenly jolted from behind, a dull noise of metal on bumper. It's too light a touch to hurt anyone, but the seat belt snaps taut across Frankie's stomach, her heart rate so fast it foams over into nausea again.

Frankie stares into the rearview mirror now, and everyone else—except Ashley, the driver—turns awkwardly to look out the back. Jimmy leans out of the window, pointing the gun back down the road and firing. The girls drops Frankie's hand to cover her eyes and ears, curling her body into the brace position. Ashley slows.

"Don't fucking stop, dickhead," shouts Sandy.

"You can outrun this twat," says Jimmy. He leans out with the gun again but the bumpy lane jiggles his arm around and he doesn't fire. This time.

Ashley lurches forward then, much faster than before, slingshotting into a turn at over 50 mph. Frankie wraps her arm around the girl as the truck spins around another corner but is then slammed from behind.

As Ashley grapples with the wheel, Sandy shoots forward. He knocks the back of Jimmy's head with his own, the hollow sound of two coconuts colliding, and then slumps back down in the back. Jimmy continues forward from the passenger seat, slicing through the windshield, leaving a man-shaped hole in the middle, just as the truck collides with a huge tree and something else slides into them from behind.

Chapter Thirty-Nine

MRS. DABB

He had taken her home in a truck the next day. She'd forgotten that until today, but now it all comes back. The mud-splattered step up into its body, the cab filled with boys-y smells and detritus. Paper bakery bags, made see-through with oil. Dank smells from strong cigarettes, butts spilling from an overstuffed cigarette tray. Discarded work hoodies along the back seat. Stink on stink on stink. She'd forgotten it all.

She still can't remember the color of its exterior, only the mud and the smell threatening to make her sick, her belches rising in a final indignity. He was a stranger again in the morning. A name known by reputation and already a regret.

She'd asked him to drop her off in Chagford instead of at the cottage, not wanting to be seen. And he knew why, a brief wave of hurt passing over his face. To think, she'd once felt sorry for him, as she tucked her Saturday night tail between her Sunday morning legs and slunk home.

The truck slows ahead of her. Inside, a collection of heads bob up and down with the camber of the road. She speeds up to get a closer look, but then it indicates left and carefully turns. As she zooms past, she can see no one inside that she recognizes.

His place is just over the brow of the next hill. How had they got there that night, from Chagford? Vague recollections of a car, maybe a lift from another drinking buddy, themselves beer-breathed and swaying? Country rules. They all thought they were untouchable. They were, until they skidded over that line. Before he killed someone she loved and turned her life inside out, the raw flesh of it still exposed.

Fuck. *Fuck.* Bunny knew his name, knew his reputation, the stories, and still . . .

Because she didn't know the most crucial bit, and what's more alluring than being handed the missing piece of your own puzzle?

She is trying not to think of Bunny being pecked at by what's left of that family. But if there's any possibility she's there . . . Are there any good ones among them? Any women . . . an aunt or grandmother who might keep her child safe? Especially if they value their own blood so much.

Well, half their blood, but loved with her mother's whole heart. She drives faster as the little car whines its way up the slope toward the dark valley on the other side.

21 MINUTES UNTIL IMPACT

Chapter Forty

CARRIE

"Are you okay?" Carrie asks Grace uselessly, as their feet slap hard and fast along Kennington Road.

"Are you for real?" Grace says, but then her voice softens. "Yeah, I'm okay. I'll be okay, thank you for . . ."

"Of course. Do you want to talk about . . ?"

"No," Grace says quietly as they finally turn into Elm Walk.

Grace speeds up as they pass a squat block of flats, three lockup garages in a row, and a small cluster of houses. As they approach Grace's block of flats, she breaks into a run, Carrie trying to keep up. Most of the windows are covered with curtains or blinds, one or two with big bedsheets. The communal entrance door is closed; above it a row of thin windows flicker with movement. Just as Carrie and Grace reach the front door, it flies open and a woman runs out.

"Mummy!" Grace shouts, bursting into tears. The woman is maybe forty, a little taller than Grace, slim, dark-skinned, crying, and wrapped in a chunky green cardigan. The woman does not look at Carrie once, just grabs Grace and pulls her in so suddenly that Grace nearly falls over. Her mum peppers Grace with kisses, forehead, cheeks, the crown of her head, breathing her in.

"Where's Josh?" Grace says, muffled by her mother's hug.

"Upstairs, he's safe," her mother says and only then does she pull back and look at Carrie, standing motionless next to them.

"My god, thank you so much," Grace's mother says. "Do you need to shelter with us?"

Just like that. As if that's not an enormous offer, as if that's not offering the whole world to a stranger.

Carrie shakes her head. "Thank you, but I need to get back to my own family." Grace hugs Carrie, wordlessly. Grace, so reserved and cool, is now so clearly a child. Carrie can feel her small fingers gripping her coat. The forceful hug slackens and she moves away so Grace's mother can take her place, pulling Carrie into a tight embrace.

"I won't ever forget this," she says into Carrie's shoulder. "I'm sorry, I don't know your . . ."

"I'm Carrie, Carrie Spencer."

"Beverley, Beverley Morrow."

"Your daughter is . . ."

"I know, I know she is."

Some of the streetlights flicker as she runs back down Elm Walk but some are still dead. She'd not considered that things might stop working ahead of six o'clock, but maybe it will be a disintegration first and then . . .

She thinks of what else Grace said. About these last minutes. Is it true what she was hinting at? Will they all just be wiped out as soon as the missile strikes . . . the whole city? The whole country? And would that be better than surviving anyway?

Grace is only a kid, can she really know?

She pictures Clementine and Emma waiting at the window the way Beverley had been, unable to leave her much younger son to hunt for Grace. On the days Carrie picks Clementine up and takes her home, they often look out of the window for "Mama" when she's due back. Watching for Emma's bright-red hair, her graceful neck, and her giant tote bag filled with snacks and life rubble.

Emma and Clementine are rarely in the window looking out for "Mummy" on the days that Emma does pick up. They're usually knee-deep in a puzzle when Carrie gets home. Or they're curled up on the sofa with a bowl of cheese cubes, watching *Bluey*, which Emma likes even more than Clementine. Clementine is just happy to cuddle up and laugh along.

So they'll be okay, she thinks suddenly. If Carrie doesn't make it back but her family survives somehow . . . they will be okay. Without her. Because it's Carrie who will miss out. And that's the most unbearable thought.

Chapter Forty-One

FRANKIE

Frankie's whole head *whoomp-whoomps* like a siren. Everything is on backward and in the wrong place. She is rag-dolled.

The engine in the crashed truck has cut out, the radio is off, and cold air screams in through the hole in the windshield.

The metal nose of the truck, so solid and threatening, is now concertinaed, folded up as if pinched by a giant hand. The tree is right there, its rough bark a fingertip away from the front of the cab, like it's trying to get inside. A halo around the truck flashes orange, on and off, on and off, illuminating the road and hedgerow. Hazard lights, she thinks. Her mind allowing only bare essential realizations to form. One at a time, pearls on a string.

Frankie is sitting bolt upright, held in place by a seat belt. She feels idiotic in this pose, grotesque, while all around her bodies slump and contort. Her chest and abdomen hurt like she's winded.

Oh god, the baby, the poppy seed. And Otis. And the fucking missile.

The girl is also sitting upright now, her breath fast, her eyes screwed shut and her hand still gripping one of Frankie's fingers. "Keep your eyes closed, all right? I'll help you out," Frankie says, looking at the mess of a man next to her. "Just . . . just keep your eyes properly closed."

The girl whimpers but does as instructed. Sandy is slumped next to Frankie in a shape that a human body should not be capable of forming. She knows where Jimmy went—the hole in the windshield tells that story. The driver, Ashley, is still in situ, a fat airbag between him and the steering wheel, stinking of burned rubber. Deep dark blood gushes down the side of his head where his brother must have hit him on his journey out through the windshield. Now Ashley lolls slowly to the side, his body settling against the door in a drunken slump.

Frankie fumbles for the seat belt buckle and disentangles herself and then reaches over Sandy for the door handle. His back is bent over, his face hidden. She reaches down to his drooping neck like she's only seen people do on-screen. His skin is warm but there's no pulse. She looks at his bent back, no breaths in or out. He is undeniably dead.

"Oh fuck, oh fuck!"

"What?" says the girl.

"Just keep 'em closed, I'll come and get you out."

She grips the door handle and shoves. It doesn't swing open properly, wedged against something outside, but she has enough space to push Sandy through. He slithers to the tarmac, leaving a trail of blood and fluids on the seat and carpet that she can't bear to think about. The air is thick with the smell of iron and piss. As he lands, a *hmph* sound bubbles from his mouth, and she gasps. "Are you . . ." she starts to say. But he is not alive, this is trapped air. She can tell because a significant chunk of the front of his head is missing.

She climbs up onto her knees, losing her other boot in the process, and scrambles along the seat toward the open door, climbing down next to Sandy's motionless body. She cannot catch her breath and her neck is aching but she is out in the cool air, no longer trapped.

Exhausted and in pain, she feels her way around the back of the truck to the other side and pulls open the door. Reaching inside, she unbuckles the girl—her eyes still screwed tightly—and helps her climb down.

"Face this way," Frankie says, but the girl doesn't seem to be listening, sagging on the spot like a marionette, so Frankie manually turns her from the truck. "Now open your eyes."

They both look at the road behind them. The mist is continuing to lift, and a few meters away, half-eaten by the hedge, is the blue-delphinium smear of Otis's car.

Chapter Forty-Two

MRS. DABB

The siren still cries in the distance but the fog is lifting whip-quick now. It has left a trace smell of burning, a motor smell that you don't get as much these days. Rubber and steel, diesel even, smearing slick rainbows on the silver tarmac. The fog picks up nearby fragrances, amplifies and spreads them. Normally it's sweetened with gorse, but right now it smells as sour and man-made as everything else happening today.

She reaches the brow of the hill and takes a sudden breath at the sight. Down there, in the dark blanket of fields, sits a small cluster of lights, all alone.

What must it have been like to grow up there? Cut off, banded together, and fed from birth with stories of family glory. All tooled up with weapons they didn't need, looking for a fight they'd been bred for. It was only going to end one way.

As she starts to speed down the hill toward it, a helicopter swings into view along the horizon, blades chuntering as it sweeps its searchlight across the fields. She sucks in a breath and tries to block out the sound, the vibrations shaking her skull as it zooms directly over the car and away.

It used to be a working farm but it is skeletal now, large outbuildings reduced to shells, the moon peeping through their patchy roofs. There are no crops in the overgrown fields. Weeds sway tall in the wind with no animals to stomp and chew them. As her car slides quietly closer, she can see a pole flying a bright Lest We Forget poppy flag next to the main farmhouse, the only building that seems relatively intact. It was Remembrance Day on Monday. But every day is Remembrance Day for her.

When she was last here, the pole was hung with a huge flapping

Devon Militia emblem hand-painted by one of the wing nut cousins. She had ducked under it on the morning walk of shame and flinched when it touched her. Oblivious to her distaste, he'd proudly explained the origins. All of his family were members of the militia. Well, all of the male relatives. *What the fuck am I doing here*, she'd thought, even as she was making her escape.

A security light flickers on now as she pulls off the lane and into the overgrown farmyard. Is anyone looking out for her? A sudden thought: *Is this a trap?*

The air outside the car smells stagnant, years of agricultural smells baked into the stones and still leaking back out long after they stopped farming.

There are no visible vehicles here but there were loads when she first saw this place. Working trucks, vans, old Land Rover Defenders stripped down, their bones picked for parts. Where are all the vehicles?

The security light is still blazing; there's nowhere for her to hide and time is marching. She has no choice but to walk into this wasp's nest.

"Bunny?" she shouts, rushing toward the crumbling farmhouse. The dusty windows are shoddily blocked up from the inside, but an electric glow sketches the edge of each frame. She bangs on the glass, hard as she dares, but nothing happens, so she moves toward the wooden front door, fist raised.

18 MINUTES UNTIL IMPACT

Chapter Forty-Three

CARRIE

Carrie's on Kennington Road now. A bus lies on its side that wasn't there earlier, felled like big game. Some people scramble out of it but others lie motionless inside. Ahead, she can see another roadblock. Blue lights pulse from askew police cars, but she can't see any officers now. Are they taking cover? She imagines them, uniformed and severe, inside nearby houses.

As she heads toward the roadblock, a car judders out of a side road and then, nosing into pockets of space between abandoned vehicles, drives directly at the police cars. Gunshots crack. The car swerves, then crashes into a nearby abandoned van. No one gets out.

She cannot run that way. Armed police are outside. Who knows what orders to shoot they might have? She scrambles across the road and sprints into Walcot Square. Bold-red postbox, neat iron-fenced communal lawn, window boxes, and Georgian terraced houses. A "Disney bit," as Emma calls them, these fancy parts of London that look like backdrops to *101 Dalmatians*.

"How long do we have?" she shouts to a man running toward her wearing a navy suit and shiny brown brogues, a flap of blond hair over his strong-jawed face. A Disney prince.

"Eighteen," he shouts without slowing.

"Thank you," she calls. "And good luck." He ignores her.

Two helicopters zip noisily overhead, not the usual controlled machines that slide along invisible traffic lines from the city's financial district to Battersea. These judder and swing over rooftops as if joyriders are behind the controls. Maybe they are.

Ahead of her, the huge spike of the Highpoint apartment block rises up from Elephant and Castle. There are forty-six floors, she knows because she googled it while walking past a few weeks ago. Until today, that's what her phone was, in the main. A mobile search engine for any whim. A meme-distribution device. But now she needs it for the basics. Time. Calls. And it's no good for anything.

Carrie nearly tips over as she skids into St. Mary's Walk, which curls back on itself like a mistake. The houses have two stories aboveground but lower ground floors too; some of them are separate flats, others—those belonging to well-off families—used as playrooms and home gyms. As she runs, scores of eyes peer up at her from these subterranean spaces, watching expressionless as she thunders past.

Electric cables crisscross overhead, their buzzing taking her back, briefly, to the tube rails, the suicide pit, the feeling that she might be going in the wrong direction, screwing herself into the Embankment. At least she's out of there and heading for home. And Grace, lovely Grace, is back where she belongs.

Toward the end of the road, the houses on the right peel away and the road forks, a little communal garden nestling in the V-shape.

A woman sits on the bench there, ramrod straight. In her lap she has a white plastic bag from which she's tugging hunks of bread, tearing them into pieces and throwing them for pigeons.

"Madam," Carrie shouts, always unsure how to address the elderly.

"Leave me be," the woman shouts back primly, without looking over.

"But don't you know there's—"

"I know very well. Now, fuck off."

Chapter Forty-Four

FRANKIE

The mist is lifting fast. As Frankie fumbles her way on cold, socked feet, the outline of Otis's car grows clearer. The hood is open and bent, the front grille hanging off from where it hit the truck. The windshield is impossible to see through, cracked and bubbled. She sucks in a breath, holds her aching stomach, and moves closer. The girl hovers uneasily behind her.

"Otis?"

There is no movement, and no reply. She is by the passenger side now and presses her face to the window. Otis is sitting in the driver's seat, pulled forward as usual. She cries out for her old-lady boyfriend with his sweet careful driving. He is motionless, his head supported by an airbag she didn't dare hope this old Mercedes had. As it shrinks, his head slumps forward with it but his seat belt holds his body rigid. His chest rises and falls.

"Oh my god, Otis, you're alive!"

The internal light pops on as she climbs into the passenger seat and reaches toward him. He has burn marks on his face, that same smell of burning rubber in here as in the truck, but there's no blood. She reaches for his shoulder, shakes it gingerly. His eyes are still closed, his mouth falls open.

"Otis, please wake up. We've got to get inside."

The dashboard clock says 5:43 p.m. They have seventeen minutes to find shelter, and now she's responsible for this girl too. She climbs back out of the car and looks around. The girl's face is blank with terror, her school coat still on. The mist is clearing fast but it's pitch-black beyond the truck's hazard lights. No house lights are beckoning them and she can hear no other cars. No siren now.

"Do you know where we are?" she calls.

"Somewhere near Chagford," the girl says, her voice nearly lost to the wind.

"Is there anywhere else around here, another village or a . . . I don't know. Any houses?"

"I don't know," the girl says.

"You live round here, you must know. Which is the quickest way to get to a house? Come on, think."

"I don't know," the girl cries, visibly shaking. "It all looks the same in the fog, I couldn't see where we were going!"

Frankie looks down at her own body and realizes she too is violently shaking. Despite that, she feels like she's burning up. It's the adrenaline, it must be. Her teeth chatter as she makes her way to the driver's seat and pulls open the door. The skin on Otis's face and neck goose-bumps as the cold air hits him but he doesn't stir.

"Otis, please. Oh god, please wake up."

She strokes his face, but he's unresponsive. She picks up his arm and it droops like a weed, heavier than she'd realized. She feels for his pulse. Fast. Very fast. What does that mean?

Frankie unclips him carefully and tries to slide her arms under his body, as if she could scoop him out and carry him to safety. But Frankie can't even get her arms under him. She starts to pull him toward her, but he is a deadweight and will fall to the floor, maybe injuring himself more.

"Come and help me," she calls to the girl, who walks tentatively nearer, repeatedly looking back at the truck.

Frankie turns the key in the ignition. If they can shunt him across to the other seat, she could drive them back to Chagford and all three might stand a chance. The key clicks but nothing happens. She pulls the handbrake on, pulls out the key and puts it back in, closing her eyes as she tries again.

Nothing.

"Please, please wake up, Otis. We have to find somewhere to shelter."

From inside the truck, Ashley makes a groaning noise from the driver's seat.

"They're awake," the girl hisses, grabbing Frankie's arm and pulling on it. "I can't let them get me again."

"But Otis, my boyfriend—"

"You don't understand, you don't know the Curtiss family."

"But—"

"I'm sorry, I can't stay here, I have to get to my mum!"

The girl runs. Her legs fly in the direction they just came, coat flapping behind her. She doesn't look back, doesn't wait for permission, she just runs. Sixteen minutes to get to Chagford, with youth on her side? Maybe.

Frankie looks down at her socked feet, filthed by mud and grit. Absolutely zero chance.

Chapter Forty-Five

MRS. DABB

She can hear movement inside the crumbling farmhouse.

"Bunny!" She bangs and kicks so hard the door shakes in its frame. Who is behind that door? How many of them still live here? Where the fuck are all the vehicles?!

"Bunny!"

"All right," a strong Devon accent shouts back, female but low. "Keep yer wig on."

The door swings inward and an elderly lady in a pinafore apron—four foot if she's an inch—is staring back out. She has a face of gentle ruin but her eyes are warm. "You've lost your rabbit?" she says, sympathetic but bewildered.

"No, my daughter, is she here?"

The hallway behind the old woman is filled with work boots, waxed jackets, and old puffy coats, but Bunny's is not among them. The smell of baking competes with the smell of cheap synthetic logs burning somewhere else in the belly of this house. But she cannot smell any trace of her daughter, nor see or hear her.

"There's no one here, love, they're all at the church or out . . ." She lowers her eyes. ". . . out looking."

"Please, if you've seen her—just please say. She's thirteen but she's tall, she was in school uniform but she might have changed. She's got dark hair and—"

"But why would she be here, my love?"

"My daughter is a relative," she says uneasily. "She's related to the family who live here." The woman frowns, as if trying to read the face in front of her for signs and similarities.

"Well, I'm not a part of the family that live 'ere myself," the woman says, "but I'm an old friend of Mrs. Curtiss and I've just brought food over for . . . for afterward, you know." Her eyes are watery now. "When the time comes. Someone needs to help out. I know the family's not everyone's cup of tea, but I watched those boys grow up and—"

"I don't have time for this and they don't bloody deserve you, or her, so if you have any idea where they might have taken her, whichever of these scumbags have been sniffing around, giving her things and trying to take her from me, then—"

"Oh, love," the woman says, "come on, don't upset yourself, this is a hard day for everyone but we're all in this together, especially if you're related, so let's—"

"I'm not related!" she shouts then. "All *my* relatives are dead except for Bunny and that's all down to the Curtiss family!"

The woman recoils and her face changes in an instant. She knows. She has recognized, from the court, from the news.

"Your daughter's not here," she says firmly. "And I don't know where she's got to but you need to get away from here right now."

"But—"

"It's not safe for you here. I know who you are and I'm sorry for your loss, but you're a liar, aren't you? All this time . . . And I'll be telling Mrs. Curtiss about this, I promise you that."

The door is slammed closed; a faded sign that reads CURTISS swings on its nail and slides to the floor. "Bunny!" she shouts. "If you're in there, come out!"

From behind the wood, the little woman shouts, "You need to get out of here right now."

15 MINUTES UNTIL IMPACT

Chapter Forty-Six

CARRIE

Carrie passes a community care center that has an amputee rehabilitation unit inside. Have all the doctors and nurses stayed with their patients or fled to be with their own children and loved ones?

A little way up the road, a man's lifeless body swings gently from a tough little cherry tree. At his feet, a book lies open, the wind ruffling its pages. Carrie gasps but she does not slow down.

Carrie staggers down Bird Walk, a narrow path between the tall, terraced houses. She comes out by a primary school, where what looks like an after-school club of children is cowering in the hall, its windows still uncovered. A man who has been running alongside her, barely noticed, peels away and jumps onto the fence, shouting his child's name: "Reuben!" He monkeys up and over the wire fence like it's nothing. As she runs on, chest tightening and throat so dry she's open-mouth coughing, she hears a little voice from inside the school shouting, "Daddy!"

She thinks, of course, of Clementine. Of soft brown curls whorling out of a double crown, the thumb she sucks when she's tired. The sweet smell of her when they wake her up, the way she wipes the sleep from her eyes like a baby animal.

That little cub is too young to remember this lovely life.

Clementine will never know how good we had it.

Cars line both sides of this street. How are there so many cars when no one in London drives? Her feet are on fire, soles aching from thumping along the pavement in fashion sneakers.

She thinks of Grace and draws strength from the memory. How Beverley must have thought her daughter wasn't coming home and yet she waited, watching, hoping... and it paid off. Now Grace is home, with her mum and little brother. So it's not impossible. Which is proof that Carrie can reach Clementine and Emma.

How many times in her life has she run like fury to the comfort of Emma and her house? When her mother Janet's grief rose like damp up the walls of their home and Carrie could do nothing to help. Poor Mum, how hard it must have been to be suddenly alone. Dad had been Mum's best friend, to lose a love like that...

I have a love like that. I cannot lose it. She cannot lose me.

Because Emma *is* home. More than Carrie's mother's house is home. Clementine and Emma are home. And they're home together. They're home together. They're home together.

The mantra settles alongside the rhythm of her painful feet on the pavement as she runs past apartment buildings with boxy balconies; on one, a huge malamute dog paces around the small space, his howls more human than animal.

They'll bring him inside before... won't they? Surely? She's stopped without realizing, looking up at his big wolfy face as he stuffs his snout through the balustrade.

Yes, they will bring him in, she decides, sucking in a deep breath, running on and then vomiting. No warning, just a sudden surge, the hot slap of it hitting the ground followed by an acidic aftertaste. It's as if her body knows she's nearly home and everything it's been holding on to is loosening.

But I'm not home yet, stupid body.

"You all right, darling?"

Carrie looks around but the street is empty.

"Up here, love."

She steps away from the apartment block and looks up.

"That's it, bit farther."

She looks up again. To the balconies running along the third floor. A woman of at least seventy, maybe more, sits on a deck chair. She wears a cream fur coat and bright-blue rimmed glasses, her lips bold red against powdery pale skin. In one hand she grips a tall glass with a cocktail umbrella and in the other is a thick cigar.

"Better out than in," she says, and takes a puff. "You wanna come up?"

"What?"

"You wanna come up and have a drink, a bit of company? Use the loo?"

"Oh, thank you so much, but—" Carrie turns away, looking in the rough direction of her home.

"You got people?" the woman calls down.

"I have."

"Nice people?" The woman's accent is born-and-bred Lambeth and Carrie loves it.

"The best," Carrie says, and allows herself a smile.

"S'what it's all about then."

"Do *you* have people?" Carrie calls up.

"I had the best person in the world for nearly fifty years," the woman calls down and takes a long sip of her drink. "Can't say fairer than that."

She puffs her cigar. "I'm going to drink to him and watch the fireworks. Sure you don't wanna join me?"

"I need to get to my people," Carrie says, "but thank you."

"Then I'll drink to you too, love. Godspeed, darling."

Chapter Forty-Seven

FRANKIE

The girl has disappeared around the kink in the road. From the front of the truck, a few meters away, comes another groan. The driver is alive but in what condition? Frankie shuffles around and climbs into the passenger seat of the Mercedes beside Otis, ducking out of view—she hopes—from the truck. Is Ashley going to climb out and find her? What will he do to them? He can't make it anywhere in his truck, that's smashed to pieces. And Otis's car is no use. He didn't look in shape to run back to the village. Maybe he'll just kill her and Otis, because he has no other options. Because he's a fucking animal.

She waits, holding Otis's limp hand and counting to ten but then carrying on to twenty. Nothing. No more sound, no movement. She thinks of that great gash on Ashley's head, all the blood. Surely he's not capable...

The mist has nearly gone now. How quickly it's disappeared after causing all that trouble. She climbs out carefully, head still thick with pain, body still shaking, and looks around. The vehicles are wedged against a muddy, tree-lined bank on a narrow lane, in the apex of a gentle bend.

She knows what lies in the direction they came, and it's all too far away. Instead, her throbbing eyes follow the curve of the road in the other direction. The road not yet traveled. She paces around the corner a little way, looking behind her constantly in case Ashley has followed or somehow Otis has sprung to life or the girl has come back. But nothing happens.

She takes another corner, and another, and a third. And there, ahead by maybe a hundred meters, sits a building with smoke coming from its chimney. She looks behind her, the car and truck blocked by curves in the road, and she looks ahead. Shelter.

She rushes back to the car as fast as she can manage through the pain that is getting worse in her head and her body, her cold, unprotected feet. Otis is still unconscious, his pulse still far too fast.

"Otis, I've found somewhere we can go but we need to get there right now."

He doesn't react. She pulls his arm, shakes it, kisses his face, sweeps his hair out of his eyes, jiggles his knee with her hand, and then grabs both shoulders and shakes him so hard she worries she'll break something. Nothing works.

She has thirteen minutes. Thirteen minutes to get to that building, convince them to help her get Otis and carry him back inside too. That has to be enough time, they have to agree to help. They have to. But to make sure of it, Frankie creeps silently toward the truck. Ashley is still in the driver's seat and as she opens the passenger-side door, he groans again. But his eyes are closed and he doesn't move, even as she carefully reaches into the footwell and pulls out the gun.

Chapter Forty-Eight

MRS. DABB

She's back in the driver's seat, gunning the engine. She can't remember opening the door, climbing in, or starting it. She races straight back up the hill, surging out of this dark valley. Now that she knows Bunny is not at the Curtiss place, she wants to get away as fast as she can. The little woman will tell the matriarch, of course she will, but will she then tell the others? And if she does, when and how will they come for her? Because they *will* come for her.

And did she risk all that for no reason? Maybe Bunny really did have a doctor's appointment, missed the bus, and made her slow way back? Maybe she wanted contraception, a sickening thought but not . . . not impossible. She would do that in secret, wouldn't she? And the phone . . . maybe it was from a boyfriend and she gave Jasmine a made-up story. Or Jasmine was covering for her. That is what friends do.

Of the options left—going into the village and banging on random doors, trying to drag a different truth out of Jasmine, or going home and hoping Bunny's there—going home seems the least reckless. Mary should be there by now and Bunny would want to be home for 5:59. If it's within her power to get there, she'll get there. They must be together. The alternative is unthinkable.

These lanes were not designed for driving fast but she stamps on the accelerator anyway, flying through sharp turns, to hell with the risk. This economy car was not built for speed either, and it slides and rattles in protest. Forty miles an hour, forty-five, fifty. It whines and whines. The car tries to take control, to slow itself down, so she turns it to full self-drive. It instantly feels more chaotic, but at least she can go faster.

The fog has totally gone, the air crisp and clear. She presses the accelerator again, chewing the road up underneath the narrow tires and pulling herself forward, nose closer to the windshield. As she reaches the top of the hill—Chagford fizzing with light ahead of her—the car judders into a pothole and bounces back out.

She doesn't slow down. If the tires are damaged, she'll drive on the bare metal rims if that's what it takes. She has to get home.

12 MINUTES UNTIL IMPACT

Chapter Forty-Nine

CARRIE

Carrie cuffs her eyes on her grimy coat sleeve. Vomiting back there has left her throat sore and dry, and every few steps are stumbled by coughing. Less than an hour ago she was standing on the concourse at Waterloo, coat clean, worry-free, looking forward to a takeaway and family weekend. Now she's bruised, filthy, unable to stop stumbling when she should be running. Her life has been dismantled in less time than a spin class. And this, right now . . . this is the best it will ever be again. Everything ahead of them is worse to a multiplication number she can't even picture.

Even a confirmed optimist like Carrie is prone to daily complaints, London all but requires it as an entrance fee. And to think what she usually complains about. The injustice of a late train. Outrage at her favorite Pret sandwich running out. A tantrum when the supermarket order arrives with silly replacement items. Sesame bagels instead of cinnamon and raisin is not a real problem. This is a real problem.

In Reedworth Street, she can see a Tesco home delivery van, sitting diagonally across the road. All its doors are open, like its pockets have been turned out. Blue crates strewn and empty. She and Emma got their last shopping delivery on Wednesday night. If only they'd known. The order contained no bottled water, no canned vegetables, only four rolls of toilet paper, those bloody bagels. Emma had added a jumbo bag of Haribo Tangfastics, and separately, without realizing it, Carrie had added the same. Two kilograms of sweets is no help now. They learned nothing from 2020.

The first day of the Covid lockdown, she and Emma had been too late to get any toilet paper before the shelves were picked clean. They'd been forced to use washcloths and strips of old towels, dropping them into a bucket and repeatedly putting the washing machine on. Extra detergent, high heat. That had all seemed so uncivilized, at the very edge of what was humanly tolerable. "We're basically cave people," Emma had said. Carrie would take that over what's coming in a heartbeat.

As she reaches the Tesco van, Carrie sees a puddle of dark blood on the floor, smaller blots trailing away. No one is around, the whole street empty like those first bewildering weeks of the pandemic. But that . . . that was not this. And that was nothing like what could happen next.

Maybe a direct hit is better than what the survivors will face. Maybe she should hope for that. This rational thought curdles because humans strive to keep going, no matter what. And she, Carrie, maybe more than most.

She's never been truly depressed, and rarely sad. Her dad's death was the worst thing that ever happened to her. The worst thing, she thought, that ever would happen. And she was dogged in pursuing gratitude even in her grief. Being glad for the time she'd had with Dad. Glad for who she still had (Emma) and accepting that her mum, while a bit of a nut at times, kept her clothed and fed. And loved her, definitely.

What's coming will be the worst thing anyone in this city has ever faced. There will be no food and water after impact, that's what the radio said, no emergency services. What does that even look like? Even scenes from war-torn countries have some survival stories. Babies hoisted out of rubble. White hats. Red crosses. She thinks of Chernobyl, the TV show anyway, which happened before she was born. The genetically altered dogs still roaming the abandoned radioactive no-go zone. Will that be London's future?

There are no curtains twitching in any of the flats lining Reedworth Street. No sound of kids playing outside, none of the usual wild abandon on bikes and scooters, no one pushing a stroller. She turns into the Cotton Gardens housing estate, knowing she can cut through and come out on Kennington Lane, moments from home.

But now she hears people again. Lots of people.

Chapter Fifty

FRANKIE

Now that the mist has drifted away, a full moon is visible in the clear night sky. Frankie's head aches so deeply the pain has turned into a sound; her face is slick with tears and blood. The gun feels grotesque and surprisingly heavy. But if she has to use it to get someone to help Otis, so be it. What does she have to lose now? Twelve minutes before everything changes. Life and death. Fuck. Like, actually life and death.

She thinks of the teenage girl, running like crazy in the other direction. If she called her back, told her there was shelter, would she hear? Frankie doesn't even know what name to call out. And would Ashley hear instead?

Frankie makes no sound. *The girl will make it*, she tells herself, *but she's on her own now.*

A cloud slides in front of the pitted gray moon, and everything dissolves to a deep black again. She doesn't dare use the flashlight on her pocketed phone, not yet, not with Ashley sitting meters behind her.

The lane twists ahead of Frankie, the going uneven. It twists again, and when she looks back, she can't see the wreckage of the truck or car, just the glow of the hazards in the sky. She finally puts on her light. It lights very little. All she can really see is the mud at the side of the road, the great grooves chomped out of it by hundreds of horse hooves.

Is that a Dartmoor pony?

She can see the cottage easily now, silhouetted by the moonlight, the smoke guiding her. Her skull feels explosive with pain, her stomach churning, but she tries to run, gripping the gun and pointing it away from her, distrustful of everyone.

As she draws closer to the building, she can see wisps of light in the windows, at the edges of curtains. Or maybe barricades. The stone is not black, as it first appeared. It's honey-colored but darkened by a great beard of ivy.

Shelter.

In the driveway sits an old 4x4, its skirt muddy, its tires enormous. If she could use that, she could drive to collect Otis in it, drag him into the back. The front gate opens with a squeak and she grabs at the door knocker, slams it down. The metallic thud rings across the fields, around the pig's-tail lane. Maybe the keys are reachable through the letterbox; she tries to push her hand through but there's only space for her fingers and she feels nothing but air.

And anyway, then what? Where would they go in the 4x4? The holiday cottage has nothing in it, barely any food or water. That man Robert outside the shop said that food and water was the difference between living and dying.

She bangs on the door. "Please open up, I really need your help!"

Nothing happens. She rattles the door handle, but it's locked. Of course it's locked. Frankie bangs on the door with her fist now, the sound conducting through her aching skull—more feeling than sound.

She pries the letterbox open again and peers through, but she can just see an empty set of stairs.

There are ten minutes left. There is not enough time to find anywhere else, it's here or . . . nowhere. She bangs the knocker again and then, when that doesn't make a difference, she tramples barefoot through one of the little flower beds that sits in front of a wooden window and starts to bang on the glass. "Please, I'm pregnant. I'm alone. I need your help!"

She clumps her way back to the front door and starts to count as she bangs and slaps the door.

One.

If they don't open up by the time she reaches three . . .

Two.

. . . she looks at the gun.

Chapter Fifty-One

MRS. DABB

The lanes are empty, she cannot see or hear a helicopter now, and even the siren seems to have stopped. As if all those official efforts are being packed up and folded away while she is still out here, legs shaking with adrenaline and terror. For herself, for everyone else, but mostly for Bunny.

If Bunny is not at home, there is nowhere to turn. Anyone in a uniform will be far too busy. Any potential Good Samaritans will likely be tucked up inside, eyes glued to the screen, or arms threaded through other arms in the village church, candles lit.

Her pulse is liquid in her ears. Her fingers drum on the wheel in agitation. She can smell her own fear, sour and curdling. In the back of the car, something works loose and clatters back and forth across the seat as she swings into the bends. An old coin or a token for something, something snapped off from an old gadget or purse. Things just fall off Bunny, inky pens soaking into upholstery, cheap earrings stabbing their heels from the middle of the rug, bus passes wedged in unlikely places. The driver always lets her on anyway, she knows that and is grateful, although it was no help today.

She glances at the dashboard clock and taps the pedal to go just a little faster. She pictures Bunny at home, Mary too, tucking into the piles of food without waiting. The fire is on as the clock counts down, Bunny wearing her pajamas and precious dressing gown, a gift from her late godfather. Soon she will be home too. Please, please let Bunny be there.

And if she is—*when she is, have faith*—maybe they can just batten down the hatches, switch off the lights, and eat scones and cakes until they run out, then ransack the cellar shelves. Maybe they can hide forever, maybe they never have to have a conversation about the phone, or the bunking off, or Bunny's biological father. Never have to look this one in the eye. What will it matter, so long as Bunny's home?

9 MINUTES UNTIL IMPACT

Chapter Fifty-Two

CARRIE

Carrie is on her guard, as she runs toward the sound of people. She has not heard a static crowd since Waterloo and that crowd was penned in by armed officials. Is this one the same? She emerges from Cotton Gardens onto Kennington Lane and is faced with a swarm of people's backs.

They're gathering outside the old pub that's now a community hub of some kind. At first she thinks they're all trying to get inside, but then she sees that the movement of the crowd isn't them pushing their bodies forward, but passing things toward the building. Shopping bags, bottles of water, blankets, toys. The faces inside stare out, wide eyes in little faces. Most are children.

"Pass it all down, that's it," a warm voice at the front calls out. As people let go of their goods, they start to peel away, breaking into shuffling runs or at least determined walks to nearby streets and homes.

"Thank you, gorgeous," another voice calls. "Love you all."

An elderly woman approaches the back of the crowd dragging a shopping cart, full of blankets and soft toys. She's hobbling slightly, wonky like she has an old injury stiffening one side. She passes the cart to a gray-haired man near the back of the crowd. "Get these to the children," she says.

"How much time do we have left?" Carrie asks, but the old woman just shrugs. "Don't want to know, doesn't really make any difference to me." The woman looks back at the faces in the windows and shakes her head. "Just want them to be comfy."

"Eight minutes, love," an old man says as he starts to jog awkwardly away in stiff trousers. "Get cracking if you've somewhere to be."

She heads down Kennington Lane where some of the beautiful old buildings have been carved up into flats. She thinks of the people living on the top, first to be hit. And if not hit, because she has not one clue what actually happens in a missile strike no matter what Grace hinted at, then the first to receive a blanket of fallout. Right? So they're screwed. And maybe everyone is, but they're the most screwed. Have their downstairs neighbors let them into those lower flats? Surely they must have?

During the pandemic, this road had been filled with people clapping for the nurses, putting their children's rainbow drawings in the window, and shopping for their neighbors. And those people back there, outside the community hub . . . yes, she tells herself, of course the downstairs neighbors have let the upper-floor neighbors into their flats. But she can't bear to look up just in case she sees any stranded faces.

Around the slight bend by the bottom of Chester Way. The Kings Arms, her local since she first moved into Pepper's building. Even though it's not strictly her nearest pub, the actual nearest one being fancier and more expensive. The shutters at the Kings Arms are closed but the hum of people inside still reaches her. Faces she'd recognize, bar staff and customers. A proper pub, as her dad would have said. Real ales. She can see the green felt of the pool table in the corner window, flipped on its side to cover the shutterless glass. She imagines the solids and stripes rolling between legs.

The pub has been here since 1800. Pepper—who goes every Thursday for his gin and bitter lemon—still calls it the Little Apple, as it was known in its days as a gay pub. Over a century before that, it had a theater license. She's always loved collecting little scraps of history like that. She hopes those little scraps will be preserved somehow. But god knows how.

She runs across the road to the secret archway between two huge Georgian houses, their stucco bottoms cream-dipped. As she passes between them, she can hear a dog going bonkers, a baby crying.

Carrie's feet feel wet. Blister-pus, blood, sweat, and street slop. But it's okay, it's all worth it, because Grace got home to her family and so will Carrie. She can't be more than two minutes away.

She runs along the back of the Georgian villas that line Kennington Lane. She's always thought of this as seeing behind the velvet rope.

Backstage. The brick is unpainted at the backs of the houses. The scruffy rough-wood fences and overgrown lawns of homes that are new-pin-perfect at the front. The expensive-looking tree house in one of the gardens—painted in Farrow & Ball Whirlybird—that always makes her feel bad for Clementine, for whom she will never, ever be able to afford to build a tree house like that.

Through some gates, she can see piles of black trash bags. If there are any survivors here, these bags will surely mount in the coming weeks. Although, will they even be able to leave their homes to get rid of rubbish? Open the window and lob it out or . . . or live with it? With the disgusting remnants of how they live. The maggots. The cost of doing business, of life, laid out and stinking.

I read a lot about this. . . . I don't think it's going to go how people think.

No, people will find a way to make it all work. It won't all be for nothing. It can't be. People are fundamentally good, innovative, and helpful. They will find a way.

Chapter Fifty-Three

FRANKIE

Wisps of smoke curl slyly from the chimney. But the people who live here have still not opened the door. People are fundamentally selfish, she's always said that, but the secret soft heart of her hoped it wasn't true.

Frankie's right hand hurts from slapping against the wood, her left aches as it curls around the gun. She bangs on the door again, hard.

She takes a breath and counts again from the beginning.

One.
Two.
Three.

Nothing. *Fuck!*

She looks at the gun with its mysterious metal levers and ice-cold barrel. She knows it was loaded because it was fired earlier, but how many more bullets are in it? How many times has it been used today? She has no idea how to check. Maybe it's empty. But if it is, the people inside sure as hell don't know that.

She creeps around the side of the cottage, brushing her hand along the powdery stone to guide herself. God, her head hurts. The banging and shouting has only made it worse. The bones in her face hurt, her eyes.

Will they melt if I don't get inside?

Eight minutes, Otis out there in the dark, that girl running for her life. And Ashley . . . has he woken up? Frankie has to get back to Otis, drag him to safety, whatever form that takes. She cannot do that without help, and if people won't help willingly then they've only got themselves to blame.

The back window of the cottage is covered by something makeshift but she can see tiger stripes of light through it. She knocks on the window and tries to peer through but sees nothing.

"Are you in there?"

She moves to the back door, a solid oak thing split across the middle. She bangs on it with her right fist, then taps it loudly with the nose of the gun gripped in her left hand, already becoming a part of her.

No answer.

"Please help, I'm pregnant and I'm desperate." She pauses, tries to sound calmer, like she's a safe person to let in. "It's just me by myself. Please, I need help."

Nothing.

"Please! Please!" She's screaming now, and still no one stirs. She could smash her way inside with the gun. Could push through that window, knock the shards free, and climb in.

She turns the gun around so the fattest bit is facing forward, lifts it onto her shoulder, and walks back to the window, her cold toes curling into the ground. She raises the gun, ready to smash the glass, but then comes the sound of a bolt being slid open.

Chapter Fifty-Four

MRS. DABB

It's not cold but she shivers in her coat, hands shaking on the wheel. In nine minutes' time . . . A moment that spins out into the past and the future, but that pins everyone in place now, sealing them in amber. Will the survivors ever truly get over whatever they had to do in the last, terrible scramble?

In the far distance, hazard lights throb on the horizon. It's unusual to see flashing lights like this out here, these are city things. Neon skies and emergencies. That's what people come here to escape.

Home is in sight and she speeds toward it, pulling into the driveway next to the old Land Rover, the gravel sighing under her tires.

The lights are still on behind the curtains and the cottage glows softly like a Christmas decoration. The kind of gingerbread cottage that fairy tales are written about. But Bunny's face is not pressed to any window and Mary's car isn't here yet. She's probably taking ages wrapping up the food to bring over. Or maybe all this is simply too much for Mary and she's run aground.

She rushes to the front door and pats her pockets for the keys, fumbling and nearly dropping them. Shoving the door open, she calls out, "Bunny?"

No reply.

She paces down the hallway to the kitchen, where the cakes and scones still lie in neat rows, untouched on the cooling rack. The fire has nearly gone out in the living room, a dank smokiness in the air like the day after a bonfire.

She throws off her coat and searches frantically in all the places that haven't been hidden in for years. She looks behind the sagging sofa, its back fabric torn like an old sweater, ratty underwear showing through. She checks in the space next to the bookcase, barely big enough for a human, from which rivers of dust cascade as she struggles back out and knocks into the armchair, sending an abandoned mug spinning. A trail of cold tea sprays upward—briefly beautiful and captivating as accidents are—and lands in a beige line across the floor.

The frozen downstairs bathroom is empty. A relic from decades earlier, its corners encrusted with spiders no matter how many horse chestnuts lace the small windowsill. Bunny prefers the new bathroom upstairs, they both do. She runs up to check it now, the most luxurious room in the house, smooth where the other rooms are crumbling. It's empty, no misting on the shower door, no trace of bubbles in the bath, no towel dumped on the floor. God, how she misses wrapping up her tiny, wriggling daughter after a bath. Rabbit ears on the hooded towel, bubbles sliding off chunky legs. She'd always been told baths relaxed babies, to include them as part of a bedtime routine. Not her kid. Baths drove her frothy with excitement until she was way too keyed up to sleep. What a relentless joy she was then.

All those promises she made that little kid, while she washed her hair or scooped bubbles from the bath to put on the end of her nose. She meant every one of them. But now look.

She sits down heavily on the toilet lid, head in her hands. The cottage has never felt more empty. This date has been a day of mourning for so long that she thought it couldn't get any sadder. That grief could not hollow her out any more than it already has, because there was nothing left to take. But there was. Because Bunny is not here. Nor is she with Jasmine, nor at school. She's not even at the Curtiss compound. Today she'd have been almost too relieved to care. Now she has no idea where to find her daughter and it's nearly six o'clock. She has failed her child.

Exhaustion rounds her spine and deflates her lungs. She sags so low she might just slide to the floor, through the tiles, into the dirty creases between the ceiling beams. She might as well just die there.

Loud knocks from the door downstairs startle her.

Down the stairs, along the hall, toward the kitchen, where the bangs are coming from the back door.

"Bunny?" she calls, but if it were Bunny, she'd just let herself in. Has that old woman told the Curtiss family already? Is there a mob outside? She grabs the biggest knife from the drawer as she passes it, then pulls back the bolt on the back door.

6 MINUTES UNTIL IMPACT

Chapter Fifty-Five

CARRIE

White Hart Street is never empty, never silent. But now everything is hushed, voices trapped inside by whatever is covering their windows.

This street is parallel to her own road but the chunky Kennings Estate sits in between, with its four solid blocks of flats, each seven stories high. She can't see her road, but she knows it's right there. Clementine, Emma, and Pepper are right there.

All of Kennington used to belong to the Duchy of Cornwall but now just a few slivers of it sit in the royal purse. She didn't believe it at first, when Emma's stepdad told them they were leaving a part of Devon largely owned by Prince Charles (as he still was then), only to move to a bit of the capital owned by the very same. When she told her mum, she seemed to perk up. The only bit of Carrie's London plan that she did like. "At least I know who's looking after you."

"Does she think Prince Charles roams around Kennington fighting crime?" Emma had said. "Like Batman?"

She's never really cared before, but today the circular nature of it all feels like some kind of message. Or maybe she's just looking for meaning on a day when, in mere minutes, all meaning could be destroyed.

With no idea of time and no sense of what it will feel like when time does run out, Carrie skids into the grounds of the Kennings Estate. She can see more windows than she can count, heart hurting at the thought of just how many people, how many children, are lined up in there, under beds and behind sofas. People praying, howling, saying what they need to say. Repenting. Loving. In the end, what else matters but love?

And then it happens. A roaring sound from above that feels close enough to slice the top of her head off. She falls to the ground, covering her ears as the sound radiates toward her, soon followed by an explosion somewhere. Over her? Next to her? She can't tell, it's more feeling than sound, but it's louder than anything she's ever experienced before. She scrunches up her eyes. The air above her is sucked, chopped, a tornado licking at her. Is her skin being peeled off? It feels like it, like it's being tugged away from her bones, her skeleton picked clean.

I am too late.

She is so close to her people but she is too late.

She stumbles to her feet and runs anyway, faster than she's ever run, even as a black shadow covers the dimly lit lawn she's running across, its metallic sound mighty and unrelenting. Her arms pump by her sides, her ears uncovered and no longer working. No sound, only feeling, as the missile shudders across rooftops all around her, the air churning, ruffling the coat that is somehow still on her body. Pieces of grit fly up and hit her neck, face, and hands. Maybe it's not grit. Maybe it's poisoned detritus falling on her. Maybe she's already dead. But still she runs.

Down the narrow pathway that only locals know, reaching a darkened Prince's Square, she sprints for the communal garden at the center.

She was so nearly there. She *is* so nearly there. And she's not giving up, even as the great shadow thrashes around over her, spinning, taunting her, shaking her bones and rippling her scalp.

Who knew missiles could do this?

Who knew I'd still be able to think while they did this?

Carrie skids through the rosebushes, scratching cat-claw chunks from her legs and arms, slashing through her jeans and coat. The power from above chops great globs of soil up, spraying it meters into the air. Stones, tree branches, and garden gates are tossed up and scattered everywhere. She ducks as a metal watering can just misses her forehead. A whirligig clothes dryer whistles past her. The air is dense with dust and smoke, she can barely see.

And then comes the bang, heard not in her damaged ears but in her very bones.

Chapter Fifty-Six

FRANKIE

"Please, my boyfriend, he's—"

A woman of seventy or so peers out with quick darting eyes. Then she yanks open the door and pulls Frankie inside the homey kitchen. Bolts slide, a key turns. Before saying anything else, the woman pulls Frankie into a hug. It's so disarming that for a moment, Frankie closes her eyes and says nothing. The gun hangs limply in her left hand. If the woman has seen it, she's not letting on.

This woman is five foot nothing. Short gray hair that's fuzzy like a peach. She wears jogging bottoms and thick knitwear. She's slightly stooped but looks exceptionally capable. "Did I hear that right, you're pregnant?"

"Yes, but that's not . . ."

The woman cocks her head, like she's hard of hearing, so Frankie raises her voice. "It's my boyfriend, Otis, he's . . . I need your car. But I can go alone if you can't—"

"We're not going anywhere, love. Not together or alone. Whoever is still out there . . . there's nothing we can do for them."

"No," Frankie says, and she lifts the gun in a way that feels pantomime, "you're not listening to me, you have to—"

"If you're going to shoot me you should get on with it," the little woman says, walking into the belly of the kitchen. "There's only five minutes left either way. I'm Janet, by the way, Janet Spencer. And you are?"

"Frankie," she manages to say as Janet pulls a huge green first aid kit from a stuffed cupboard.

"I would like to look at that head wound before you pull the trigger, though," Janet says.

"What?" The gun trembles in Frankie's left hand; she secures it with the right but it feels ludicrous now, silly.

"That's a lot of blood. What happened?"

"Car crash," Frankie says, feeling the pinch of tacky blood in her hairline now, the sting of it in her eyes. "And my boyfriend was injured too. He's alive but he's unconscious and we're running out of time."

"Let's get this stitched up quickly in the good light and then we can settle ourselves in downstairs." Janet gestures for Frankie to sit at the table, pulling out cotton wool, a little bottle of disinfectant, and some adhesive bandages.

Frankie grips the gun to her body. "But my boyfriend is still out there," she says, even as she follows to the table, her filthy feet leaving a trail of mud across the tiles.

"We all have people out there," Janet says quietly.

Frankie has a sudden need to not be standing or moving. Has she ever felt so tired, in so much pain? The gun still trembles in her hand and she hugs it to her like a baby as she sits heavily on the kitchen chair. It's so warm after the outside that she feels a sudden sweat coating her. Janet dabs disinfectant onto a cloud of cotton wool. "This'll sting a bit, Frankie."

It stings like hell, but Frankie stays silent. She grits her teeth as a large Band-Aid is applied to her throbbing forehead and an even larger gauze pad somewhere near her crown, wrapped loosely in place with a long strip of elastic bandage, flattening her hair.

The small hand of the kitchen clock moves audibly. "Oh god," Frankie says. She places the gun on the table and moves her hands from it. What good is it now? There are four minutes left, not enough time to drive back to Otis, drag him into a vehicle, and get back here. *He's gone.*

"He has," Janet says softly. Frankie must have said it out loud. The two women clasp hands, and Frankie gasps as she's pulled gently to a stand and led into the hallway, stopping in front of an open cellar door. "But we haven't, and I think we'll be best off down here."

Frankie has to duck, her head throbbing harder as she lowers it. The dusty stone stairs are lit by a bare bulb, but more light glows below and as she reaches the bottom step, she can see that the cellar is probably as big as the footprint of the house, a shadow version of life on top. Drums of water, cans of food, jars of god knows what line up like infantry troops along the wall. It seems designed for this very occasion. Janet passes her a bundled pair of thick socks from a shelf of clothes. She takes them gratefully.

And that's it. That's all it took for her to leave Otis out there, in the mist and the rain, the fire and the incoming fallout. Three minutes since Janet opened the door. That's all it took. How will she ever forget that?

Chapter Fifty-Seven

MRS. DABB

"I couldn't get my key out," Mary says, shuffling into the kitchen, arms filled with Tupperware and tinfoiled plates. "Is Bunny back?"

"No, she's not, Mary. What the hell am I going to do?"

"Oh darling." Mary struggles over to the old oak table and dumps her cargo. Every anniversary, the same routine. A mountain of favorite food to mark the loss, most of it left uneaten. Usually Bunny would be taking slabs of cake to school for a week after. Usually.

"It's nearly six o'clock, Mary. It's nearly . . ."

Mary pulls her in and rubs her back. "Come on, it's okay, she'll be here."

She shakes her head, burrowing deeper into Mary's soft shoulder and her old waxed jacket. "I think she found out about her biological father, I think he's got to her."

"But . . ." Mary starts, and then sucks in a breath. This is the one topic they never touch. "You must have known this could happen if you didn't warn her?"

"What?" She recoils from Mary like she's just been shot. "Are you serious? Bunny is missing, I don't have a clue where she is, and instead of helping, you're blaming me? *Me?* For trying to keep her safe?"

"I don't know if it was optimism or denial, but this was a ticking time bomb," Mary says. "It was always going to happen. You couldn't keep the truth from her forever, and now it's blown up in your face." Mary covers her eyes, the wording so poor that neither can address it. Instead, Mary starts to lay out the plates and open the Tupperware, as if that's the most important thing to do right now.

"It's not just you that . . ." Mary starts, peeling back foil on a plate of bright jam tarts.

"It's not just me that what?"

Mary shakes her head, shoulders bunched, tugging off the last lid: coconut snowballs, far too festive for November.

"Leave the bloody food! It's"—she looks up at the kitchen clock—"five fifty-five, it's minutes—"

"You think I don't have a clock in my head, counting down to it. . . ." Mary never shouts but she is now, and her voice, unused to the volume, cracks and gives out.

White light fills the kitchen. The noise of the helicopter following, suddenly close. They look at each other then.

The sound recedes a little but the kitchen still glows an unnatural white from the searchlight. The food on the table is lit like a neon tableau, a ridiculous still life. The light creeps away, the kitchen dims again.

"I'm sorry," Mary says, "it's just too much."

"It's far too much," she manages to say, reaching for Mary's hands.

A noise outside.

"Did you hear that?" Mary says, but she doesn't answer, running instead to the front door and grappling with all the bolts and locks.

It's the sound of fast footsteps, of a young girl's voice calling out in total panic. She pulls the door open, and a blur of school uniform rushes inside.

Part Two

ATTACK

Chapter Fifty-Eight

CARRIE

face in dirt

scalp crawling

air slammed from lungs

wood
concrete
glass
brick

scattered under you
over you
around

you're not dead yet but
maybe you are dying because you're watching a

zoetrope of

                                                    your life

tiny carrie with fat hands and shaking knees stumbling toward

dad

                                   dad smell and dad strength and

mum
not the sadness from after but the

                                                        softness before

                                                                and

   new stiff shirt scratchy collar
   biff and chip
   and the dinner lady has made a tiny dinner on a milk bottle top because you are scared and feel so small and you brought mr. mouse even
   though mum said no don't take mr. mouse because what if you lose him

                            only heat no sound
                  pieces of the buildings have ribboned like nothing

   year three

   a new girl with a wicked bump in her red hair that your stupid hair is
   too thin to achieve it just flat-falls and you reach out to touch hers and
   that's weird really to do that but emma laughs and says she doesn't mind
   and shows you how to back-comb just that front bit and bobby-pin it
   nicely
                                eyes gummed
                        iron taste behind gritted teeth
                  stone and concrete chunks press into your skin
                         you know you should get up
                                 be inside
                             but you can't quite

      re m e   m   b   e   r
                                why

                    flames behind and above you

   teen years
   vodka and jeans and a nice top

i love this song and i love you
just us always
spit shake on it
kiss on it

                                          but the next day
                                          you tell emma
                    you don't know if you love her like that
                                                  not yet

                 heat behind you
                    above you
                 and seconds left
            fractions of time left to

                                             years pass and
            you catch on to yourself just as she stops waiting
                        and it was only ever her for you really
                             but she got sick of waiting and
                           found someone else to love like that
                                and you storm off bratty
                                  and fuck indiscriminately
                                    and after all that
                                    you tell her anyway
                              i love you i love you i love you
                                      finally says emma

and the timing could not have been better or worse

                                                 you got people
                                                 nice people
                                                     the best

you are still alive somehow but you won't be for long and you have to
get inside but your body is blanketed by shards and chunks and slabs

positive pregnancy test gripped in your hand
just four weeks into this new old love
this lifelong buildup suddenly realized
but emma says okay emma says we can handle anything emma says we
will have a baby then
just like that

"CLEMENTINE!"

your sound has disappeared but

your legs and elbows collapse as you find your way to hands and knees
stuff slides off your back
your whole body trembles
but you have to
G
E
T
T
O
Y
O
U
R
C
H
I
L
D

flames
is this it
surely you should be dead

there must be more bombs coming because you and the street and the
city and your thoughts and the air should not still exist like this

and I don't think it's going to go how people think

blood in your eyes
one long whine in your ears
you get up and fall and get up and fall and get up
stumbling over the everything that is lying around

you run the way you know your home is no matter how blind or deaf or
injured you are
moth to light
you to home

but someone grabs you now
and you whirl on the spot cartoon legs off the
end of a cliff not falling for a second too long
but
falling to the ground all the same

NO NO PLEASE

they fall on top of you and the soil hits your teeth and up your nose and
their weight pins you and they have no smell but soil

and you
buck
scream
beg
cry
they are not moving now
they are not letting you up
and it hits you like a punch
even now
even in this

you think suddenly of mr. mouse
his fat belly and the stuffing coming out of his legs and
your hand-stitching on his ear in too-thick thread
and how he made you feel safe

but you are not safe

still blinded and deafened
you feel around
amid the stone and wood mess
through the black smoke
until you find a large brick
furred with churned soil
they squirm
and your elbow pops and grinds but

you swing

THUD

they slacken
and you finally shake them off.

Chapter Fifty-Nine

FRANKIE

Along one cellar wall is an ancient futon, piled high with blankets and towels, one of its armrests hanging loosely from the joint. They sit together on it, like strangers in a waiting room.

And all she can think of is Otis.

And his heart as fast as an injured fox's.

And the hole in the truck's windshield.

And all that blood.

"Here." A nearby bucket is slid between Frankie's aching feet warming in Janet's socks. She retches but nothing comes out. She must block out thoughts of Otis, of how she just abandoned him. She has to think about something else, anything else . . .

"My daughter, Carrie," Janet says suddenly. "And my little granddaughter, Clementine . . ." The words dissolve into a slow moan as she grips Frankie's hand in hers.

Frankie can't bear it. She wants her mum. Her brother, Sebastian. Even her sly, volatile dad. She wants them all. Wants them to fold around her, absorb her, keep her and her baby safe. And more than anything, she wants Otis back, wrapped big around her and her poppy seed middle.

Frankie is not this woman's daughter, this woman is not her mum. None of this is good enough, and it's all they have.

Hopefully, Frankie thinks, astounded by the clarity of this, *hopefully Otis has already passed and won't suffer what is coming.* But still she pictures him waking up. Out there. A cascade of questions overtakes her. Was the car radio still on? What about the dashboard clock, was it smashed or will he know, if he wakes, how much time he has? Could he have woken already, gone looking for her? And what about Ashley? Could he be outside now, could he—

Under her leg, something vibrates.

"My phone," she says, grappling for it as it makes its second loud, unusual shriek today. She stares, unblinking. Not able, at first, to believe the words.

NUCLEAR MISSILE THREAT AVERTED. REPEAT. NUCLEAR MISSILE THREAT NO LONGER IN EFFECT.

"Oh my god, Janet. Look."

They both stare at her screen but cannot dare to believe it.

"Is that true? Is that message real?"

"Do you have a radio?" Frankie asks Janet urgently. "A TV?"

"It's Dartmoor, not the Dark Ages."

Before Frankie has stood up, Janet is up with a knee-crack and a wince but she scrambles up the stairs as quick as a mountain goat. She's in the kitchen already when Frankie walks in, flicking on an oily radio near the stove. Frankie holds her breath as the radio crackles to life. It's not a great signal, like Frankie's phone with its one precious bar of 4G, but they can hear the bewildered voice shouting out from its speaker, the same woman from earlier, the DJ from Pirate FM.

"And I repeat, missile strike averted. Missile strike averted. Oh my god, we're going to be okay. Lily, if you're listening, Mummy loves you. I love you all. I repeat, missile strike averted."

Chapter Sixty

MRS. DABB

She's hit with the frantic body slam of a hug. "I'm so sorry, Mum." Bunny is sobbing so violently that her rib cage shakes through her coat.

"It's okay, it's okay." It's all she can say, the words running together. Because Bunny is here, she's alive!

"You're just in time," she manages to gasp out, but the tears are coming now, thickening her throat as she takes in her daughter's buttoned coat, her messy hair, her laddered tights.

"I'm so sorry," Bunny sobs, breathing hard. "It's all my fault."

"Nothing is your fault. You're home. That's all that matters." The words come out as a series of exhausted exhalations that drain the last of her energy with them. She could collapse in relief. She could actually collapse. She clings to her daughter to stay upright, her face wet with tears.

"Bunny!" Mary shuffles out into the hallway and grabs the girl, peppering her with kisses while her mother double-locks the front door. Bunny looks up from Mary and watches the bolt as it's slid across.

"There are some really bad people loose out there today," she says, shaking the door now to test it even though this is a tungsten bolt, strong enough to hold back a lion.

"I know there are," Bunny puffs, struggling free from Mary and wiping her eyes on her sleeve. She's still breathing hard, her face pink and sticky with sweat. She's clearly had to run to be here.

"You're safe now," Mary says, receding into the kitchen and leaving mother and daughter alone. They sit on the stairs, side by side.

"I'm really sorry but I think my key fell out somewhere," Bunny says, her red eyes fixed on the door. "Someone could find it and—"

"Even if someone found your key, that bolt is the best in the business."

"Are you sure?"

"Double sure."

Bunny sags.

"Are you okay?"

"I feel sick," she manages to say before Mary appears again, placing a bucket in front of Bunny as her head drops between her knees.

"You stay here with her and I'll put the television on," Mary says quietly. "It's nearly time." The weight of today is visible in the way Mary carries herself. Shoulders sloping and face pinched.

Bunny spits into the bucket, her head drooping just like it did when she was little and they'd push her home from nursery. Mrs. Dabb keeps her arms wrapped tightly around Bunny's shoulders.

"I was out looking for you," she says, squeezing her to test she's really here.

"I'm sorry," Bunny repeats, her voice weak and her head still flopping.

"I've never been so frightened."

"Never?"

"Well, this was . . . it was *as* scary. Different scary but as scary."

Bunny snaps forward and a spray of vomit hits the bucket.

She waits for the heaving to stop, rubbing her daughter's back gently. "Okay?"

Bunny nods but she's whimpering slightly, her face drained of all color.

"Better out than in."

Bunny sniffs. "I didn't mean to scare you, Mum. I really thought I'd be home in time. I was gonna get the 118 back to school and then get on the usual school bus and you'd never have to know. But I got the timing completely wrong and then the police came along and locked everything down and they were shouting at everyone and no one could leave and I was stuck and it was ages before they let any buses out."

She wipes her eyes. "I'm sorry, Mum."

"Oh, Bunny Rabbit, I know you are. I'm sorry too. So sorry about . . . about whatever you had to face today." *The 118 bus? Where does the 118 go from?* But it doesn't matter now.

She looks at her old watch. "Hey, Dejav who," she says, and Bunny frowns. "What?"

"Your joke, you have to finish it."

Bunny smiles then, finally. "Knock knock."

"Who's there?"

"No, Mum." Bunny laughs. Just a little, her cheeks growing pink. "That's the joke. You said *deja vu* and I said—"

"You two, come in here!" Mary calls from the living room.

Chapter Sixty-One

CARRIE

Before Carrie can make it to her front door, Pepper has flung his open and is beckoning her. He's breathing heavily from running down the stairs to the foyer—a "dignified trot" is usually the fastest he'll move. Carrie can just make out the burgundy sheen of his self-dubbed smoking jacket through her swollen eyes, still stinging. *How are we still alive? How is the building still standing?*

He points upstairs, so they must be in his upper-floor flat, surely the worst place to be. "What time is it?" she shouts, tapping her wrist where a watch would sit and shoving her body through the outside door, slamming it closed behind her. "How long do we have?" But she can't hear his answer anyway, her ears are still whining. He tries to hug her but she fights him, there's no time for this, she needs to get her family downstairs. He won't let her past and he's trying to tell her something, his mouth moving as she tries to get up the stairs. Why won't he get out of the bloody way?

As she finally gives him the slip and starts to run up, Pepper grabs her bad elbow. She cries out in pain and shakes him off, but he shoves his phone at her. An old brick of a thing that she and Emma like to wind him up about. It is sheathed in the burgundy sequined case that they bought him for Christmas. She can barely see the screen in the dimly lit hall.

NUCLEAR MISSILE THREAT AVERTED. REPEAT. NUCLEAR MISSILE THREAT NO LONGER IN EFFECT.

"Really?" she says, grabbing the phone and staring at it. He nods, mouths the word *really*, and then struggles to catch her as she folds over, slowly collapsing.

But the fire? The deafening sound and the smoke and the heat? The bricks and stones and tree branches tossed around like paper airplanes?

Sitting in a heap on the stairs, Carrie points back toward the communal garden, mimes an explosion, but Pepper shakes his head, throws his hands into a swan dive like something crashing down from the air. It would be funny under any other circumstances. His arm over his head like a blade now. A helicopter. A crashed helicopter.

She doesn't understand what this all means, though, can't grasp hold of these thoughts. Everything is choked by the deafening whine in her head, the smoke coating her eyes and throat. Have the missiles just gone elsewhere? Are there burning white skies over some other city and the scientists or the army or whatever got the warning wrong? Or have they been canceled entirely? Turned around and sent back to . . . she doesn't actually know where. Nothing makes sense.

She has fought her way across London, literally fought people, lost her hearing, seen things she will never forget. All to be back here, with her loves, just in time. Every atom of energy has burned out. She is empty, exhausted, gripping the banister with her good arm and wobbling her way up each step like she's a hundred years old. Barely able to keep up with seventy-five-year-old Pepper and his dancer's gait.

When he turns back to look at her, she's never seen eyes so sad.

Chapter Sixty-Two

FRANKIE

"I have to go back to Otis," Frankie says.

"Just take a minute." Janet sits down in the kitchen chair and rubs her temples, as if in pain. "Let's just have a sit-down, take a moment. I can't . . . I can't make sense of all this."

"I really have to get to Otis and I need your help. I need your Land Rover and I need you to help me get him into it."

"And then what?"

"Hospital."

"You won't get to the hospital, the roads will be chaos."

Frankie slides the gun from the table and holds it. "I'm not just leaving Otis there."

"I'm not saying to leave him, we can bring him back here and I'll do what I can while we wait for an ambulance." Janet looks older in relief than she did in panic.

"If everyone's inside sheltering, why would the roads—"

"Look at where we are, love. Everyone from Exeter and Plymouth will have tried to come here, to get away from city centers, and they'll have jammed the main roads. The cities will still be locked down. Turn on the TV and see for yourself if you don't believe me."

"No, I believe you, I'm just running out of time."

"Can we just take a minute to be relieved, love?"

"He might not have a minute," Frankie says.

But then the bang comes on the front door. A loud, angry bang. A man's bang. As Janet gets up and starts to walk toward the hallway, Frankie grabs her arm.

"Wait, what are you doing?"

"It could be your boyfriend," Janet says. It could, Frankie thinks, but he had not looked on the brink of waking, let alone walking.

Chapter Sixty-Three

MRS. DABB

Relief never feels as it should.

She can't settle, standing next to the fireplace trying to warm herself, pacing to the window to straighten the curtains again, glancing at the television, squeezing Bunny's shoulder, scratching herself. She feels encircled; the helicopters are still flying over, the air still feels thick with threat.

"Sit down, love," Mary says, patting the sofa next to her, but she shakes her head.

"Too wired." But that hardly covers it.

Mary has made them all tea "strong enough to stand your spoon up" and grips hers tightly in her lap, in hands that have still not stopped shaking. Crescents of tea dot her beige trousers but she doesn't seem to have noticed.

The television is showing footage from around the country, most of it captured on people's cell phones. Poorly lit, badly framed. Feet run up and down stairs. People fight over boats, buses, planes. A shaky video shows a family jumping off the Dartford Bridge, soundtracked by gasps from unseen mouths. Cars slide under one another like old penny-pusher machines at an arcade. Footage of the skies around airports in Europe and Ireland shows diverted planes that had been meant for England, circling and circling, waiting for a precious spot elsewhere. And the plane that ran out of fuel, pirouetting down.

They watch this as punishment. Collective, media-curated survivor's guilt.

Bunny is curled into the corner of the sofa, an old blanket they've had her whole life pulled up over her school uniform. She should go and shower, brush her teeth, throw out the tights, get into her clean comfies, and slough the day off. Then she will feel like herself. Bunny has literally never still been in school uniform past six o'clock before. But she seems utterly beaten, crushed by her own guilt even though no one has told her off or even asked what she was playing at, why she bunked off, where she went. *Where does the 118 go from?* No one has mentioned the phone. None of it matters, not now. Not yet.

Chapter Sixty-Four

CARRIE

On the middle floor, Carrie tugs off her filthy shoes, slicing blistered skin off with them. Her hands are foul but Pepper leads her by one of them anyway. She's shaking violently as she walks down the familiar hallway lined with black-and-white photos, theatrical posters, and a huge ornate mirror. She looks in it without thinking.

The woman in the reflection is filthy. Black mess from the tube, blood from her head, grass and soil from falling over so many times. It's all gummed together into a kind of mask, her bleached hair now bog-colored. Soon, she thinks, will come the most heavenly shower of her life. The clean hot water, a gift from the gods that she will never take for granted again. All her lovely bubby things, the shampoo, the fruity shower gel. Things she didn't even consider but nearly never had again.

But first, Clementine and Emma. Above anything else. Against the odds. Her family.

She casts one eye back to the small landing window. She cannot see the crashed helicopter from here, or the damage it did, only the black smoke that still fills the night air.

She reaches the open-plan living/dining room, expecting to be knocked over by her people, but nothing happens.

Pepper's flat looks completely normal. He has prepared nothing. No buckets of water, no gathered cans, no covered windows. On the table sits a plastic IKEA cup and two cocktail glasses, rimmed in gold. And finally, oh god, finally, there is Clementine. Curled almost invisible into a cushion nest on Pepper's velvet sofa, her ever-present soft rabbit in the crook of her arm, bought for her by Emma before she was even born.

A nearly finished bowl of żurek sits on the table with a plastic spoon. They must have fed her even as they thought the world was about end.

"Baby!" she says, in what she hopes is her cheeriest, mummiest voice, even though she can't hear it properly under the whine in her ears. Clementine turns coolly, frowns at how filthy one of her mothers is, then looks back at the television. Full preschooler nonchalance.

They have protected her from it all, she realizes, as she sits gingerly next to her daughter and gently pulls her into a hug with her good arm. They have protected her from everything, and she is so grateful that now, finally, she starts to cry. Hard sobs that she hopes are silent. It's hard to know with the siren sound still in her head. She presses her face into Clementine's beautiful soft curls and sobs until Clementine wriggles free, her sweater now streaked with grime from Carrie's coat and hands. "Where is Mama?" she asks Clementine, but Clementine doesn't help, she's too interested in the TV.

"Where is Emma?" she calls to Pepper, her aching throat the only confirmation that she's made a sound. He is fussing around in the kitchen, bashing about clumsily, movements she's never seen from him before. He can usually make emptying the bins look elegant.

When she walks over to him, he stops moving and stands there, staring back.

"What is it?" she says, apparently sharp enough that Clementine looks up in surprise. Still he stares. "Where is she?" Carrie might be shouting now. But she's been back minutes on a day when seconds are a lifetime, and Emma, her Emma, her twin heart, her wife in all but name, has not emerged. And maybe Carrie knows. Maybe she knew straightaway. Maybe the moments and the knowledge had accordion-folded inside her, and now they are expanding as he tells her what she already knows, with his sad eyes and his clamped mouth which never normally stops. Maybe she will burst.

She steps forward and clutches his dressing gown, bunching its slippery soft fabric and staring dead straight into his eyes, begging for an answer she doesn't really want.

He is breathing fast and she is breathing fast too, and Clementine has turned from the TV to watch this, two of her best adults locked together in an unspoken conversation she cannot understand.

"Where is she, Pepper?" Carrie manages to say. He finally opens his mouth but she points to her ruined ears. He pries her fingers from the fabric and points to the little table, a notepad and pen on it. He is always writing there, "catching up with his correspondence" to old theater friends who have mostly left the city in their old age. To his disgust.

She walks to the table and sits heavily, the adrenaline that got her home seeping away, leaving nausea and pain behind. He follows her and picks up the pen like a condemned man.

He holds the nib in the air for too long and she must growl in frustration, as Clementine cries and he tries to go to her, to comfort her, but Carrie grabs his hand with her own good hand and pulls him back to the chair. He must tell her, he has to tell her, she cannot live in this limbo for one more second.

He starts to write.

Chapter Sixty-Five

FRANKIE

"I need your help!" The man's voice through the door is loud, desperate, and familiar.

"Oh no," Frankie whispers, crouching as if he can see her. "It's Ashley."

"Ashley?"

"He . . . he and his brothers grabbed me, they hurt me and they took another girl too."

"Ashley? Ashley *Curtiss*?"

"He's out for blood, his brothers are dead, and he'll blame Otis, he'll blame me!"

"Please," Ashley shouts again. "I'm begging you, I need shelter."

"His brothers are *dead*?" Janet says, raising a hand to her mouth but flicking her eyes at the door. "What happened to—"

"Never mind that—he can't come in here and see me." Frankie lifts the gun and points it toward the woman's birdlike chest as she stiffens. It feels like playacting.

"Tell him it was all a false alarm," Frankie says quietly, her voice steelier than her insides. "Say that he doesn't need to shelter anymore."

"You're not going to shoot me."

"He's dangerous," Frankie says. "Properly, actually dangerous. And if you try to let him in, I will shoot you."

"I know he's from rough stock, believe me, I know all about him. But we're not animals."

Janet walks toward the front door. Frankie follows, her legs shaking and her head banging. The gauze prickly on her head.

"I mean it," Frankie hisses. "That man will hurt us both."

Janet steps forward, slower this time. Ashley must hear her footsteps because he starts to cry out: "Let me in, please! I need help, my brothers . . . my brothers . . ." The rest is lost to tears. A gruesome, gargling sound. The woman's nimble fingers reach for the bolt.

"Don't you dare!" Frankie whispers, pushing her own finger into the crook of the gun, the trigger vibrating slightly as she trembles.

The bolt is pulled back, just a little. Frankie steps closer, gun still rattling in her hands. "Please," she hisses. "Please don't do this."

But Janet has already opened the door, and Frankie was never going to be able to stop her. Ashley stumbles into the hallway as Frankie cocks the gun. "You," he says, his voice slurred with pain. "What are you doing with my brother's gun?"

"Ashley," Janet says calmly, "you need to sit down, you're in a terrible state and you need looking at—"

"We don't have time for that," he says, "a missile is coming, I need to get to HQ. My . . . my . . ."

He sits heavily on the wooden stairs, his head in his hands. "Ah, there's no fucking point," he says. "It was them that cared about all that."

Frankie points the gun uselessly at him.

"Ashley," Janet says carefully. "You need to know that there is no missile."

"Bollocks."

"It's been called off. Honestly. Love, give him your phone."

Frankie shakes her head. "I'm not giving him anything, he's the reason my boyfriend is bleeding to death out there."

"Your boyfriend?" Ashley roars. "The prick that smashed into us?"

"Because you fucking kidnapped me!"

"We saved you!"

Ashley stands up, staggering a little but stepping heavily toward her. The gun shakes in Frankie's hands. Minutes ago, she had stood outside this cottage prepared to shoot her way inside. Janet not yet a person to her, just a barrier to safety, a gatekeeper. Minutes before that, she had been willing to leave Ashley to die in his truck. Hopeful, even, that he would die. Willing to leave Otis, to her deep shame. When there were minutes on the clock, what did any of it matter? But the clock has been rewound, the clean slate smeared dirty again. She looks at the gun and wills herself to be that Frankie again. The Frankie who was capable of pulling the trigger.

But it's too late, Ashley has snatched it.

And now he's pointing it at her.

Chapter Sixty-Six

MRS. DABB

"I know there's stuff we need to talk about," Bunny says cautiously, chewing her nails.

"It can wait, Bunny Rabbit."

"It really can?" Oh, her voice. She is still a little girl, deep down. Still the same child who would strike out on some caper and then need picking up and carrying home. Still cuddly even now she's at secondary school.

"That can all wait. I'm just so glad you're home and safe. Especially"—she swallows, the words hard as marbles in her throat—"especially on a day when so many people didn't make it home."

The television screen cuts between carnage from around the country and the preparations for a service from St. Paul's, just about to start. A BBC voice-over somberly reads the numbers, the accidental deaths, the suicides, the murders. Mary's chin trembles with the effort of containing her despair.

Outside the cottage, an engine growls past, and Bunny sits up, alarmed. "Who is that?" Her voice is the same as when she was little and woke with a gasping nightmare.

Mary eases herself to a stand and pulls the curtains open a crack, peering out. "There's no one there now." She smooths the curtains back together and sits down with a sigh. "It was someone just driving past."

The screen shows politicians and dignitaries picking their way to the doors of St. Paul's in long black coats. Many of the same grim faces who stood at the Cenotaph last Sunday, the poppies still in their lapels. No King, of course, he is in Greece, where he will stay.

Mary isn't watching. She is staring at her granddaughter, who flinches and looks behind her, just quickly. "Bunny," she says, putting her mug down with a slop onto the carpet. "Bunny, look at me."

Bunny turns her head slowly but avoids her grandmother's eyes.

"I think there's something you're not telling us."

"Mary, don't..."

Mary keeps her eyes on Bunny, who is paling like she could vomit again. She suddenly flinches again and whispers, "Did you hear that?"

"Hear what?"

Bunny is rigid with fear again, but then she shakes her head. "Nothing," she says.

"Bunny," Mary says, "what's going on?"

"I'm just scared," Bunny says. "Because the bad people are still out there."

"You locked the back door after I came in, didn't you?" Mary says, turning to her, a wave of panic spreading through the room. *Did I?*

Bunny catches her expression and looks terrified, burrowing deeper into the corner of the sofa, but Mary has already bustled out into the kitchen. The sound of the key being turned and the bolt sliding across are audible even over the horrifying television commentary.

"The whole house is locked up now, Bunny. I promise, you've got nothing to worry about."

"Are you sure, Mum?" she says, her voice small. But before she can reply, Mary comes back into the living room and sits right next to Bunny.

"Listen," Mary says, so firmly that Bunny shrinks back and closes her eyes.

"Bunny, look at me." It takes ten, maybe fifteen seconds before Bunny slowly unscrews her eyes and looks at her grandmother. Her expression is steeped in shame and fear.

"What aren't you telling us, girl?"

Chapter Sixty-Seven

CARRIE

Pepper writes carefully.

Emma was watching for you out of the window, Carrie.

Carrie stares at each word as they form the sentence. Grammatically perfect and precise, even as the pen shakes between Pepper's index finger and thumb.

When the helicopter crashed, she saw you fall.

"What?"

He stops, avoids her eye, fusses with the pen. He is stalling, and she can't bear it.

"Please, Pepper!"

She went out there. There wasn't long left and she went out to help you inside.

"No . . ." Carrie shakes her head. "No."

I tried to stop her.

He pauses. The whine in her ears has faded just a little. She can just make out the wails of fire engines, police, and ambulances. It sounds like make-believe. Like TV.

I saw her trying to help you but you both fell over. I saw you fight her off.

He stops and looks up at Carrie, reaching up and cupping her filthy chin so gently, so sadly, that she cries out. Then he takes a sharp breath and writes the rest.

You could not have known it was her.

Now Carrie is running on her shaking legs, her damaged arm swinging. She is down the stairs.

She is at the front door.

Pepper is coming after her and as she yanks the door with her good arm, he pulls her from behind, tries to turn her face to his. She shakes him off. She has to find Emma, to tell her sorry, to tend whatever injury she has. To tell her they should move to Brighton, eat candy every day, just be together with Clementine forever and ever.

To tell her over and over again that she didn't know it was her. She couldn't see, couldn't hear. Would never have—

Oh god.

The air outside is still thick with smoke from the helicopter, sour and dank. Rubble and detritus are strewn like Legos. The huge, burned-out carcass lies on its side, blades limp like dead dragonfly wings. The flames are lazy now, just a few licking along the outline of the machine.

On a bench nearby, a man lies still, arms crossed. Carrie will later find out he took all his insulin at once and lay there to die, unable to make it home to his family in time. Right now, he looks like he's sleeping. People don't pay much attention to him as he slowly fades away.

Several figures squat down behind the trees, pausing to look at something and then hurrying away. She strains to see. Her eyes are still sore and puffy, but she can make out a shape between the tree trunks. There is something there that troubles passersby but not enough to keep them from their own people. Maybe nothing could stop a person tonight, unsure whether to truly believe that their world—flawed and beautiful—has survived.

Her eyes are leaking, half-closed, but she steps outside and moves closer, dodging the hazards, only realizing that she's still barefoot due to the pain. Shards of glass slice through her soles as she moves closer to the place where Emma grabbed her, and where she struck out.

She wipes her eyes with her scrubbed and raw hands and tries again to make out the shape on the ground.

She must be screaming, even if she can't hear it, because Pepper is outside now and he's grabbing her, pulling her into the house away from the flames and the people.

Away from Emma's body and the huge, bloodied brick next to her beautiful, damaged head.

Chapter Sixty-Eight

FRANKIE

"Ashley," Janet says, as Frankie instinctively puts her hands up and backs away from him, her back against the front door, her hip brushing envelopes off a little shelf nearby. If she could think properly, if she could follow a thought, Frankie might reach behind and open the door, take her chances and run. But she cannot think, her brain is a whiteout.

"What are you doing?" Janet is saying, her voice drifting through Frankie's mind like flotsam, nothing taking root.

"No missiles?" he says.

"That's right, we're saved, we're okay."

"My brothers aren't saved," he says quietly. He stares between them both, eyes glazing. He wipes his nascent tears roughly with the heel of one hand, the gun still gripped on his shoulder with the other. His forehead is streaked with blood, but it folds with thought. Calculation.

"Ah, shit," he says. "Now I'm really fucked. It would have been better if the bomb had landed. Now everything we did looks really bad. Everything *they* did, it's all on me."

"No," Frankie says, her brain snapping alert. "We can say it was just them, or I can say I got in willingly, that it was all a misunderstanding."

"A misunderstanding?" His voice is so low now that it rumbles through her body. "So you'll just . . . you'll lie for me?"

"I will," she says, holding out her hands in an offering of peace. "I will. And I'll tell Otis that I thought he'd gone off and left me and you guys just offered me a lift."

"You'd do that?"

"I would. I just want an end to this. I just want to go and help Otis, that's all."

"Bollocks," he says, and adjusts the gun on his shoulder. "I will never trust another woman, you're all liars."

"If you shoot me, they'll know it was all on purpose, because why else—"

"Ashley, for your mum's sake," Janet says softly, "think about what you're doing."

"My mother turned her back on us."

"There must be someone, someone you're—"

"I've got no one left, and I'm not having this bitch telling tales about my brothers, twisting things, getting that girl to back her up too."

"You do have someone," Janet says. Her voice is unsteady, infused with something that Frankie can't decipher. Fear, but maybe guilt too.

"What are you talking about?" He turns so the gun is now trained on Janet's forehead. She recoils, scrunching her eyes in fear, but then opens them, wide and deliberate.

"You . . . you have a child."

"No," he snorts, almost amused. "I don't."

"You do, you have a daughter."

"What the fuck are you talking about? I don't have a kid."

"You have a little girl. And if you do this, you'll never stand a chance of seeing her. But if you surrender, they'll understand this was an extreme situation and they'll make allowances. I promise."

He shakes his head. "I don't have a daughter, woman. You've lost your marbles."

"Her name is Clementine, she's three years old, and she has your eyes."

"A clementine is a fucking orange."

Janet flinches and slowly reaches toward a framed photograph on the wall of the hallway. Two smiling women a bit younger than Frankie, one small and blond, one tall and redheaded, and a dark-haired girl in a stroller, holding a rabbit teddy, on holiday somewhere white and blue. Frankie gives what she thinks is a passing glance, too frightened to take anything in, but she will never forget their faces.

"A woman called Carrie?" Janet says, her voice breaking slightly.

"Carrie Spencer from primary school?"

"That's my daughter. She came to visit me, about four years ago now. She was having a hard time and we had a bit of a tiff about it, so she went out for the night." Now Janet adopts a brisk tone. A nurse's tone. "You met up in a pub and you had sex."

Something changes. He has softened, his face, his stance. Even his voice. "We . . . maybe. But—"

He holds the gun loosely in his right hand, and reaches for the photo with his left. A loud bang comes on the front door.

The photograph falls to the floor; the gun slips from Ashley's grasp and as he snatches it again, pulls it back to his shoulder, curls his finger through—

BANG.

Chapter Sixty-Nine

MRS. DABB

"Bunny," Mary says again. "What aren't you telling us, girl?"

For a long moment, Bunny doesn't reply. Instead, her eyes fill and tears brim over her dark lashes, trickling down her heart-shaped face and dripping from her chin. "I'm sorry," she says. "It's the prisoners from Princetown."

"What about them?"

"I think one of them is coming to get me."

"Oh, Bunny, why?"

"Which prisoner?" Mary presses. "And why would he be coming here?"

"My biological father," Bunny says.

"What?" She stares back at her daughter. "What are you talking about? We've never . . . you don't even know who—"

"I know it wasn't someone you met on holiday abroad because I've seen your passport, the old stamps. You didn't go on holiday the year I was . . . made."

"But why do you think it's someone in prison?" Skin burning, ears beating with pulse. *She can't know. She can't.*

"Mum," Bunny says, with the gentle tone of a doctor delivering bad news. "I know who he is and I know he's in prison."

"And he's not due to get out," Mary cuts in, "for at least another year."

"That's what I'm saying," Bunny says, "that's who the siren is for. He's the one that escaped, the one all the helicopters are looking for. I'm sure of it."

"How could you know this?" Mary asks. "They didn't name anyone on the TV, you must be confused—"

"Because I was there," Bunny says, covering her face with both hands. "And this is all my fault."

"What do you mean, you were there, Bunny?" Mary tries to pull Bunny's hands away but she just shakes her head.

Bunny draws her knees up to her chin, folding over herself. "I did something really bad. And you will both really hate me." Bunny snuffles.

"We would never ever hate you," she says, even as she remembers where the 118 bus goes from. Even as her chest starts to hurt.

"I used Mama as an excuse," Bunny says, so quietly that Mary holds her breath and leans closer. "I used the tenth anniversary of Mama dying as an excuse to get out of school. I said we were all going to the big service in London, but I went to Princetown instead. I went to see Ashley Curtiss. To see my dad."

Chapter Seventy

CARRIE

Pepper places a mug of something on the nightstand next to the bed, the sound as loud as a gunshot in this silence. Her eyes stay trained on the ceiling as if they're nothing to do with her, and she's nothing to do with whatever he's just brought in.

"*Kochanie*," he says. "Your daughter needs you. I went downstairs to get her some things but I don't know if they're right. She's not impressed with the clothes I chose, she is asking for her mummy." He lowers his voice, hesitant for once. "And for her mama."

Carrie rolls over slowly, her body tender. She faces away from him, her eyes trained on the window, the red curtains almost black in this light.

She misses the whine in her head from earlier, which would have snuffed all this talking right out. Misses the tears of relief that came so easily. Before she knew. Before she was cursed to always know what she had done to Emma. The love of her life.

Now she is crisped, dried of all emotion. A brittle hostage to that blank ceiling, that black-red curtain. Pepper's incessant speech grates on her ears, missing any of his usual humor, his spiky barbs.

"Come and tuck Clementine in," Pepper tries. The curtain billows, just for a second, bellying inward. A breeze that she doesn't feel.

"I killed Emma," she says. Her voice is dry and flat. But time must have passed, because he has gone. The curtain hangs limp. The room is cold. Clementine must be asleep in the other spare room, cuddled up to Barnaby, her rabbit teddy.

Her nickname in the womb was Bunny. She had twitched her little nose on the twenty-week 3D scan and that was it. Bunny. Long before she was born, they'd bought rabbit bedding, a rabbit mobile, a rabbit-eared baby towel. "How can this be so tiny?" Emma said, and then sobbed all over the fluffy fabric so they had to wash her mascara out of it.

Just before the birth, when Carrie was finally on parental leave and spending her days peeing endlessly and watching old films all day, Emma came home with Barnaby the soft rabbit.

Barnaby was placed in the plastic cot on the newborn ward and has never left Clementine's bed since. They were still debating calling her Bunny for a first name on the walk to the register office to make it official. "But what if we ever move back to Devon?" Carrie said. "People there don't have a London tolerance for wacky names."

"I can't see us moving back to Devon," Emma had said quietly, a shadow passing over her face. "Not with you-know-who there. And anyway," she'd said, smiling, "you know full well we'll move out to Brighton when we're sick of this city anyway. We could call her Whizz Bang Banana Pants and no one would give a monkey's in Brighton."

In the end, as they wheeled the giant stroller through the doors like it was made of fragile glass, they decided that Bunny would be her middle name and she could choose whether or not to use it when she was older. "She'll probably change her name to Jane no middle name Smith," Emma said, "and take out a restraining order against her mad mums."

When Carrie gets up now, her knees buckle as if they've forgotten their business, muscles weak and trembling. She staggers to the window and slips behind the curtain, slamming the window down to shut out the breeze. She wants to spoil and grow stale in here. She wants to rot.

She rests her forehead on the cold glass and looks out. Under the glow of the ornate streetlamps, she can make out Pepper sitting stiffly on a bench amid the mess and rubble. He wears a hat and scarf, the collar on his tweed coat stiff around his jaw. At his feet, something bulky is wrapped carefully in one of the thick throws from his settee.

She presses a hand to the window but it's too much. It's all too much. She fights her way back through the curtain and into the room, half falling onto the bed in haste, and wraps herself tight in the eiderdown, tighter still, face under, mouth full of satin, an unbreathing thing. As close as she can be to being the body out there, her twin heart stopped. But not close enough.

Chapter Seventy-One

FRANKIE

Someone is thumping on the door. Janet lies in the hallway with a ragged burn hole in her forehead and her eyes wide open. She is motionless, but blood trickles from her nose, down her cheek, and drips quietly, *tap-tap-tap*, on the wooden floor.

Frankie and Ashley stare at each other, for a moment united in panic, but then he drops the gun and runs for the back of the house, his movement unsteady on his injured limbs, the kitchen door banging open as he goes. Frankie drops to her knees beside Janet, as the front door thuds grow ever more insistent. She presses her fingers to the older woman's soft neck, crying out as she makes contact. It's very obviously too late.

Frankie's hands smear blood on the door as she pulls it open and blinks out at the faces. Pale panicked face of a man in his forties with kind eyes. Just behind him, a teenage girl. *The* teenage girl.

"Juno here came to our house for help," the man says. "We came to help."

"Juno," Frankie says, dazed. "I never asked your name."

"I ran across some fields and found their house, I told them about the crash," Juno says, staring not at Frankie but at the body of Janet. The man is looking at Frankie's hands, and the gun lying behind her.

"I didn't . . ." she starts.

"Help me!" another man's voice calls, somewhere near the road.

"Nathan," the man shouts, rushing in the direction of the cry.

Juno steps forward, grabs Frankie by the wrist, and guides her out of the house. "I told them what the Curtiss brothers did to us. They're here to help your boyfriend."

In the road, next to a Jeep seemingly filled with writhing greyhounds, the two men are holding Ashley Curtiss down. The light from the Jeep's headlamps pools around them; all three men look wildly out of their depth.

She hears Ashley say, "I'm sorry." The words are muffled, his lips pressed into the tarmac. He is limp, exhausted, and no longer fighting. The blood from his injuries now a dark red.

"This was all my fault," Frankie says, turning to look back into the cottage, but Juno shakes her head. "Don't look back," she says to Frankie, pulling a tissue from her coat pocket and wiping the blood from Frankie's hands, so gently that Frankie starts to weep.

Ashley bucks his body one final time and then appears to pass out. "This was all their fault, not yours," one of the men says, gesturing to Ashley without loosening his grip.

"And we'll make sure the police know that. I'm Mark, by the way, and this is Nathan."

With one hand and a knee still on a felled Ashley, Nathan pulls his phone from his pocket. The dogs watch with mild interest from the Jeep windows.

"The network's back!" He dials 999 and then looks at Frankie. "It's ringing. Tell me where you crashed."

Frankie should not be sitting here. Frankie should be with Otis. Wherever the doctors have put his gurney while they try to fix him, that's where she should be.

Although neither of them should really be in this chaotically busy hospital, where walking wounded like her sit in shocked piles anywhere they can find floor space, staring at nothing or trying to make contact on devices with hardly any battery, through networks that keep collapsing under the strain. Whispering calls to find out who made it, urgently thumbing screens.

Frankie and Otis should never have come to Devon. They should be at home in their flat, milky brew and trash TV, maybe a book in the crook of her arm. Toast. Lots of toast. And crisps. *Life can't be that bad if we've still got crisps.*

But there are no crisps, nor tea and toast. The vending machines were emptied during the 59 minutes, a nurse told her, the kitchens turned over. A local warehouse has promised to bring supplies, but nothing has arrived. Frankie thinks, stupidly, of the oat bar back at the cottage, the fancy soap. She's so hungry, she'd eat them both.

When will they let Janet's daughter know? And her granddaughter?

There is a TV in the ward, turned up high to do battle with the crying and the low moans of pain that permeate the whole hospital. It's well past midnight but no one will be sleeping tonight. All those crammed into the ward stare at the screen bringing news from around the country, tributes and promises from across the world.

Earlier, the television news said the North was "relatively unscathed." This has already turned out to be very relative because, by most normal measures, it was extremely scathed. But compared to the gridlocked Midlands with the multiple fatal pileups on the M40, the M6, and the M1, compared to the South where people jumped into their cars out of habit and slammed into each other, with nowhere to actually go, the North was lucky.

As Frankie drinks tap water from a paper cup, the Manchester mayor is interviewed. In the coming months, the statement he just made will become an ironic T-shirt slogan and reframed as multiple memes: "The North is all right." But no one is laughing yet.

Time has become doughy, hard to measure. She knows she has asked repeatedly about Otis. Where is he? When can they leave? Can he be transferred to Withenshawe or the Manchester Royal Infirmary or St. Mary's or anywhere up there, anywhere but here? But no one can say.

The police got to Ashley quicker than the ambulance got to Otis. She'd gone to wait at the car with Juno, holding Otis's limp hand, while Mark and Nathan stayed outside the cottage. Otis didn't wake up. So maybe he is dead, and they're just not telling her. By leaving him in the car like that, alone and damaged, maybe she killed him. Just like she killed Janet by leading that man to the cottage. Maybe no one is safe from her.

Chapter Seventy-Two

MRS. CARRIE DABB

**November 14, 2035
Ten Years After the Alert**

Mary stands up so fast she nearly tips over, but when Bunny offers her hand, Mary brushes it away. "Let me get this straight, you told the school we were all going to London for the memorial service? You used the death of your mama, *my daughter Emma*, as an excuse to bunk off school." It's not a question.

"I'm sorry," Bunny says, but Mary shakes her head and walks out of the living room and into the kitchen. Still the old footage fills the screen, as it does every year. A reminder, as if anyone could ever forget.

"Mum, I'm sorry," Bunny cries. "I didn't want to hurt you and Gran, I thought you never had to know."

"You thought we wouldn't find out that you'd lied to the school about us all going to London so you could sneak off to Princetown?" Carrie says. "So you could go to a bloody *prison*? How could you do this?"

"No, it . . . it wasn't at the prison. The ones who'd shown good behavior, the prisoners, I mean, the ones they didn't think would run away . . ." Bunny pauses, as if trying to find the words. "You know how there are services all over the country for the people who died in the alert, Mum? Because it's ten years, it's a big anniversary?"

"Yes," Carrie says quietly. "I'm well aware."

"Well, some of the prisoners got to go to the service in Princetown church. And he was one of them. My d—Ashley."

"That man was allowed out of prison to go to a *church service*?" Carrie says, the words sharp and salty on her tongue. "A church service for people like your mama."

Bunny puts her face in her hands and nods.

"A church service for people like my mother? My mother who *he* bloody killed. Your dead grandmother!"

"I'm sorry, Mummy. I'm so sorry. As soon as I saw him in there in the pew with the others, I knew it was a mistake. I got up and left and he watched me and he looked . . . sad. Like, really, really sad. And then when I was waiting at the bus stop, the siren went off. The prison siren, I mean. And someone said that meant there'd been an escape and I knew. I just knew it was him."

"How could he have even known it was you in there? How would he have recognized you?"

"His mum sent him pictures. She's the one who told me about the service."

"You actually met up with her?" Carrie thinks of that isolated compound, the crumbling building with its blocked-up windows. For years, teenagers would drive out there and put stones through the windows or spray-paint the walls. She almost drove there herself once, set the whole stinking thing on fire. Pepper, still alive then, had talked her down from his flat in London: "You're no good to your daughter if you're banged up for arson, *kochanie*, and I'm too old to come and break you out." In reality, she couldn't bear to go there again, took circuitous routes to avoid that dark valley. Blotted it from her mental map.

The Curtiss mother had apparently moved back in, years after she first left. With her other sons dead and Ashley in prison, it was her right. Or maybe her penance.

"I only met her once," Bunny says, and there's a defensiveness to her tone. "She hates what he did, like, she didn't go to the service herself, but he's all she's got left. Apart from m—"

"You're all *I've* got left!" Carrie cries. "You're all Gran's got left! Ashley's mum can't have you! There's plenty of wing nut Curtiss cousins still around, she can have them!"

A door creaks somewhere in the house. Carrie had thought Mary would go and angrily bash plates around, throw herself into laying out the buffet or clattering teacups around. But there's no noise from the kitchen. It sounds . . . that doesn't make sense. It sounds like Mary has just opened the cellar door, but why would she go down there? It's still laid out just as Janet Spencer had left it, the pickles and preserves, the dusty futon, the rolled-up clothes for an apocalypse that never came, but also did.

"I just wanted to know what he was like."

"You know what he's like because you know what he did!"

"Yeah, and I have half his genes, so if he's bad then maybe I'm bad and I just wanted to know if . . . if there was any good in him. I know you hate him, Mum, and I know you didn't want me to know the truth but I do. The match was ninety-nine point nine percent, it's like . . . it's undeniable. So I needed to know for myself."

"What do you mean, the match?"

"An online DNA test. It's just a checkbox for parental permission and I knew you'd never agree so . . . I just checked it myself."

"But how did you—"

"His mum gave a sample. My . . ." She looks toward the kitchen and whispers, "My other gran, I guess."

"Jesus, you've not just met her, you swapped fluid samples?!"

"She's not how you think, Mum. I told you, she hates what they did."

"But she gave you a phone and arranged a DNA test."

"I needed to know where I got this from," Bunny says eventually, reaching up to her thick curly hair. It's long and out of control. Carrie longs to be allowed to brush it again. To tease a ribbon of it loose and twirl it in her hands.

"And my eyes, Mum. 'Cos yours are blue."

"Emma, your mama, she had brown eyes too."

"You know what I mean, Mum. It doesn't mean I didn't . . . It doesn't mean anything bad about you and Mama. Wouldn't you want to know the truth, if you were me?"

On the screen, against a blue-paneled TV studio backdrop, a man in a Campaign for Nuclear Disarmament T-shirt is arguing with a woman in a suit.

"There would have been no incentive for them to hack the system like that if there were no nukes to threaten each other with," the man on-screen says as the woman rolls her eyes.

"Be realistic," she cuts in, as the host in the middle battles a small smile.

"People like me are the only ones who are being realistic. No matter how much suspicion the mainstream media throws at us, we're still the only ones willing to say on camera that it was the state of R—"

The screen cuts away to old footage.

"Sometimes," Carrie says, "the truth makes everything worse."

The Guardian
November 15, 2025

59 MINUTES: Death Toll Rises to 542
Road traffic accidents account for majority of known deaths. Suicide, self-defense, and assault also responsible for loss of life during "false alert."

Early indications suggest the death toll will climb higher in the coming days, a joint spokesperson for the emergency services said today. The loss of life during yesterday's false nuclear alert is the highest experienced on a single day in England during peacetime. Volunteers and retired emergency staff are . . .

Chapter Seventy-Three

CARRIE

November 15, 2025
The Next Day

Carrie snaps awake. Clementine has climbed onto the bed next to her, Barnaby wedged into the crook of her little arm. What time is it? It's dark out and the bowl of stew Pepper brought her earlier is congealing on the bedstand. Its meaty smell twists her stomach.

"Mummy?"

"What?"

Her voice, an unpracticed bark, does not sound like her own. Clementine must think so too as she bursts into tears.

"Oh," Carrie says. For a moment, she watches her daughter cry into Barnaby, his furry neck strangled in her plump little hand in the soupy gray of the room, yellowed by the streetlight outside. Tears rain down on pajamas that are too small and that she meant to weed out and put in a charity bag. For a moment, the sadness on the little screwed face does not touch her, the smallness of her daughter does not affect her as it normally does—with a constant base level of shock that anything so small can be autonomous, have thoughts and feelings. She thinks then, suddenly, of the moment her own mother came into the family room at the hospital, after Dad died. How teenage Carrie had stood waiting, shaking with grief, but her mother had not touched her. Had not comforted her. Had entirely collapsed under her own sense of loss.

Carrie reaches for Clementine and pulls her in. She softens her voice and smells her daughter's hair, the days-old trace of shampoo.

"Sweetie," she says, "my little bunny rabbit, it's okay." Clementine grips Carrie's clothes—what clothes?—Carrie looks down and realizes she's wearing Pepper's pajamas. When was she helped into those? She has no memory. Oh god, Pepper. He has kept her human. "It's okay," she says, the rough edges of her voice falling away. "Mummy's here. Mummy will always be here."

The Sun on Sunday
November 16, 2025

BLOOD ON THEIR HANDS
Government sources say ANTINUKE NUTTERS could be responsible for terror hack hoax as death toll hits 2,000.

Antinuclear activists may be to blame for Friday's devastating hoax, an anonymous government source has exclusively told *The Sun on Sunday*. The deranged agenda to stop the expansion of nuclear weapons may have led to hackers seizing . . .

Chapter Seventy-Four

FRANKIE

November 16, 2025
Two Days Later

"Yes, moderate brain injury," Frankie says, the phone hot against her cheek even as she shivers in the hospital parking lot. The November air is crisp out here, her breath fogging. Frankie is desperate—surprisingly, inappropriately—for a cigarette. The craving is so extreme and sudden that she can taste the smoke in her mouth, feel her teeth furring with it. She says a silent apology to the poppy seed in her belly, for the fact that she would *without hesitation* snatch a cigarette if one were in front of her right now, light it up, and suck it down to the filter.

"Thank god," Otis's mum says down the line. "Moderate is . . ."

"It's better than it could have been," Frankie says, "but it's not good. It's not *mild*."

"He's awake, though?" Jo says.

"Yeah, he's awake, but he's not really with it. He was out cold for four hours, near on. And they've—"

"I'm coming down, love."

Frankie shivers, tugs her hair out of its bun with her spare hand, mindlessly fidgeting with her painful hairline. She feels Janet's deft fingers patching her, caring for her. She closes her eyes, but the memories remain.

"The hospital is crammed, they wouldn't let you in, Jo."

The ER and the ICU are still teeming, just like Janet warned her they would be. Car crash victims sardined in corridors, bruised parents shushing wild-eyed offspring, doctors and nurses with war-torn faces. Otis and Frankie were lucky to have been in the first wave of casualties to arrive here, before the motorways were scraped for survivors. Now people are being turned away or chucked out early. Relatives sent to plead with cottage hospitals and health centers to provide emergency care they're not equipped to give.

"And how are you, Francesca? Are they looking after you?"

"I was very lucky," Frankie says, after a long pause. "They discharged me this morning, let me go to sit with Otis in ICU. Hopefully no lasting damage . . . to me." She puts a hand to her stomach, roiling with nausea.

Frankie had asked them to check her belly, to give her an ultrasound. They refused. It was an early pregnancy with no blood loss, hardly an emergency. Every ultrasound machine was being used, stretcher queues snaking through corridors as they waited. "If you start to bleed, go to the early pregnancy unit," a doctor had told her as he walked away, calling back over his shoulder. "But it'll be a long wait."

"I just don't understand why Otis crashed his car," Jo says now, and Frankie can hear the rasping wheel of her lighter. It's torture. "He's always such a careful driver."

"They weren't normal driving conditions," Frankie says, more snappily than intended. "It was misty, we were in the middle of nowhere and on the brink of nuclear war."

"Oh, that was never going to happen," Jo says, taking an audible drag. "Fake news."

Frankie says nothing; she has not told Jo that Otis saved her life. That he believed that "fake" alert enough to drive his car into a truck to stop three psycho brothers stealing her away and doing fuck knows what with her and teenage Juno during nuclear winter. That he must have known he might kill himself and still took the risk. For her. For their baby. People died because he made that decision.

"I'll give him your love, Jo." She hangs up.

Chapter Seventy-Five

MRS. CARRIE DABB

November 15, 2035
Ten Years Later

"I just didn't think he'd do that," Bunny says, picking at a hole in the blanket that Carrie has bodge-sewed twice already. "Escaping, I mean. He only has a year left until he has a chance to get out and he was trusted and now—"

"Well, you don't actually know that it was him who escaped," Carrie says, trying to keep her voice level while her insides whirl and churn, her heartbeat wild in her temples and chest. She takes a steadying breath. "And whoever it is has probably already been caught."

Bunny looks skeptical but doesn't argue.

"It's pretty hard to get away with escaping custody."

"There have been, like, loads of escapes from that prison."

"Not in your lifetime, Bunny. Not even in mine. And they all got caught and so will this person. And whoever it is will be locked up for a lot longer because of this," Carrie says. "And that's no bad thing. If it was him, he's clearly nowhere near ready to be released and trusted out in the world. And someone probably got hurt during all this."

"He wasn't even handcuffed, Mum. He was just sitting in a pew with some other prisoners and someone in uniform at each end."

"Yes, and at least one of those uniformed men probably got bashed when he broke away. Other people too probably."

Bunny cringes, but Carrie doesn't stop. "Jasmine's dad works at the prison, doesn't he—he could have been hurt."

"He wasn't there, it was other prison people."

"Is that okay then? For someone to hurt other people in the . . . in the panic of a moment? I don't think that's okay. I think anyone who . . . I think that's something that should never be forgiven." *I will never forgive myself.*

Bunny looks down at the blanket.

"If it was him, then he's really not reformed at all, because that's exactly what he did ten years ago. To your—"

"I know!" Bunny cries. "And I know it was him that escaped and I know it was my fault because he was trying to follow me."

On the screen, the procession from the city's remembrance walls to St. Paul's is finally underway. A torchlight parade, forty-eight people, each nominated to represent their individual county's losses. Some of them too young to remember. They weave slowly along dark pavements whose streetlights have been dimmed for tonight. Alongside the swollen Thames, higher than it was ten years ago. Past the illuminated little boats that row, chug, and punt solemnly parallel to the foot parade, many of them renamed for tonight to honor the boats that sank, or from whose slippery sides people tumbled. For once, the screen has no soundtrack even with the sound up. For some things, only silence is enough.

"Is Gran angry?"

"Yes."

"Are you angry?"

Carrie pulls her daughter into a hug. "No," she says softly, kissing Bunny's crown. She smells of outside. "But I really wish you hadn't gone about it like this."

"I know." Bunny's voice is muffled against Carrie's sweatshirt, still traced with the flour from today's baking.

"But you know . . . if you really think he's the one who escaped, then I need to call the police and let them know you've been in contact. I need to do that right now, actually." *I should have done this as soon as she told me.*

"I'm going to go and have a shower and get into my comfies," Bunny says. Her voice is light but she moves heavily, pulling herself from the sofa and plodding out with Carrie right behind her. In the kitchen, Mary sits at the tired old table.

"I'm sorry, Gran."

Mary does not look at her. In front of her, among the Tupperware and cakes, her hearing aids lie where she has wrenched them from her ears.

"You go and have your shower," Carrie says to Bunny, gently pulling her into the hall. "I need to make that call."

Fear has animated Carrie's body for the last ten years. She has been coiled, filed down to a point of hypervigilance, ready to spring at any danger. Taking out a restraining order against any Curtiss in a ten-mile radius, refusing to accept DNA tests or letterbox contact, or anything asked of her. Once such a people pleaser, she has turned herself into a shield, stopping any advances dead. Anyone offering friendship could be working for them, any of Bunny's school friends could be a distant relative. She has traced, followed, and maneuvered to avoid this. She has refused to let Bunny have a phone, and she herself will never have one again. The trouble they cause is insurmountable.

But the thing she's been most terrified of all these years has happened anyway. Not the prison break, not even Bunny going to see him. That's horrifying, absolutely devastating, but nothing is as frightening as Bunny defending his mother just now. Talking about his family members as if they are real human beings, as if they are her family. Or could be. Bunny will never have a parental relationship with the man who murdered her grandmother, but she could be slowly nibbled at by the rest of the family until they have consumed all her goodness. Until there is nothing left. No trace of the girl she and Emma created from the mess that she and Ashley made.

She hears Bunny's footsteps in the bathroom upstairs, the thud as she steps heavily into the shower, the shudder of the old pipes as they're asked to give it their all. This old cottage constantly creaks and sighs, rhythms she steadily relearned after moving back in. Pepper pleaded with her to stay in London, but London was a crime scene. He offered to help her sell this place, to move somewhere brand-new and safe. But that's not what she wanted either. Dartmoor is penance and peace. The last place that everyone she loved was alive. Mum, Dad, and Emma.

She picks up the landline and wavers. It feels like a 999 situation but it also feels like panic. She is back in Waterloo, gasping fish-mouthed, worried about making a fuss, even in the face of *that*.

Her fingers brush the number 9 but she doesn't commit.

Upstairs, there's a heavy creak from Bunny's room but the shower gushes on. The house is cracking its knuckles in the cold.

She dials.

The Sunday Times
November 16, 2025

PM LAUNCHES INQUIRY INTO "ALERT"
Independent body to consider how emergency systems were compromised and why fail-safes did not prevent disaster.

Foreign powers, state-sponsored hackers, and domestic terrorists are currently being considered as possible agents behind Friday's catastrophe, which saw the government's flagship Emergency Alerts hacked, along with public transport information, missile detection systems, and civil defense systems.

Despite early attempts by some in Whitehall to blame antinuclear and environmental activists, official sources say it is too early to tell who was behind the hack . . .

Chapter Seventy-Six

CARRIE

**November 17, 2025
Three Days Later**

She knows that Pepper called Mary and told her about Emma. And then told the story again to John, Emma's stepdad, because Mary could not speak. Carrie had not been in the room. Could not be in the room. But now, as she zombie-trails Clementine into the living room, Pepper gestures to the phone in his hand. "John again," he whispers, covering the handset. "They just want to know what happened."

"No," Pepper says quickly, seeing Carrie's face whiten with shame, "not that . . . just when we found her, and what happened next. Details are all they can cling to, *kochanie*."

"I can't talk to them," she says, and stares at Clementine, who has picked up a wooden shape puzzle, brought up from the flat below by Pepper. Jauntily painted rabbits with pegs in their backs. What could Carrie say to John that would help? That Emma's body was just one of hundreds littering their part of London, one of two in the communal garden alone.

That bodies are still being found, let alone collected. Covered by bedsheets and blankets from nearby houses, frost silvering the fabric shrouds each morning.

That the person Emma loved most was the one who killed her? That Carrie will never forgive herself. That if it weren't for their daughter, she would want to be buried alongside the woman who should have been her wife.

While Emma lay under Pepper's best throw, he had guarded her body at night, unwilling to leave her flesh to the foxes and the screaming birds. The dead helicopter lay felled on its side in the center of the garden all that time, the smoke fading to a dank trace. Yesterday morning, before they brought a crane to collect it, two laughing kids from number 26 climbed on its metal carcass, meters from Emma's body.

No police came to investigate, just a collection van staffed with exhausted volunteers, who slipped on a toe tag and handed Pepper a paper receipt. As Carrie watched from the window, her palm pressed to the cold pane, the van beeped its jolly reversing warning, then rumbled away to collect the next reported corpse from the Kennings Estate. Someone she must have run straight past and not even seen.

Pepper had locked himself in the bathroom afterward but it was futile, she could hear his sobs rack through the flat. She had never heard him cry before.

Pepper ends the call with John and replaces the phone on its cradle. It immediately rings again. She stares at it. "I wish they'd stop calling," she says again, and he wavers, leaving it for another ring, another ring, but then snatches it up.

"Peplinski," he says warily. He looks ten, twenty years older than he did last week.

He listens to the caller, looking over at Carrie in alarm. "Can I relay the message?" he asks, but whoever it is says no and so, reluctantly, he holds out the phone.

"I'm so sorry, *kochanie*," he says, resting his hand on her shoulder.

A soft voice is at the end of the line, calling from the big police headquarters at the Middlemoor roundabout in Exeter, where she'd failed her driving test two of the three times. They have been trying to reach her, found this number among her mother's things.

"My mother?"

The police officer, whose name she pays no attention to, then tells her gently that Janet died during the 59 minutes, shot by an intruder she had tried to help. A man named Ashley Curtiss.

The Independent
November 18, 2025

"EXPRESS" MURDER SENTENCES AND "GET OUT OF JAIL FREE CARDS"
Emergency laws expected to pass through Parliament today will allow "59 minute killers" who plead guilty to serve "micro" terms known as "Hail Mary sentences."

People who committed murder and other serious offenses during the 59 minutes will be eligible for drastically reduced sentences or for community service, rebuilding damaged areas and clearing road wreckage. Prison spaces will be freed through early release schemes and cancellation of all personal use drug offenses, as well as sentences for shoplifting and other minor crimes. All non–life term prisoners with fewer than six months left to serve will be released.

Justice campaigners argue that express sentences "cheapen life," while domestic violence charities warn that abusers who killed partners and children during the chaos are now able to hide behind an "ill-conceived scheme."

A Number Ten spokeswoman said that . . .

Chapter Seventy-Seven

FRANKIE

November 18, 2025
Four Days Later

Otis still sleeps most of the time and Frankie is glad of it. Whenever Otis wakes—thrashing against his tubes and wires, moaning suddenly, eyes bewildered—she watches him frowning and fumbling for answers, for words that he can't always find.

He looks older. His face pinched, puckered, and lined in new ways. His gold hair has been shaved close by doctors, and his days-old stubble looks deadened and gray. When he sleeps, his face slackens like a popped balloon.

The ICU has thinned out over the last day or so due to a combination of deaths, transfers to wards, and a handful of discharges, but it is still twice over capacity, beds and gurneys wedged where staff normally move, drugs and dressings frequently running out.

Frankie's not supposed to have stayed in there up until now, semi-sleeping in a wingback chair at night, staring into space by day or wincing as Otis wakes occasionally and the whole performance starts again. The staff themselves are ragged. They sleep top and tail in the family room or lie in the corridors, the cleaners' hands raw, the porters staggering. But Exeter has nothing on what's happening in London. The television news, spoiled for scenes to show across the capital, has played footage of St. Thomas' that looks more like helmet footage from rubbled hospitals in war-torn countries thousands of miles away. The confirmed death toll keeps climbing, hundreds or even thousands by the day it seems.

Now the screen is playing a current affairs panel show, guests from binary sides arguing over these new "Hail Mary" sentences. "It mocks the very foundation of English law, which says there must be mandatory life sentences for murder," a man in a gray suit argues.

"How can anyone be accused of intention to murder under these circumstances?" a woman in a navy suit responds. "That's like accusing soldiers of murder when they're at war. Normal rules do not apply."

"And if a violent man used this as an excuse to go on a rampage or to kill his family in an escalation of domestic abuse, then he gets out in a year too?"

The woman shakes her head and makes a scoffing sound. "I never thought I'd see the left arguing for longer prison terms."

"Anyone can say they made a mistake due to the pressure of—" the man starts.

"The prisons will overflow if we treat these crimes in the normal way," the woman says. "No, it's only right that in cases where accidents occurred or poor decisions were made under extreme conditions, and, *crucially*, guilt is admitted, people get a second chance."

The man folds his arms and shakes his head.

Someone in the ward tuts, but Frankie can't tell which side of the argument they're on.

Killers out in a year if they admit guilt and blame the madness of the 59 minutes? Is that what will happen to Ashley Curtiss? One calendar year for all the damage that he and his brothers caused, to Otis and to Janet? That's not right. He does not deserve a second chance.

If it were up to her . . . *Well, it isn't.* She stands up and clicks her joints, stretches her back. She needs to freshen up, although all that's possible is a spit bath. As she reaches for her tote bag—a cheap job picked up at the nearest supermarket for carrying all her tat around, her new toothbrush and face wipes—a volunteer nurse walks toward her.

Round and kind, she has curly blond hair in a bun and a dachshund brooch on her uniform. Despite everything, she even smiles sometimes. But not now. "The police are here to see you, love."

People spill from the family room as the two young police officers approach it, Frankie trailing behind. Children gripped to hips, haunted speechless adults look at her briefly, eyes crinkled with lack of sleep, with worry. They must think the worst for her, assuming she is receiving more of the kind of bad news that brought them all here. They leave their plastic bags and magazines, their paper cups. No one rubbernecks misery anymore, she notices. It seems everyone has had their fill of it.

The officers—both neat-haired boys with trimmed fingernails and shining shoes—hold the door open for her. "Would you like a tea or anything?" the shorter of the two says, and his words suck her inside the room like a tractor beam, snap the door closed behind her.

"The machine's broken," she says, amazed her voice still works. "Ta, though."

Frankie didn't catch their names or ranks. She has not asked to see a badge, though maybe the nurse did. The two of them sit on the dated sofa, just the wrong side of comfortable, and gesture for her to sit as well.

"We need to take a statement about what happened to Janet Spencer," the taller one says. He has a long, sharp nose like a cartoon character, barely real.

"But I already told . . ." Who did she tell? Maybe it was just a nurse, maybe it was no one.

"We can do it here or you can come to the station. Here is nicer," the shorter one says. When he smiles, his eyes turn into quotation marks, nearly disappearing into his flesh. He must have been an adorable kid, she thinks. His soft face is at odds with the uniform, but his skin is lined with tiredness just like everyone else's. How long have these two been working?

"We've taken statements from everyone else involved, but now we need your side of things."

"My side? There's only one side." She pictures it all in her head, a mad collage. The kidnapping, the look on Juno's face in the back of the truck, the fear as they were whisked away, Otis permanently damaged by saving her. And Janet.

"Has he . . ." She thinks of the panel show, the express sentences. "Has he admitted guilt?" she says.

The officers look at each other but don't answer.

"Ashley Curtiss deliberately shot Janet Spencer," she says firmly. "And if he says otherwise, he's a liar."

Chapter Seventy-Eight

MRS. CARRIE DABB

November 14, 2035
Ten Years Later

Carrie's call has been passed to someone important at Devon and Cornwall Police and her whistle-stop backstory has been met with an "I see."

"So is it him? Is Ashley Curtiss the one who escaped?"

It can't be real, can it?

In the breath-space between question and answer, she can hear industrious muffle. Keys being tapped and screens beeping and conversations just out of reach. Expectation burns in her chest. She has been suspended here before, in the Venn diagram center of fear, hope, and disbelief. A glass ceiling ready to shatter over her.

. . . the rows of screens showing destinations start to flicker, the train times disappearing, the list of stops wiped . . .

"I'm not strictly supposed to release that information over the phone," says the woman, whose name and rank have already slipped out of Carrie's brain. "But we can see the address you're calling from and your voice has passed the rudimentary verification match, so I will tell you that, yes, Ashley Curtiss is currently unaccounted for."

Every screen in the station is now black.

"So he really could be coming here? He could be heading to my home to try to snatch my daughter?"

"Mrs. Dabb, I trust you to remain calm and to keep this information restricted to yourself and the other members of your household. We don't want to start a panic among neighbors."

"I don't have any neighbors," she manages to say, but her voice is coming from deep underground. She's stepping onto the tracks, listening for the sizzle.

"I have dispatched a patrol car with specialist officers and they're on their way to you right now. I'm sure you've already done this, but I would like you to check all of your doors and windows again. Double-lock them where possible and stay inside."

SEEK IMMEDIATE SHELTER.

"And if you have any of those old sash windows that—"

"No," Carrie says, coming back to the surface. "None of my windows open from the outside. The whole cottage was fitted out after . . . after Mum."

"You should both stay at my place," Mary says, appearing in the doorway, her hearing aids back in her ears.

"Could we go to my mother-in-law's home?" Carrie asks.

"It's really best you stay exactly where you are; our helicopter will be passing over in under a minute and the patrol car is already en route."

"What do we do if he turns up before the police?" Carrie says.

"Just remain calm, stay inside, and do not answer the door to anyone except uniformed officers who arrive in a Devon and Cornwall Police patrol car, do you understand?"

"Yes," she says. *But no, no, I don't understand anything. Nothing about what's happening today, or what happened ten years ago.*

"If we need to contact you, we will use this number, so make sure you keep the line clear."

She replaces the handset and looks at Mary, who stares back. "I don't know what to say," Carrie says. Upstairs, the shower shudders to a stop and they both look up at the ceiling.

"What was she thinking?" Mary says.

"You know exactly what she was thinking." Carrie flops down on the bottom step of the stairs. The toe of her slipper boot touches an invisible tideline on the wooden floor and she snaps it back. The cleaning company that Pepper arranged had removed all trace of her mother's blood, tidied away Janet's last meal, scrubbed the mud and road mess dragged in by Frankie Drake's feet; all the other damage, the horror, was neatly tidied away. But she can see it anyway, lit up neon.

"You warned me years ago," Carrie says, thudding her forehead with the heel of her hand. "You said I had to tell her something or she'd fill in the blanks by herself. And I made up something stupid about meeting someone on holiday before me and Emma . . ."

Mary puts a hand on her shoulder. "You did your best," she says. "That's all any of us can do."

The bathroom door opens on the floor above them, the fan noise switching off with the light. Bunny plods along the landing, one step, two steps, three, four, five to her little bedroom. The same one Carrie slept in every night until she left for university.

Her bedroom door creaks open, rattling the bags, coats, and hoodies hung on the back of it.

They hear a gasp, a muffled cry, and then the growl of a man's voice.

Part Three

AFTERMATH

One Year Later

DISPATCHES FROM LONDON: "THE WALLS"
By Maria Fortescue for *The New York Times*
November 14, 2026

For some, the memorials at the seaside mean the most. Every port, cove, and promenade sent its waves of little boats out, swollen with people, to take their chance on the open water.

Overfilled vessels, swaying wildly, captained by amateurs or overpowered fishing folk. A few bottles of water as their only defense, no room for food, hardly enough life jackets. Better that small chance of survival than a certain death. Waiting on land that would poison them, if they weren't burned to dust by the air. Maybe not immediately, but soon.

Now every port, cove, and promenade has an engraved list, some with names in their hundreds, while tiny coastal villages may have just one memorialized name. Either way, grief is quotidian in these communities.

For some, London's suicide wall gets the flowers. A long, gray, wispy structure, running alongside the Broad Walk in the famous Regent's Park. Around the country, people drank bleach, or swallowed all the painkillers in the house. Parents laid their children out in their beds, and then lay down next to them. Anything to avoid the terror of what came next.

The majority of London's suicides jumped into the Thames. Many were washed out to the estuary, resurfacing in Essex waters some forty miles due east, or not at all. Some were sucked into the thin gray mud that fringes the old river to be later found by mudlarks, a different bounty from their usual coins and old bottles. This is how many Britons learned that the Thames is tidal.

It's not officially called the suicide wall, of course, it is called the Wall of the Lost. But nobody uses that name. The site of the Broad Walk for this memorial is either particularly poignant or particularly pointed, depending on one's outlook. It was here that the King, the Queen, and various appendages were collected by army plane and zipped away. Through air that was about to spoil, away from ground that would soon be scorched.

The belly of the plane surged over the roof of the little Regent's Park café, stuffed with people who, at that point, were still busily upending tables to push against windows and were not yet crushing one another into the back wall in the scramble for space. A memorial plaque is now mounted on the wall nearest the serving hatch where fistfuls of ice creams and popsicles will be distributed in summer.

But even before those commemorated people had died, the royal plane had already zoomed up to the top of the country. At Aberdeen Airport in Scotland, it landed in a fenced section away from the (mostly) men offering what was left of their oil money and everything else they owned, for a seat on a plane out of Britain. Not always for themselves, often for their children, wives, or girlfriends. But yes, sometimes for themselves. The warnings had said that missiles were headed to the South of England. But oil men, rig men, they know wind. They know weather. They know how disasters travel, that even the sea can catch on fire. And so, they were as desperate as any southerner for escape.

But the King and his entourage did not have to see those men because the King and his entourage were already being collected from their special fenced-off section by an unmarked black helicopter. They were whisked up and over the rough sea, over the tumbling little boats, and out to join the *Hebridean Duchess*. Not a royal yacht, but a commandeered passenger vessel, emptied of normal people who instead crowded on the shore and begged at the airport. It was heading toward Greenland when the good news came through and the ferry began its slow turnaround. The royal family remained intact for another thirty-seven days.

The King's last action before public grief crushed any hope of rehabilitation was to establish a Royal Commission inquiry into what went wrong. And, in invisible parentheses, why none of what happened was his institution's fault. The prime minister at the time responded by establishing a public inquiry into how the country's missile detection and civil defense systems were so comprehensively infiltrated and why Britain's NATO partners did not promise to launch a retaliation. And, in invisible parentheses, why none of what happened was his cabinet's fault. Several NATO partners were quick to release statements saying that they could not threaten a retaliatory strike when no state had been identified as launching the missiles, because the missiles in question did not exist. That the rogue actors were technically unaffiliated with any state, no matter what some intelligence may now indicate. (And it wasn't our fault.)

The oval-shaped "murder and accident" wall, iced with polished brass that glints like a blade, sits near the center of London's St. James's Park. Officially the Wall of the Fallen, it is constructed on a large plinth rising from the middle of a pretty lake. A belly button equidistant from Buckingham Palace and Downing Street, so loaded with names, more and more pouring still from the emergency courts, that the architects had to revise their plans a second, third, and fourth time, to fit the never-ending list of people in type large enough to read, while leaving space for more.

There is no wall for the rape victims. Partly because there is no official record of how many spent their perceived final 59 minutes that way. And besides, whose name would be chiseled? No. There is no wall for the rapes.

The (now former) prime minister wasn't in Number Ten Downing Street when the warning came; the prime minister was on the way back from a ceremonial ribbon cutting of a new center for Border Security Command.

Despite the liveried cars, bikes, elephantine Range Rovers, and even some uniformed police on bicycles surrounding the car, it took twelve minutes to get the prime ministerial cargo to the nearest helipad. By the time they arrived, all but two police bikes had been swallowed up along the way.

According to sources, this time lag was a failing in the plans, a "learning," but at least the stilted journey had allowed the prime minister to record a message for distribution to all broadcasters, who were told that the prime minister was speaking from a secure location rather than an entourage nosing through the same clogged roads as everyone else. The country will continue, the message suggested, even if you people listening are cauterized from its surface. If it was reassuring at the time, no one says so now.

From the helipad, the prime minister and their team were choppered up and down in just three minutes, arriving at the entrance to the Ministry of Defence Pindar Bunker under Whitehall.

The underground broadcast studio was readied for further speeches to the country, and the prime minister was all set to deliver exactly the right tone all over again. But then a new briefing began.

And still, it took twelve further minutes to tell the country there was no missile.

Six hundred and twenty-two of the names on those walls died in that time.

Chapter Seventy-Nine

CARRIE

St. James's Park
One Year Later

The sun will not rise for another two hours but here it is always light. Pale-pink bulbs have been strung along the little bridges connecting the main park to the memorial wall at the center of the lake, and tiny pinprick lights are dotted among the names like constellations of stars. The polished brass, which runs along the top of the large oval structure, glows in the lingering moonlight.

From this distance, the thousands of tiny names are impossible to make out. But Carrie cannot will her legs to move closer yet. She stands at the lake's edge and watches the wind toy with the surface of the water that surrounds the murder and accident wall. Or, to give it its official title, the Wall of the Fallen.

People in small somber clusters sit on the many benches, their plaques named for the donating families. Others, like her, stand cautiously, as if awaiting permission. But from whom, she couldn't say.

Flowers slump along the bottom of the wall, as if washed there by a tide. She feels stupid in her empty-handedness. She left the Airbnb in Clapham in a hurry before dawn, unsure she would be able to face coming here at all, rushing out before her nerves failed.

The streets had been busier than expected, grim-faced insomniacs pacing through Battersea Park wearing headphones or staring out at the Thames from Chelsea Bridge, newly gilded with memorial plaques. The pavements running around Victoria were peppered with ghosts, watched over by empty buildings, their tenants moving out to Birmingham, Manchester, or Glasgow, or simply unable to coax traumatized staff back into huge glass buildings.

Carrie herself never went back to work, never even contacted them. They paid her for a few months and then stopped. A letter was probably sent, or an email—she hasn't thought to check. She wonders now, for the first time, how many staff her agency lost. Either during the 59 minutes or after. People she once ate lunch with, worked late with, talked about behind their backs. To think she'd ever cared about that work, that any of them had. After the alert, ad campaigns for cat food and credit cards seemed suddenly as important as they really were, which is to say not important at all. She has enough from her inheritance, her mum's solid NHS pension, to live simply without work for at least several years.

She would be incapable now anyway. Getting up each day, living a guilty widow's half-life while trying to be a whole parent, that takes every part of her.

She only opened her laptop once in those last London weeks, drifting automatically to clunky web versions of social platforms, awash with all the footage and thoughts no one had been able to share during the network blackout. She closed her computer with a snap after a few minutes of exposure. It now lies furred with dust under the bed that used to be her mother's. She is not exactly a member of the growing smartphone liberation movement, but she doesn't ever want to look at a cell phone screen again and she would never believe what is written there.

Back in Clapham, her daughter sleeps on in the double bed they slept in together last night. For the last year, they have shared a bed every night. Clementine clinging to Barnaby, her little forehead frowning in sleep, while Carrie watches, unable to sleep, until it's nearly morning. Clementine sometimes still cries out for Mama when she wakes, but far less often than before. Which somehow hurts more.

Clementine has started asking to be called by her middle name, Bunny. A victory Emma has missed out on, among so many others. It will probably just be a phase.

Carrie plans to be back before she wakes but knows that Pepper, sleeping in the second room of the benign all-white apartment, will feed and distract her daughter if she wakes early. Jam sandwiches for breakfast or sugary cereal, no one cares much about these things now. When he visited Carrie last month, he had asked, "Would you like to stay at my place when you come, *kochanie*?" He needed no explanation when she shook her head.

Although Carrie has not been in the city for many months, she knew the route here instinctively. Infected with the knowledge that all Londoners, whether émigré or native, find it hard to ever shake. In her final few weeks in the city, before leaving for Dartmoor, Carrie had barely left Pepper's flat, screaming into his pillows or trailing needfully after Clementine, grabbing at her, hugging her until she fought to get away. Carrie did not go out onto the street unless absolutely unavoidable, and then walked a pretzel route to avoid certain spots. She has certainly not been this close to the center until today. Too many people. Too much London. Too many memories.

She has promised to visit Grace and her family, to take Clementine for lunch at their flat on Elm Walk. If she can stand to get that close to Prince's Square. And then, the long train home and back for bedtime in the cottage. Where she will lie next to Clementine's sleeping body and replay those last seconds, fighting for her life and ruining it at the very same time. More than replay, relive. Nausea sweeping over her, her hearing faltering, forgetting to breathe or breathing too fast. But right now, she is numb.

The names on the wall are alphabetical. She crosses the bridge for D to F.

Chapter Eighty

FRANKIE

St. James's Park
One Year Later

Frankie has parked somewhere stupid. The kind of place people who live in London would know not to park in. A side street, but with lines she's never seen before. Zigzagged red? Can't be good. She'll find out when the ticket arrives.

A little bird dances on the top of a dog waste bin. He stops strutting and looks at her, head tilted. For the last year, she's struggled to look at birds. Imagining, every time, their wingtips in flame, their bodies popping in midair and just disappearing. More than people, more than animals, it's the birds that get her. They would have all vanished, just like that. Yet this little bird, with his proudly puffed stomach, fluffy feathers cuffing the tops of his pencil-line legs, he just goes right on living. He doesn't even know that there are things in the world that could end all life, including his. She watches him in envy, forcing herself not to look away, but he loses interest in her and flies off. She takes another step.

This park is grander than it looked on TV. The scale of this place, the length of the lake, and that huge slab of misery in the middle seem extraordinary. Like a blockbuster setting. Ideal for a disaster movie.

At the far end, the specter of Buckingham Palace recedes into the background, weird without its Beefeaters and horses. The flags along the nearby Mall are lowered to half-staff, drooping like fuchsias. A few people are here already, moving uneasily in little clusters, squatting on benches or behind windbreaks, staking claims to parcels of land ahead of the crowds. It reminds her of the Coronation a few years ago, which she'd observed through rolled eyes. As a small-business owner, she did not even benefit from the day off.

She wonders if any of the royal dregs will be watching from Greece and America, or if they are too busy penning groveling explain-alls or practicing for *Dancing with the Stars*.

On one of the nearest benches, a man and woman sit together. "Poor Mum," the woman sobs, over and over. The man sits in silent concern, not quite touching her. Siblings, perhaps, although Seb would be hugging her back, probably crying too. They would have missed Mam, even if now she's driving them mad. Practically asking to move in with Frankie and Otis, to help with the baby. Luckily flights get more expensive by the month, keeping her at bay, but only somewhat.

There were no hotel rooms available to book when Frankie decided, just yesterday afternoon, to come down to see the wall. Of course there weren't any beds. Millions of people are expected to pour into the capital today, the highest number since November last year, and hotels have been grub-handedly upping their prices since the great grief jamboree was announced.

Otis didn't understand her sudden decision, but they were used to navigating that. Gaps that were without feeling for him had to be explained, smoke holes where memories should be. When she told him she wanted to pay her respects to Janet Spencer, he understood, but he did not feel the same need. He was sad for her and her family, but he blamed the Curtiss brothers for everything. Otis carried no guilt for what had happened during the 59 minutes, and did not understand why Frankie did. He'd never even met Janet, never saw her house, and seemed never to think of her unless Frankie brought it up. But if Frankie hadn't gone to Janet's house, Janet would still be alive. Her daughter and granddaughter would not have lost her. She cannot ever stop thinking about Janet, it's literally the least she can do.

Thorne Junius Drake is only four months old and it seems *insane* that he is currently hundreds of miles away. She can feel a physical pull to him, as if the umbilical cord were tangled around Frankie's spine, tugging. But he is safe. Right now, he is in his warm home. In theory, he is being looked after by Otis, but with Otis not-quite-recovered, maybe-never-recovering, he's really being looked after by Otis's mum, Jo. They'll be elbowing each other over who gets to give the morning bottle.

Frankie had always intended to breastfeed, but when Thorne was born, she just couldn't do it. When pushed, she told her health visitor it was fear of the discomfort, but this was not true. As she'd held his little mouth to her chest in those first tender moments, she was seized by the thought that she would pass poison to her baby through her milk. A mangled cultural memory from long before she was born, the Windscale nuclear plant fire and fears over atomic milk from nearby cows. A nightmare she knows is not true. There was no bomb. It didn't just *not go off*, it never existed. And despite the British government's attempts to blame eco-activists and anyone else it suited, it has become clear that it was a hoax designed by an enemy state and enacted by state-sponsored hackers to cause their rival to destroy itself.

But she couldn't shake the fear. When she looked online, tumbling down the Mumsnet rabbit hole, she learned she wasn't the only one with this phobia. Which helped and didn't. Otis has an ongoing tremor and Jo plays fast and loose with measurements, so Frankie made up more than enough bottles before she left last night. Looking at them lined up like little soldiers almost stopped her going. Saying goodbye took hours and she finally stopped crying around Stafford.

Chapter Eighty-One

MRS. CARRIE DABB

November 14, 2035
Ten Years Later

Carrie is running up the stairs, Mary following slowly, creakily behind. "No," she hisses down the stairs at her, "call the police back, call 999." Mary ricochets back down to the hallway as Carrie reaches the landing.

"Bunny!"

She pushes at the bedroom door but it doesn't open. There's no lock or bolt; something or someone must be pushed against it.

She presses her ear to the old wood, some part of her expecting it to have a heartbeat. She can hear the scuff-muffle of feet on carpet, the sound of whispering or maybe . . . maybe a mouth covered by thick, rough fingers, trying to cry out.

I want my mum.

The thought bubbles up from her chest. An ancient well, sprung. But Mum is not here. Dad is not here. Emma is not here. Pepper is not here. *I need to save her myself.*

"Is that you, Ashley?" The name is sour on her tongue, too big for her mouth. He doesn't reply, but she hears Bunny whimper.

"I think it is you, Ashley. And . . ." Her vision is whiting out, her ears roar with fear. She is disposing of a bomb with no training. Her daughter is in there, packed with dynamite.

"Ashley?" She waits, but he doesn't reply. "Ashley, I don't know what to say to you. I don't . . . I don't know what to say because you're scaring me and I think you're scaring Bunny too. And I . . . I don't think you want to scare her or upset her."

"You lied to me."

She has not heard his voice in nearly nine years, and then it was only to confirm his name and his not-guilty plea. His legal team hadn't put him forward as a witness. She had watched from the corner of the public gallery, huddled with Pepper, trying to understand who he really was, and how she could ever have been intimate with someone who now seemed so monstrous, so gigantic.

She sucks in a breath. "I didn't tell you about . . . about the baby, yeah. So I guess I lied by omission." She braces for a reply, but none comes. Even Bunny isn't making a sound.

Oh god, what is he doing to her in there?

"And then when you found out, I admit that . . . yeah, I denied it over and over because . . . because you'd just killed my mother."

She presses her cheek hard against the wooden door, grinding her cheekbone and desperately trying to find the thread of a sound from inside. A thread she could pluck and follow, that would lead her to Bunny being okay. But there is only silence now. She waits.

"You never gave me a chance," he says finally. There is a strain in his voice, like it's costing him to find any volume. "If I'd known about her, about my kid, I wouldn't have . . . I would have been different."

"Do you really believe that?" She holds her breath; she is dealing with a wild animal and just made too-sudden a movement. Downstairs, Mary talks quickly into the phone. Above, the *flap-flap-flap* of metal dragonfly wings is moving closer. He must hear the helicopter too. She is crouching, shrinking from it. From its ten-year-long shadow. She can smell burning, but it's not real. This closed door in front of her, that is what's real.

The door opens inward so fast that she stumbles, nearly falling onto the carpet. Bunny is sitting on the bed, wrapped in Pepper's burgundy dressing gown, her beautiful dark curly hair whipped up in a towel, her face pink-scrubbed. Ashley is still gripping the door handle with one of his big hands. In the other is the knife she herself grabbed from the kitchen drawer earlier. She knows how sharp it is but Carrie rushes past it anyway and leaps onto the bed next to Bunny.

She kisses Bunny's face, puts her own body in front of her, and then turns to face him. His own curly hair is grayed and almost gone. He has Bunny's chin. Her eyes.

"I don't care what you do to me," Carrie says, "but I will not let you hurt her."

He looks down at the knife, shakes his head, and lets it droop but does not put it down. "I would never . . ." He runs out of words and slumps, scrawny in his clothes. A gray hoodie and what look like suit trousers and black clumpy shoes.

The helicopter is circling, the light flashing through the room and across the bed like a beacon. "My lift is here," he says, his Devon accent soft. No one laughs.

"You know I didn't hurt your granny on purpose, don't you?" he says to Bunny, stepping closer so she shrinks back against the wall, squashing the piled duvet, the army of teddies. She is shaking, the slippery folds of the satin dressing gown shimmering with the movement.

"You're scaring me," Bunny says.

"My mum told you that already, didn't she?" Ashley says. "She told you I never meant to hurt your granny and you said you believed it."

Bunny stares at him, then at her mother. "I didn't . . . I don't know . . ."

"I believe you, Ashley," Carrie says. "I think you would have just taken the Hail Mary sentence otherwise."

"Everyone wanted me to," he says. "But then she'd think I really did it." He's pointing the knife at Bunny but realizes what he's doing and moves it away. "And I couldn't have that."

He puts the knife on the floor beside him, his knees audibly cracking with the movement. He looks twenty years older than he is, but Carrie probably does too. A whole generation probably does.

"I heard what you said about me earlier," he says.

"What?"

"I came in through the kitchen to grab her and take her with me, force her to listen." He closes his eyes and sags, he looks exhausted, but Carrie remains rigid.

"Seeing her in the church like that, it was . . . it was a really big feeling. And then when she left, I just . . . I just want to have a chance to talk to her, to my daughter. I wanted to make her see I wasn't the man they all said I was. The papers an' that. Some monster. And I wanted her to know why I hated you, Carrie, for keeping her from me. . . ."

Carrie reaches for Bunny's hand. It quivers in her own like a mouse.

"But when I came in, I heard you talking about me and I went onto the cellar stairs to hide so I could listen. And what you said, Carrie . . . I got it. I got why you'd lied to her. I would have lied to her. And if I'd grabbed her again, if I'd taken her, I really would have been a monster. So I just needed to explain, just this one time." He swallows and looks at Bunny, who flinches.

"What do you want to explain to her?" Carrie says. "Because you have a chance now."

"I'm not good with words. You said I looked sad in church, Clementine, but I wasn't sad, I was proud. I've done one good thing in my life, even if I didn't know it. And I want to say that I'm sorry you got a dad like me but you're not bad."

Bunny stares back at him, unblinking.

"You said earlier you were half of me and that I'm bad, but none of you is bad, girl. Any good I have in me came from my mum. I didn't know that until it was too late, but it's true. But all your goodness came from your mum."

He looks at Carrie and sighs. "Of course you didn't want her to know about me."

Downstairs, the front door opens and boots thump up the stairs.

"I really am sorry about your mum, Carrie," he says, his voice thick. "She was just trying to help me." He walks slowly toward the noise. "It's okay," he calls. "You can come and get me."

Heavy boots crowd the tiny bedroom, scuffing schoolbooks and teddy bears. Two of them hold Ashley in place as another handcuffs him, a slick, calm movement. "Please don't punish my mum for what I did," he says to Carrie.

Mary has stepped inside the bedroom and stares at him now. "It's always the mums who suffer," she says.

Chapter Eighty-Two

CARRIE

**St. James's Park
One Year Later**

Emma Dabb is now level with Carrie's shoulder.

Even though Carrie knew Emma's name was on this wall, even though her mum and John came here for the official unveiling last month, she is still stunned that it's true. That Emma, *her Emma*, has been immortalized in this way. A pseudo celebrity. At once publicly infamous and one of too large a group to ever be truly known. What's the Stalin quote . . . *A single death is a tragedy, a million deaths are a statistic.*

But Emma's absence *is* a tragedy and she doesn't belong with these neighbors—these Dabrals, Dabengwas, Dangs, and Davids—people she never met.

Emma Dabb, eight dead letters unequivocally chiseled into the wall by a hand steadier than Carrie's. She lifts her fingers slowly to trace the letters, but she can't do it. Can't bear to touch this evidence. Her arm aches like a warning as she drops her hand limply again.

She and Clementine are both full Dabbs now, changed by deed poll. It's not much, but it's something to call herself Mrs. Dabb, for both members of the parenting unit to be represented by name. She wears Emma's ruby ring on her wedding finger, a ring given to Emma by her mother and John for her eighteenth birthday, plucked from her body by Pepper before thieves came for it. A sentence that is so horrific it must be fiction but is somehow truth. She spins it now, slightly too big but she cannot bring herself to have it adjusted. It must remain untouched.

A man approaches the wall. He's wearing a Ban the Bomb hoodie, with a Campaign for Nuclear Disarmament logo she's seen a lot during her brief return to the city. Until recently, she hadn't seen a CND badge since childhood, and even back then it was retro. The man wavers, as if looking for the right section of wall, then walks around to the other side. At his side, a small bunch of flowers he's gripping tightly is shedding petals.

Carrie came this early to avoid the crowds, with which she has not been good since last year and can't imagine ever trusting again. But there are already more people here than she expected.

A group of protestors assemble near the drinking fountain in woolly hats and puffy coats. They stamp their feet and blow into cupped hands. Some have reusable cups, others clutch single-use bottles of water, which aren't sold anymore in Chagford, where she now lives. The protestors' heads huddle as if in conference, the glow of streetlights from Birdcage Walk illuminating the bobbles of their hats like Christmas decorations.

Some protesters have signs that dangle by their sides, or sit propped against trees. A mixture of ages, genders and ethnicities, they wear jeans, baggy leggings, or joggers, stuffed into sneakers or boots. Probably expecting to be on their feet for hours, but they'll be lucky to last an hour unhampered once the sun comes up. The Met have made no secret of plans to arrest protestors again, according to Pepper, who worried she'd be mistaken for one. Carrie can't make out most of the signs from here, but a middle-aged woman in a mustard scarf twists her placard around and the black block letters sit in stark relief to the white backing board.

STOP THE GET-OUT-OF-JAIL-FREE CARDS!

The emergency Hail Mary laws were only applied to people who pleaded guilty, and Carrie did not plead guilty to anything. She has never told the truth to anyone but Pepper. She took that truth away from Emma's family, and no one but them ever looked for it. Even Mary has stopped asking.

The police initially warned her that Ashley Curtiss would likely be eligible for an express sentence, but he has refused to plead guilty. Instead, the woman and the girl that he and his brothers kidnapped will have to come to court to relive that day, and autopsies and statements about her mother's last moments will be pinned up and pored over by a jury.

Ashley Curtiss has asked for her to visit him in remand prison repeatedly; his solicitor has sent several letters that she has burned without reading. He is pleading not guilty, claiming it was an accident. Some people are not brave enough to admit what they have done, and it turns out she and he are birds of a feather in that respect. And yet, the child made from their combined genes is the kindest, most caring girl. She can never know who her biological father is, can never be forced to wonder at the blood sloshing through her, and the poison it could carry. This will be Carrie's sole focus from now on.

Chapter Eighty-Three

FRANKIE

St. James's Park
One Year Later

It should have taken four and a half hours for Frankie to reach London, but the southbound motorways were filled with tentative traffic, people heading to take up those prebooked hotel rooms. As she drove slowly and cautiously down the M6 and M1 last night, she tried to forget the death toll claimed by those roads, whose banks are still dusted in memorial flowers. She turned the radio on but it was a gobshite phone-in, tinfoil-hatters blaming 5G masts for the false alert, others who still believe that a missile did strike offshore and that everyone in the UK is slowly being poisoned. The reality, it seems, is too plausible to be true.

Around midnight, eyes raw from concentrating on driving, she pulled into London Gateway services, tucked the car into a dark corner away from the trucks, and climbed into the back seat, sleeping—sort of—until four. When she woke, she headed straight here.

The memorial wall runs almost the full length of the lake, stopping just before the empty playground at one end and a little island with a cottage on it at the other. Here, more than any other part of London she passed through this morning, she can begin to imagine what the city must have looked like during the 59 minutes.

There were undoubtedly children playing over there, snatched suddenly out of swings, pulled off still-spinning merry-go-rounds, by parents and grandparents, nannies and au pairs, with tourists and Londoners screaming in a million languages. She's seen enough of that kind of footage to picture it, the videos taken by shaking hands, with no way to upload it then, just recording while they still could. She's watched it all, read every memoir, bought fattened newspapers and magazines for photos of the first baby born who had been conceived during the 59 minutes. A whole crop of them within a four-week window, from the early labors to latest, the earliest born prematurely a few weeks before Thorne. She's read everyone's accounts, everyone's confessions, searching for some insight, some path to follow. But they're all on a different track from her.

Maybe it would have been easier in the city. A simple, bloody fight for survival. Unlike Dartmoor, so shrouded in mist, literally and figuratively. Even now her memories are gray, faces and moments blanked out, dreams filling in the details sometimes, but wrong, distorted. More gruesome, less. More unlucky, more deliberate.

Frankie is swaying. She keeps doing this when she's not holding Thorne, rocking handbags, coats, Seb and Nicole's cat, who loves it. Her hands feel stupid and empty without her baby, and she fills them without thinking whenever he is asleep or with Otis in the bed, or having a cuddle with a cousin or a grandparent.

Now the light, bristly weight of the dried flower bouquet has taken the place of her warm baby. And worse, she's got that zoned-out staring thing going on, which apparently, according to both Seb and Otis, she's been doing a lot.

Ahead of her, the monolithic memorial wall is one great mass. The individual names so plentiful that they are invisible to her, blending into the surface.

Behind her, a group of protestors have picked up their signs and pulled on big white matching T-shirts over their coats. The fronts of the T-shirts say THEY'VE GOT AWAY WITH MURDER. A woman turns around and on her back it says CANCEL HAIL MARY SENTENCES.

If Ashley Curtiss had pleaded guilty, taken one of those sentences, he'd be getting out soon. Would he have come to find her and Otis? To find everyone she loves and punish them too? He blames her and Otis for everything, the police have made that clear.

Instead, by refusing to plead guilty and thus forcing a court hearing, he joins the queue. Now all of them must wait in limbo to be called up to give evidence. She worries most about Juno, whom she talks to constantly on WhatsApp, the only other person who knows what it was like to be in that truck. The brave girl who came back for her, brought help, and saved Otis's life and maybe Frankie's too. Mark and Nathan, the witnesses to the aftermath, the men who stopped Ashley getting away, they will have to come to the stand, eventually. Otis won't. His memory problems are considered too severe for him to be of any value. He knows she's nervous about reliving the "ordeal" and has fussed around her and tried to help. It has only made her feel more guilty.

Ahead of her, a woman stands gripping the handrail as if it's the only thing holding her up.

Chapter Eighty-Four

MRS. CARRIE DABB

November 14, 2035
Ten Years Later

The two police officers who remain at Carrie's cottage politely eat their way through the scones and the cake. They are too big for the seats, bulked by their padded vests and tall in their masculinity. They hold Carrie's mother's best teacups carefully in their thick fingers.

Synchronized, the officers both press a finger to their ears and look at each other.

"What is it?" she says, her back pressed to the sink, watching.

One officer nods to the other, who says, "They just picked up the cousin."

Ashley had said it wasn't premeditated, but his cousin Flynn had been outside the church right on cue. When the side doors flew open and Ashley ran out, he was able to get straight in and slide under a blanket in the back. Ashley was dropped off near Chagford as requested while Flynn went to his girlfriend's house to cobble together an alibi. Which, the officers say, has already fallen apart.

The service rattles on in the other room, unwatched by Carrie for the first time. It's also the first year that Carrie hasn't called Grace on the anniversary. She will call her tomorrow at Beverley's, where she'll be celebrating her brother Josh's birthday. A teenager now; Carrie has witnessed him growing up almost entirely through sound in the background of their calls.

Some years, the calls have been near silent. A holding of hands more than a conversation. Other calls over the years have been almost giddy. A sickening hysteria to their recollections. About rat man. And the people copping off on the lawn. They often talk up the idea of Carrie visiting on the anniversary, bringing Bunny and eating Nando's and Papa Johns, gulping down Dr Pepper and thick shakes. They both know that will never happen, but it's a sweet distraction. When Grace was eighteen, she nearly chose Exeter University to study for her physics degree. Carrie desperately wanted her nearby while feeling sick at the idea of regular contact and year-round reminiscences. When Grace chose Imperial College London instead, both were relieved.

Curled up with Mary in the living room, Bunny is still wearing Pepper's dressing gown. She always does when she's missing him. It was Richard Burton's gown, he claimed, though she has no real idea who that is. And of course, they're both missing Pepper more than usual today. He died nearly four years ago. Until then, he joined them here for every anniversary of the 59 minutes except when the 2029 floods trapped him in London. That was just before he was evacuated to a new build in Crystal Palace, where he saw out his days. There are tenants living there now, in the small property inherited by Carrie and Bunny. Impossible for them to live in—just the thought of London gives her a head rush—but financing Carrie's unending unemployment since her mother's pension ran out.

Pepper was the only one who knew everything that happened that day. When he died, her secret died with him. She set it down in the coffin. The notes he wrote that day, along with his favorite knickknacks, were placed all around him like an Egyptian queen. God, she misses him. He was her life raft in the deadly waters of aftermath. Bunny—then still Clementine—had clung bewildered to her remaining mother's neck and Carrie had tried furiously to kick herself to the surface, but without Pepper, they both would have drowned. He didn't know Janet but arranged her funeral and propped Carrie up throughout. And then, months later, he kept her breathing as they said goodbye to Emma.

She had known precisely what Emma wanted for her funeral. They'd talked about it, through pure chance, just a few weeks before the alert. "This is it," Emma said, when "Crazy in Love" came on in a pub where they were taking Clementine for lunch. "This is what I want at my funeral."

And Carrie had played along that day because death is hilarious when it is theoretical.

A disco, Emma said. Not even a party, not a club night, she wanted her funeral to be like an old-school disco. She couldn't have known, how could she? Sitting there with a doorstop sandwich, a split portion of fries sopping with ketchup. Two great big glasses of orange juice and lemonade and their legs just touching under the table. How could Emma have known? She wasn't magic, even though she was. To Carrie, she was.

People from school lined the pews, even Charlotte Upton, who'd broken Emma's heart and avoided Carrie's eye. Old teachers came too, people from uni, a few colleagues. Some of them had never met Carrie and she heard them whisper, "I think that's the girlfriend." When the beat of the music started, a surprised laugh rippled through them all.

Carrie sat in the front pew with Mary, John, and Clementine, who worked so hard to stay still and not fidget that she shook with the effort. Pepper sat just behind with his hand on Carrie's shoulder throughout. When Beyoncé finished, the celebrant described a version of Emma as if she herself loved her. And all Carrie could think about was Emma's flame-red hair, matted with blood.

Emma was so particular about her hair. Carrie was only ever trusted to straighten the back, and even then Emma would critique her handiwork. Oh god, and that time she went to the retro salon and they made her look like a founding father instead of a rockabilly Instagram girl. That time her mum cut her bangs and she looked like Janet Street-Porter. Always a disaster when anyone but Emma did it. But when Emma did it, she looked like a cartoon character. Like Jessica Rabbit. April O'Neil. *Who did her hair before they laid her in the coffin?*

"It's okay, darling," Mary had said, as Carrie's breathing quickened and her vision whited out and Clementine shook even more next to her. "It's okay."

"I'm so sorry," Carrie managed, the words more breath than word, her face wet with tears she could barely feel. And they had gripped one another as the celebrant woman rattled on, describing a facsimile of the girl, the woman, that Emma had been, barely able to measure the size of the hole left behind.

"I'm sorry too," Mary had whispered. "Your mum and now . . ."

"I promise I will always be there," Carrie said suddenly. "Not the same, but . . ."

And Mary had threaded her fingers through Carrie's and linked them, bone-tight. When John died, it was Carrie who held Mary upright. She told herself that's what Emma would have wanted. But living like this . . . small and frightened. Emma would never have wanted this.

Chapter Eighty-Five

CARRIE

St. James's Park
One Year Later

Carrie's vision swirls, the D, E, and F names twisting and dissolving, until she looks down at her feet instead. This oval wall is huge, a great slab of stone and metal, eye-shaped from above. She backs away, nauseated by the sheer scale.

Before she leaves, she must visit her mother's name. Her mother whose death did not stand on its own merits at first, but simply compounded the loss and guilt Carrie was already feeling so that only now, really, is Carrie starting to recognize the depth of that unique grief. The loss of her only remaining parent, the loss of a safety net, of the only two people who had witnessed her childhood close up. Her baby years.

As an orphan, albeit an adult one, does part of her cease to exist?

Now Carrie follows the wide walkway around, past the G's, H's, and I's and on through the letters, turning past M and then back around the other side. At R, suddenly dizzy, she stops and grips the handrail that runs alongside the edge of the plinth. When this wall first opened, a young man drowned himself here. If it weren't for Clementine, would she have thrown herself in the lake like that man? Yes. She absolutely would. Maybe that man's wife died that day too. Maybe that man killed her. Either way, she didn't dare read any of the coverage that followed. As the papers raked through his story, she backed away from the headlines. She couldn't take on anyone else's grief.

There was also a risk of hardening herself to other people's suffering, simply through overexposure. And that wouldn't do either.

Farther up the lake, a duck flips itself over, fluffy bum poking up and head in the water. *That is me,* Carrie thinks, *that is how I will survive.*

There is a woman hovering near the edge of the lake, holding a spray of flowers, which she cradles like a baby. The flowers are dead or dried, and this unnerves Carrie, the not-quite-rightness of it eerie in this half-light of early morning. Carrie steps closer to S, for Spencer, just as the woman steps closer to the S-T-U bridge. They both stop. The woman is swaying slightly, back and forth. A maternal sway that has never fully left Carrie either. Arms that have cradled a baby never fully forget their job.

The woman is slightly taller than Carrie and maybe a few years older. She wears a long black double-breasted military coat with gold buttons. A black scarf bursts from her neck, black-and-white Converse high-tops stick out beneath the hem of her coat. Her dark hair is in a messy bun, the stylish kind Carrie has never been able to do. She's not even sure what she looks like right now, un-made-up, pasty face, dishwater hair? She doesn't care and hasn't for a year.

She looks down at her own clothes and is momentarily surprised by her black puffy jacket and jeans. Accidentally, a different version of the same outfit she wore a year ago today. She wants to tear it off and burn it like she tore off and threw away last year's clothes. She tugs at her own sleeve, and when she looks up, the woman is staring at her, pale-faced.

"Oh shit . . . I don't believe it," she says, with flat northern vowels. "You're Carrie."

Chapter Eighty-Six

FRANKIE

St. James's Park
One Year Later

Janet's daughter recoils slightly. She looks considerably older than she did in the picture, so washed-out she's almost monochrome where she was luminous and golden in Janet's hallway. "How do you know my name?" she says. Her voice is barely audible, the same soft accent Janet had.

Frankie can barely speak. "I . . . I didn't expect to . . . I'm sorry, I—"

Carrie backs away, just a tiny step. "Who are you?" she whispers. "Are you . . . did the family send you?" She looks behind her, a whipcrack movement.

"What family?" Frankie says, frowning and looking around too.

"The—" Carrie stops and stands straighter. She steps slightly closer, reclaiming the ground she gave up. "I said, how do you know my name?" Her expression has sharpened from bewilderment to determination and her voice is crisper, as no-nonsense as Janet had been.

I would like to look at that head wound before you pull the trigger.

"I . . . these are for your mother, Janet." Frankie gestures to the flowers, ashamed at their inadequacy. "I'm so sorry, Carrie, I was there. At the end, I mean."

"You're—"

"I'm Frankie. Francesca Drake, the one who . . . yeah, I'm her. And I'm so . . . god, I'm just so, so sorry."

"Why?" Carrie says, her voice painfully quiet again. "You didn't kill her." She looks tiny, a shriveled little fist in a puffy coat. Even her long, limp hair seems too big for her.

"No, I know I didn't but it's my fault he was there, Ash—"

"Don't say his name," Carrie says.

"Okay, I'm sorry. But he followed me, your mum was helping me and—"

"Followed you from where?"

"The truck. The place where he . . . where we all crashed."

"Are you saying that he knew you were there, at my mum's?" Carrie's eyes search Frankie's face.

"I don't . . . I don't actually know."

"And he grabbed you in the first place, right? That's why you were in the truck?"

"Yeah, well, one of his brothers did. Ash . . . *he* was driving, but, yeah—"

"So would you have been at my mother's house that afternoon if they hadn't grabbed you?" The words are conciliatory but the tone is angry, accusing.

"No," Frankie says, "but I still chose her house and I begged her to let me in."

"I can't . . . I don't have the bandwidth for someone else's guilt," Carrie says. "Especially when it's misplaced."

Frankie swallows. "Okay then," she says. "No more apologies."

"Good."

The park is filling up now. People arrive with fold-up chairs and coolers; a tuk-tuk food truck selling coffee rolls along the path and settles near the playground.

"Those flowers are beautiful," Carrie says.

Frankie looks at them in her hand. Roses hand-dyed a licorice purple, dried cream lilies, dusty-blue hydrangeas, hazelwood sticks, and a binding of forget-me-nots—those waxed rather than dried—wound throughout the chunkier flowers. She sets them down at the seam of the wall, below Janet's name. They jostle for space with other bouquets for other names, all at different states of decay.

"I hope she'd have liked them," Frankie says, then winces at such a trite thing to say.

Carrie smiles, though it looks like it causes her pain. "Bit trendy for my mum," she says, "but I like them." She looks at them again, stooping slightly to see better. "Yeah, actually," Carrie says softly, "I really like them. I wasn't sure before but . . . they're special. Different."

Frankie smiles then. An uneasy silence falls; neither woman knows how to end this moment.

After a pause, Frankie asks, "Where's your little girl?"

"She's with her fairy godfather," Carrie says, looking at her wrist as if she were wearing a watch. "And I should be getting—" But then she frowns. "How did you know I have a little girl?"

"Oh god, sorry." *What were you thinking, Frankie, you moron.* "Your mum . . . she showed Ashley, sorry, she showed *him* a picture of you and your partner and your little girl, just before—"

"Why the hell would she do that?"

Why did Frankie have to pick at this scab, telling Carrie about her mother's final moments when they'd just about it made it through this accidental meeting in one piece?

"Well," she says, trying to find the words. "Your mum was . . . asking . . . begging him to stop." Carrie visibly shudders, but Frankie plows on. "She was trying to get him to think about who he'd be hurting, who he had in his life that—"

"*His* life? What are you talking about?"

"I really had no idea," Frankie says. "I couldn't believe it when Janet said it, it was such an awful coincidence."

"What was?"

"The way he was connected to you and your mum."

Carrie sucks in a breath like she's been punched in the gut. "What do you mean," she says, her eyes saucered.

"What Janet said to him, to try to stop him, you know—"

"No, I don't know, what are you talking about?"

"Did the police not . . ." But had Frankie told it all to the police word for word? Had they even asked about who said what? The statement taking and the fingerprints and the charge of murder, it was all a rush job. Even the autopsy, amid a national crisis that saw overworked pathologists joined by medical students scraped from universities and handed scalpels. This much Frankie does know.

"Please," Carrie says, "what do you mean who he was to me and my mum?" She looks frantic now.

"Your mum, it's just . . . She told him that . . ." Frankie feels her mouth watering, a precursor to throwing up. How can she be telling this woman something so intimate about herself?

"What?" Carrie's nostrils flare with anger now. "What?" she hisses, stepping closer to Frankie.

"She told him that . . . I mean, maybe it was bollocks or just the panic or something she just made up or . . ."

"Oh no, she didn't—"

"She told him that your kid, your daughter . . . she said he was the father."

Carrie recoils like she's been shot. Eyes mirroring Janet's in the split second after the bang. Frankie hadn't seen a resemblance until now.

"He knows?" Carrie whispers. "He knows about my daughter?"

Frankie nods. *Those eyes.* She looks down.

"He's been trying to get letters to me and I've just . . . I thought they were apology letters and I burned them. Oh fuck," Carrie says, her face turning a yellow-gray as she staggers backward into the handrail. Frankie rushes forward and grips Carrie's waist through her coat as her legs buckle. Under the padding of the slippery coat, her body feels tiny, her breathing erratic. "He knows?" Carrie says. Frankie nods, just once. Their faces are inches apart. She can smell tea on Carrie's breath.

"Did you tell anyone else what my mum said? The police or . . . anyone?"

"I don't . . . I don't know. I don't think so. But, like . . . isn't it a motive?"

Carrie stares back at her like she's insane. "I don't care," she says. "No one can know. He can't have my daughter, he can't . . . none of that lot, they can't have her."

"But he already knows," Frankie says softly.

"Who will believe him? If you don't tell anyone that part, then he could just be making things up."

"But DNA tests? Couldn't he . . . I don't know, like, ask for one?"

Carrie shakes her head. "Not until she's an adult. I can refuse, I asked a solicitor back when . . . when I first found out I was pregnant."

Carrie looks down at Frankie's hands on her. "I'm okay," she says.

Frankie releases her carefully and steps back. What little color Carrie had before has started to return to her cheeks. "Frankie," she says. "If you're really as sorry as you say for what happened to my mum—"

"I am, I'm so sorry."

"Then you'll do something for me."

"What is it?"

I told them he did it on purpose. Isn't that enough?

But the expression on Carrie's face is one Frankie would know anywhere. *A ladies' toilet look.* "Please don't tell anyone what my mother told him, especially the court. No matter what he claims. Please."

Frankie is standing by the church again, the voices of the Chagford Rock Choir a warm front against the cold, clean air. The truck door is opening, the men's laughter ricocheting like rifle shots. Juno is shaking her head inside. These looks, they cannot be ignored.

"Okay," Frankie says. "I won't ever tell anyone. No matter what."

Epilogue

CARRIE

January 1, 2036
Ten Years and Seven Weeks Later

It is a beautiful day for letting go.

Carrie has barely slept and feels a drunken lightness as she rises from the bed and leans over to kiss Bunny, starfished next to her with Barnaby in her hand. Neither has mentioned it, but she's slept in here every night since Ashley broke in, Carrie comforting Bunny the way she herself was once comforted. And without words, both know that this will not be necessary in the new place.

Carrie climbs out of bed carefully, avoiding the boxes and tea chests. The linen as old as her parents' wedding is now bagged for charity. They will buy bright new sheets tomorrow. She slides into a blouse the colors of a sunset, and cream-colored cigarette pants that skim her ankles. Her new-start outfit, her Brighton look. She had laid it out carefully last night, all her other clothes given to charity, or packed in boxes that rougher hands will carry out of here. She has recently started to dress in colors again. To wonder, and not stop herself as she always used to, what Emma would look like now and how she would dress too. And if she were here, would they be coloring the gray out of each other's hair? Emma finally trusting her input? Would they be clinging to youth or embracing middle age? Would they still be in London, or would they have moved back to Dartmoor? Got married here, in the little church, and slowly turned into their mothers.

No, she thinks now, they would have done what she and Bunny are finally doing. What Emma wanted to do all along. A new life all of their own, all the ghosts blown away by the salty sea air.

Downstairs, Carrie opens the living room shutters and presses her forehead to the glass. The dawning Dartmoor horizon is watercolor pink. Swirls of pale, clean mist lie across the curves of the uppermost fields like discarded lingerie.

In the kitchen, she boils the kettle and makes a proper pot of tea like Janet used to make. Leaves, not bags. Tea cozy older than her. She will have to wash all this up again, rebox it, but she has no regrets.

She pulls on her new pink trench coat and slips outside to the garden where, mug in hand, she sits on the old bench near the stump of a cherry tree she had to get a tree surgeon to chop down because she could not bear to see it every day. He was appalled at first and refused. It was illegal to destroy it, and morally wrong to slaughter a healthy tree. After her faltering voice described how the wind had rippled through the pages of the book beneath a man's gently swaying feet, as he swung from a tree just like that one, outside the community care center in London, he did the work for free.

Carrie has left the tree house she had built, which sits like a Farrow & Ball–painted watchtower in the old corner oak. The new owners have little kids who were excited to see it when they looked around. And besides, Bunny was never that interested in it, it was there to assuage an old guilt.

Fit for a finale, the new-year sun sparkles across the frosty raised beds and the fields beyond, where an ancient path traces its way to Emma's house. *Mary's house.*

The last time Carrie dared to stand in those fields, it was with Emma in a purple urn.

But now Emma sits down beside her, pulls up one knee, rests her chin on it, and waits. By her side, a bucket of pick'n'mix.

"Okay," Carrie says, as she always used to, "get ready for the download."

She closes her eyes and tells Emma about Bunny, their cozy girl. About her jokes and her messiness, how tall she is and how sweet. About the ways she is like her mummy, and all the ways she is like her mama.

Her beauty and her silliness, how she makes anything fun, even the worst day of their lives. Just like Emma would. "Knock knock."

She tells her, out loud—"they'll have me committed if anyone hears me"—about the ways the world has changed, and all the ways it has stayed the same. Especially here, where they were formed, their childhoods crystallized around in-jokes and shared songs, howling at the same moon. And she tells her that if she could do it all again, she would do it all with her. That the pain of loss was a cost she would pay, over and over, for the time they had.

The moving truck will be here soon and she is ready, finally ready, but she is enjoying here too. Cup discarded on the rickety bench, she moves through the garden one last time. Skips, twists, drops a shoulder and ducks to avoid a drooping raspberry cane stripped first by birds and finished by winter. Carrie walks carefully now across the dew-wet grass. These are her good shoes, and they're slippery. She feels overdressed, silly, but she was usually overdressed and always silly, back before . . . before everything went wrong. She has had her hair bleached back to lemon sherbet, had it cut into a bob.

"You look like the old photos of you," Bunny said. "I can sort of . . . I can sort of remember you."

She will arrive in Brighton like this, and she will match the peach Bellini frontage of their new Kemptown house. They will step into a new life already ablaze with color and sunshine.

Before they race their belongings to their new home, they have four final visits to make. To Janet's grave, to lay the last of the roses plucked during autumn, dried, preserved, and tied in a black velvet ribbon. To Mary, of course, who is still considering a move to the seaside herself. A little flat, easy to manage. Not in Brighton, "the hubbub would kill me," but in nearby Eastbourne. It's not an easy decision; her husband John and Emma are both buried here, she has a life outside of Carrie and Bunny, with a little gaggle of bustling friends. And maybe Carrie and Mary have become too entwined, maybe the guilt-glue needs to flake away a little, if Carrie is to start again.

They have promised to call in to see Jasmine, though Bunny will communicate with her through her new phone nonstop and will see her when she comes back to visit. And lastly, they will call in to the isolated farmhouse where Bunny's other grandmother lives. A cautious, breath-held meeting, Carrie hovering at the edge of her seat, everybody careful with this newborn and delicate thing. But if Carrie cannot take all the credit for Bunny's kindness, then Mrs. Curtiss cannot shoulder all the blame for her son's cruelty.

The easiest thing is to apportion blame, but the kindest and bravest thing is to forgive. And Carrie has chosen to forgive many other people. She has forgiven Mrs. Curtiss and the secret tunnels she dug to find her way to Bunny. She has forgiven the people who hacked their way into the systems ten years ago. She even forgives Ashley Curtiss, now facing another five years before he can even speak of parole, but living for the letters Bunny sends him regularly.

But the hardest thing she has ever done, is what she does now. She raises a smile, smooths down her bright clothes, and decides to forgive herself.

ACKNOWLEDGMENTS

I was writing another novel when I got the idea for *59 Minutes*. I carried on trying to write that other story, trying to care about it like I cared about this new idea. But it was impossible. Once I'd had this idea, it was all I could think about. The work in progress crumbled and I'd soon discarded it as if it had never existed. I can barely remember it now.

Deeper into the writing process, when I finally believed I could do this idea justice, I started to tell people the premise. And I found that they stopped listening to me almost immediately. "I'm sorry," they would say, "I'm just thinking about what I would do with my last fifty-nine minutes."

Everyone has an answer. And so many of those answers come back to one thing: Try to save the ones we love. More than any other book I've written, my family were in my mind the whole time. They mean everything to me, and I would do anything to save them. If we know this about ourselves then we know everyone else feels this way, which should power empathy on a global scale.

Anyway.

I'm very grateful to my agent, Sophie Lambert, who immediately seized on the concept, understood and supported me when I lurched mid-project, and championed it so brilliantly and passionately. The whole C&W team have given this book wings and I'm eternally grateful.

Ariele Fredman at UTA knocked it out of the park when she sold *59 Minutes* to the wonderful Emily Bestler. I couldn't ask for a better new home in the US than with Emily and her team.

Leodora Darlington, my new editor at Orion, has been an absolute joy to work with, helping me to whittle the pace of this story until it was so tight that my heart rate spiked when I was reading through for a final time.

Although I have used a lot of artistic license in terms of procedures and policies (in part because the real nuclear attack procedures and policies are strictly withheld from the public), a great deal of research went into the writing of the novel. Much of which never made it to the final page but has left an indelible mark on both my brain and my existential dread.

If you're interested in civil defense planning, nuclear issues, the cold war era and its ongoing echoes, I particularly recommend the podcasts *Atomic Hobo, Cold War Conversations*, the *LSE Cold War Podcast, Russia Rising, Coming in from the Cold*, and *The Cold War Vault*.

A special mention to Sacha Black, with whom I went on a trip to explore secret parts of Shepherd's Bush underground station as part of Hidden London, an experience that cracked the whole book open for me and helped me write Carrie's subterranean adventures as authentically as possible.

Beverley Morrow kindly donated to Young Lives vs Cancer to be named after a character. I hope I have done you proud, Beverley. Your character is not on the page for long, but she is one of my favorites.

In Kurt Vonnegut's novel *Cat's Cradle*, there is a fake religion called Bokononism, and within it is the concept of a karass. A karass is a group of people connected spiritually. A tribe, a gang, a network, however you want to think of it. I'm not religious, so maybe it's fitting that an element of a fake religion is the one that appeals the most, but I absolutely have a karass. My karass is filled with the people who only ever lift me, who let me be me, who don't roll their eyes at my weird obsessions or tell me to narrow my vision. I hope I do the same for them. Some are authors, some not. I have gone back and forth on naming every one of them, but I'm too worried I'll miss someone out in my haste to send these acknowledgments in on time.

If you think you might be in the karass, you almost certainly are.

And lastly, thank *you* for picking up this book, for reading to the end. Without readers, I wouldn't be a published author, and I'm really not cut out for much else. So thank you, truly, to everyone who has bought, borrowed, or read my book over someone else's shoulder and then told their friend to read it too. I appreciate every one of you.

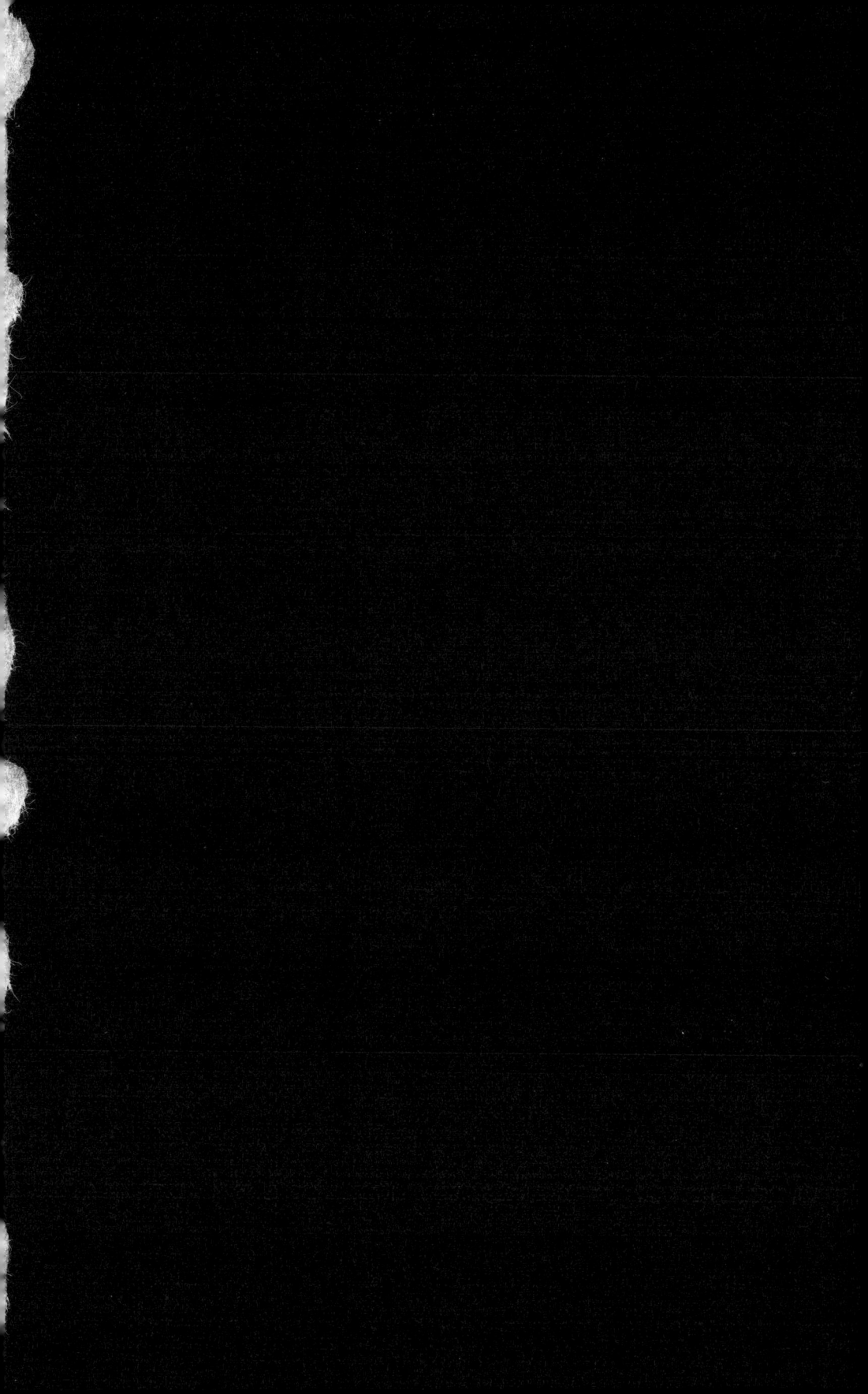